EAST OF THE WEST

EAST OF THE WEST
A Country in Stories

MIROSLAV PENKOV

Farrar, Straus and Giroux   New York

Farrar, Straus and Giroux
18 West 18th Street, New York 10011

The title story first appeared, in slightly different form, in *Orion*.
The following stories were previously published in very different form:
"Makedonija," in *Big Muddy: A Journal of the Mississippi River Valley*;
"Buying Lenin," in *The Southern Review* and *The Best American Short Stories 2008*; and "Devshirmeh," in *The Southern Review*.
"A Picture with Yuki" originally appeared in *One Story*; "The Letter"
originally appeared in *A Public Space*.

Library of Congress Cataloging-in-Publication Data
Penkov, Miroslav.
    East of the West : a country in stories / Miroslav Penkov.—1st ed.
        p.   cm.
    ISBN 978-0-374-11733-7 (alk. paper)
    1. Bulgaria—Fiction.   I. Title.

PS3616.E54E37 2011
813'.6—dc22
                                                              2010047602

Designed by Jonathan D. Lippincott

www.fsgbooks.com

1   3   5   7   9   10   8   6   4   2

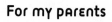
For my parents

"My soul, your voyages have been your native land!"
—Nikos Kazantzakis, *Odyssey: A Modern Sequel*,
Book XVI, line 959

CONTENTS

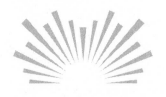

MAKEDONIJA

I was born just twenty years after we got rid of the Turks. 1898. So yes, this makes me seventy-one. And yes, I'm grumpy. I'm mean. I smell like all old men do. I am a walking pain, hips, shoulders, knees and elbows. I lie awake at night. I call my daughter by my grandson's name and I remember the day I met my wife much better than yesterday, or today. August 2, I think. 1969. Last night I pissed my bed and who knows what joy tonight will bring? I am in no way original or new. Although I might be jealous of a man who's sixty years dead.

I found his letters to my wife, from long before she knew me, when she was still sixteen. It was a silly find, one that belongs in romance novels, not in real life and old age. I dropped her box of jewelry. The lid flew to the side and the door of a secret compartment popped loose at the bottom. Inside lay a small booklet, a diary in letters.

I can't imagine ever writing the kind of letters a woman would preserve for sixty years. I wish it was not that man but I who'd known Nora, back when she was closer to a beginning than an end. Such is the simple truth—we're ending. And I don't want to end. I want to live forever. Reborn in a young man's body and with a young man's mind. But not my body and not my mind. I want to live again as someone who holds no memory of me. I want to be that other man.

·

For eight years now we've lived in this nursing home, a few kilometers away from Sofia, at the foot of the Vitosha Mountains. The view is nice, the air is fresh. It's not so much that I don't like it here. It's more that I really hate it. The view and the air, the food, the water, the way they treat us like we're all dying. The fact that we are all dying. But I suppose, if I'm honest to myself, which I rarely am, I should be glad we're where we are. It was hard to take care of Nora on my own, after her stroke. We left the apartment to our daughter, recently married, already pregnant, packed up and settled down in prison.

Since then each day is like the one before. Six thirty we wake up for medication. We eat breakfast in the cafeteria—thin slices of buttered bread with three black olives, a sliver of yellow cheese, some linden tea. Dear God, I remember eating better during the Balkan War. I sit amidst a sea of trembling chins and shaking fingers and listen to the knocking of olive pits on metal plates. I talk to no one and no one talks to me. I've managed to earn this much. Then, after breakfast, I wheel Nora up to the gym. I watch her struggle to make a fist, to hold a rubber ball. I watch the nurses massage her withered arm and leg. I watch their supple arms and legs.

The second stroke left half of Nora paralyzed, and all of her mute. Most nurses—some doctors, even—regard her as mentally challenged. She's far from that. I'm sure that in her mind all words ring clear, but they roll out disjoined, like baby talk. Sometimes I wish she'd keep the jabber to herself. Sometimes I am embarrassed by the way the nurses look at her, or me. It's obvious by now she won't miraculously learn to speak again. That part of her brain is ruined, the fuse has blown. So why can't she keep quiet? She manages to say my name and Buryana's, and if I do my best to vex her, sometimes she manages a curse. The rest is babble.

She babbles as I roll her back to our room or, if the day allows it, out in the garden, where we walk in circles. I like the

garden only when the flowers bloom. All other times the earth is
damp and black, and I cannot resist the ugly thoughts. When
we're tired we sit down on a bench and fall asleep, shoulder against
shoulder, with the sun upon our faces, and to anyone looking, I'm
sure we are a lovely sight. Then lunch. Then the siesta. Our daughter comes to visit
once a week, and sometimes she brings our grandson along. But
lately, with all the trouble she's had at home, she visits daily. She
is awful company, my daughter. We leave little Pavel with his
grandma, so she won't get upset, and in the garden Buryana talks
of how her husband is chasing after another woman. Dear Buryana, I, too, might get upset. But here I sit on the bench and listen,
because I am your father. I have no way of helping, no word of
sensible advice. Hang in there, fighter. You'll be all right. Words
mean so little, and I'm too worn out for deeds.

•

I am asleep and disconnected from what has been or is. Then I'm
awake. It seems that someone has dropped a tray outside. The
wind rattles the gutters, the trees creak and Nora breathes too
loudly. I close my eyes. But what if someone drops another tray?
What if Nora coughs or snores? I lie, anticipating sounds that
might never sound, yet all the same keep me awake. It thunders
over the mountain.

I put on my robe and sit by the window in Nora's wheelchair.
I switch on the small radio. Quiet music pours out of the speaker,
and I listen in the blue of the night, until a voice comes up to
read the late-night news. The Communist Party is great again,
more jobs for the people, less poverty. Our magnificent Bulgarian wrestlers have earned us more gold. Good night, comrades,
be safe in your sleep.

Dear God, I won't be safe. There is no sleep. And I'm so very
tired of the comrades, their all-encompassing belief in bright

future days that somehow I've started to suspect might never come. I turn the dial until I find the muffled sound of a foreign station. Romanian, it seems. Then Greek. Then British. The voices crackle and buzz, because the Party is distorting the transmissions, but at least at night the voices are strong enough to hear. I listen to the English and all the words sound like a single long word to me, a word devoid of history and meaning, completely free. At night, the air is thicker, and one foreign sound drags after itself another and they converge into a river, which flows freely from land to land.

I travel with this river. But even so, how can I resist the current of my worries? I think of Buryana. How will she pay the bills, divorced and with a little child? How will Pavel grow up a man without a father? And then my eyes seek Nora, who snores lightly on her back. I watch her face, her wrinkled skin, her crooked lips, and I can't help but think that she is pretty, still. A man ought to be able to undress his wife from all the years until she lies before him naked in youth again. Which makes me wonder if she ever lay naked for that other man, the one who wrote the letters. If he cupped her left breast in his palm. But it is Nora's breast, and wasn't he a man? Of course he cupped it.

I reach for the jewelry box and pry the bottom open. I take the little notebook and weigh it in my palm. Someone has scribbled on the cover—*Dear Miss Nora, Mr. Peyo Spasov, in his last hour, asked us to mail this book to you.* This is as far as I can read now. *Mr. Peyo Spasov.* It's hard to think of a more ordinary name. He must have been a peasant, uneducated, ignorant and simple-minded. He must have earned his bread by plowing fields, by chopping wood and herding sheep. Most likely he spoke with a lisp, or stuttered. Most likely he walked hunched over from all the work.

It suddenly strikes me I've just described myself. Of course, I hate this other man, but what if he was not a peasant like me? What if he was a doctor's son? I turn to the first letter and read.

February 5, 1905
My dearest darling Nora. I'm freezing and my fingers
hurt, but I don't want to think of such things. I'm writing
you a letter. We're crossing the Pirin Mountains and to-
morrow, if God decides, we will be in Macedonia. The
Turks . . .

My dearest darling. I shove the notebook in the box and hurry
back to bed. Under the blankets I shiver and listen to imaginary
sounds. I can't afford to read about this man. There is a chance,
however slim, that he isn't what I need him to be.

•

"So she's kept a few old letters, big deal." Buryana takes off her
sunglasses. Her eyes are red and puffy and she blinks while they
adjust to the afternoon sun. We sit out in the garden, on a bench
farthest from all other benches, but not far enough from the
sound of the cripples who drag their feet and canes and walkers
across the pebbly lanes.

" 'Big deal'?" I say.

"Big deal," she says again, and I'm terrified by how calcified
she has become, consumed by her failing marriage.

"You ought to read those letters," she says. "They might help
the boredom go away. And read them to Mother. Why not? It'll
bring her at least some joy."

Some joy! And so I say, "I won't take love advice from you." I
mean it as a joke, of course, but Buryana is in no mood for jok-
ing. And soon I wish I'd kept my mouth shut, because from that
point on it's all about her husband and that other woman, a col-
league of his from school, like him a literature teacher.

She says, "Yesterday, I followed him out of the apartment. He
met her in a café and bought her a *garash* cake. He got himself
some water, obviously he had no money for more, and while she
ate her cake, he talked and talked for an hour."

"You think he talked of you?" I say. She starts to cry.

"The worst part is," she says sobbing, "this other woman isn't even pretty. Why would he leave me for a woman less pretty than me? So what if I think that a grown man writing poetry is stupid? So what if I don't like to read? That doesn't make me a bad wife, does it?"

I put my arm around her shoulder and let her have her cry.

"This is a valid question," I say. *A valid question.* What's wrong with me? And while she sobs my thoughts drift and I imagine little Pavel, upstairs with Nora. They must be laughing, happy, both unsuspecting.

"You ought to talk to him," I say, and gather her hair in my palm, away from the wetness of her face. "You can't keep spying on him like this. It isn't right."

She straightens up. "I won't take love advice from you," she says.

•

It's night again. It could be yesterday's, or tomorrow's. A night four years back. They're all the same. I sit in Nora's wheelchair and listen to the world. I see beyond the walls, not with my eyes, but with my ears. I see the nurses, in their office, boiling coffee. The water bubbles. I hear needles clicking; someone is knitting socks. I hear the benches, the trees, the mountain. Each thing possesses a noise unique, and, like a bat, I drink the noise of all things, dead and living alike. My palate has grown a taste for sound.

I hear my grandson sleeping in his bed, my daughter talking to her husband. I hear my wife's dreams, sweet to her, but tasting of wormwood to me. No doubt she dreams of Mr. Peyo Spasov. And so it strikes me as only fair that I too should be allowed to sample the noise he's left behind. I take the notebook and read his messy writing.

February 5, 1905

My dearest darling Nora. I'm freezing and my fingers hurt, but I don't want to think of such things. I'm writing you a letter. We're crossing the Pirin Mountains and tomorrow, if God decides, we will be in Macedonia. The Turks have all the main passages guarded, so we had to find a new way through. Two of my friends slipped on ice, and were lost. The first one, Mityu, was leading the donkey with the supplies, and the donkey slipped and dragged him off the cliffs. So now we're hungry, spending the night sheltered between some rocks. The snow has begun to fall. Dearest Nora, I miss you. I wish I was by your side now. But you know how things are—a man can't stay put, knowing that in Macedonia the Turks are slaughtering our brothers, trying to keep them under the fez. I told you then and I tell you now—if men like me don't go to liberate the brothers, no one will. The Russians helped us be free. It's now our turn to help. I love you, Nora, but there are things before which even love must bow. I know with time you'll understand and forgive. Draw the knife, cock the pistol. That's what our captain, the Voivode, says. I wish you could meet him. He has only one eye, but a hungrier eye you've never seen. He lost the other in the Liberation war. He fought on the Shipka Pass, 1877, the Voivode. Can you believe that? He says the Turks were vicious then, but now, he says, we can take them. Of course it won't be easy. The Voivode says I have no father, I have no mother. My father is the mountain, my mother is the shotgun. All those back home you loved, he says, bid them farewell. It's for your brothers' blood we spill our own. But I can't say farewell, dearest Nora. And I can't hold the pencil any more. I'm cold. And please forgive. Love, Peyo.

Love, Peyo . . . Why did I read these words? I vow not to envy or fear this man. Instead, I kiss my wife's good hand and kiss her lips, as if to mark her. She's mine now and has been for a lifetime, and that is that. I listen to the nurses down the hall, I listen to the benches and the trees. But in the moonlight my pillow is a rock, and so I lie beside this rock and so the snow begins to fall. I hear the rustle of every flake on my face, the chill spreads through my traitor knees and elbows. The Voivode lost an eye in the Liberation war. My God, what an awful thing to put in a love letter. I've seen men with their eyes gouged out. Men close to me, barefooted, with wrists tied together behind their backs. Hanged on the village square for everyone to see. As I lie in bed, eyes shut tightly, I still hear the rope creaking when the bodies sway, and I can hear the sound the bodies make swaying.

•

I was born a year after my brother. When I was twelve Mother bore another boy, but it died a baby. Two years after that she had twin girls. We lived in my grandfather's house and worked his land. Our grandpa was a lazy man, the laziest I've known, but had his reasons. He sat out on the threshold from dusk till after dawn and smoked hashish. He'd let me sit beside him and told me stories of the Turkish times. All through his youth he'd served a Turkish bey, and that bey had broken his back with work enough for seven lifetimes. So now, in freedom, Grandpa refused to do as much as wipe his ass. That's what he'd say. "I have your father to wipe my ass," he'd say, and hit the smoke. He drew maps of Bulgaria in the dust, enormous as it had been more than five centuries ago, before the Turks had taken over our land. He'd draw a circle around the North and say "This is called Moesia. This is where we live, free at last, thanks to the Russian brothers." Then he'd circle the South. "This is Thrace. It stayed part of the Turkish empire for seven years after the North was freed, but now we are one, united. And this," he'd say and circle farther south, "is Macedonia. Home to Bulgarians, but still under the fez." He'd brush fingers along the lines and watch the circles for a long time, put arrows where he thought the Russians should invade and crosses where battles should be waged. Then he'd spit in the dust and draw the rest of Europe and circle it, and circle Africa and Asia. "One day, *siné*, all these continents will be Bulgarian again. And maybe the seas." Again he'd hit the smoke and sometimes he'd let me take a drag, too, because a little herb, he'd say, never hurt a child.

And now, in bed, I suddenly long to fill up my lungs with all that burning so that my head gets light and empty. Instead, I fill up with memories of things long gone the way a gourd fills up with water from rain.

Our father was a bitter man, having to kiss his in-law's hand before each meal. Father beat us plenty with his chestnut stick and I remember him happy on a single day in 1905, when we celebrated twenty years since the North had been united with the South. He sat me down with my brother, poured each a mortar of red wine and made us drink to the bottom, like men. He told us that when next we got our Macedonia back he'd fill the mortars up with *rakia*.

Father was lost in the Balkan war, seven years after. I'd like to think he fell near Edirne, a heroic death, but I won't blame him if he just chose not to return. I hope he rests in peace. When Grandpa died, it fell to me and Brother to care for the women. We worked the fields of others, cut hay, herded the village sheep. And everyone spoke of a new war, bigger than the Balkan, and that war, too, at last, reached our village. Men with guns set up camp on the square, recruiting soldiers. They said all boys of such and such age had to enlist. They said if we helped Germany win, the Germans would let us take back the land that Serbs, and Greeks, and Romanians had stolen from us after the Balkan wars. The Germans would even let us take Macedonia back from the Turks and be complete once and for all. Our mother wept and kissed my hands and then my brother's. She said, "I can't lose both my sons in this war. But I can't let you hide and shame our blood." She sent the twins to milk two sheep, then put a copper of milk before me and one before my brother. Whoever drank his copper first would get to stay home and run the house. The other would go to war. I drank as though I'd never drink again. I chugged. I quaffed. I inhaled that milk. When I was done, I saw my brother had barely touched lips to his.

Dear God. Why now? Have I no other worries? I lie and I remember and listen to the falling snow from this old and foolish letter. I feel the cold of the mountain and see my brother holding that copper still full of liquid snow. For heaven's sake, Brother. Drink.

•

After breakfast I help Nora put on her robe—the limp arm first, then the good one. I comb her hair and I talk to her like this: Did you sleep well, my dear? Did you have good dreams? Did you dream of me? I dreamed of crossing mountains and fighting Turks.

She looks confused. I help her to her feet. She smiles. Is this a loving smile? Or is she simply grateful for the help? We start slowly down the hallway, two cripples who use one another as crutches. We make a circle in the yard and then sit on a bench.

I say, "I never was a tactful man," and pull the little book of letters from my woolen jacket. I lay it on her knees. "I know about all this," I say. "I know that he loved you and that you loved him, too. This was before my time, of course, but God, Nora, I wish you'd told me. Why did you never tell me? At seventy-one, I'm not supposed to envy the dead."

I try to smile, but Nora's eyes are on the letters. She brushes the cover with a finger and it just now occurs to me that since her first stroke she hasn't held this book; that most likely, she'd reconciled with the thought of never reading his words again.

Why not? I turn the pages and clear my throat. Let this dead

lover of my wife's come to existence once more, for her sake, if
only for a day. Let me, her husband, lend him my living lips.

February 6, 1905

*My dear, lovely Nora. Today as we waded through knee-
deep snow along the Bulgarian ridge of the Pirin Mountains we saw smoke rising from behind a boulder. We
drew out our pistols, ready to spill some Turkish blood,
but instead found a man and his woman, huddled by a
tiny flame. They'd torn the man's shirt and burned strips
of it to get warm. His nose was broken and the blood had
turned black from the cold. The woman's face had been
cut by a knife. I took my cloak and gave it to her for a
while. Please forgive. The Voivode had us build a proper
fire and boil some tea and while we waited for the water
the man told us their story. They came from the other side
of the border, these two, from some village in Macedonia.
They had a small house there, a little boy of five. Two
days ago a band of* komiti, *Bulgarians like us who'd gone
to fight for Macedonia's freedom, passed through the village. Maybe afraid to anger the* komiti, *maybe out of
kindness, these good people sheltered them in their house.
The* komiti *slept, ate, drank (maybe a little too much),
gathered strength and were ready to go on their way
when, out of nowhere, a* poterya, *a pursuit party, arrived in
the village. No doubt some local coward had betrayed our
brothers. There was much shooting and much blood,
Nora, that's what the man told us. When the Turks were
finished, they dragged the* komiti *out in the yard, already
dead, mind you, and chopped their heads off just for
show. Impaled them on sticks for everyone to see. Then
they took these two people's boy and promised to turn
him Turk, so when he grew up he'd come back for the
heads of his own folk.*

Do you see now, Nora, why I've left you? Why, instead of your breast, it's stones and frozen mud and that cur the mountain that my head has to rest on? I curse the Turks, and the traitors, and all the cowards back home who choose their women before their brothers.

And with them I curse myself, Nora. I wish I, too, was a coward.

It's hard for me to finish the letter, and then, after I'm done, we sit in silence. I'd really like to see Nora's reaction, but all the same I find no strength to look her in the eye. I've always been good at looking away.

•

Our daughter comes to visit in the afternoon. Pavel is trotting behind her. He hangs on my neck and gives me a kiss. "*Dyadka*, how goes it?"

"Don't call your Grandpa '*dyadka*,'" Buryana scolds him. "It's disrespectful."

He runs to kiss his grandma.

"*Dyadka*," I call him back to my side. "Come show me those muscles of yours." Proudly he flexes his tiny arm. "Like steel," he says. And then he tells me to flex my arm. "Like jelly!" He jumps on my bed, shoes still on, and bounces off the squeaking springs.

Nora, like me, is smiling. But Buryana tells Pavel to go tell his grandma a fairy tale he's learned and drops beside me on the bed. She brushes the blanket and smooths it down. She nods at her mother. "You think we can talk?"

"As deaf as a grouse, that one," I say, "while I myself . . . I'm the ears of this world."

"Please, Father. I'm not in the mood."

That's a surprise, I think. And hush now. I, too, want to hear the fairy tale. But she goes on.

"I followed your advice and spoke with him," she says. She keeps on talking softly, and for once my mind gives up on sound. I suddenly remember how, as a little girl, she loved to ride her bike along the narrow sidewalk curb, despite my word against it. I'd make her promise me she wouldn't perform such risky stunts and she would say, "I promise, *taté!*" and only then I'd let her take out the bike. One day she stood at the doorway with a bloodied chin. She looked at me, fighting the tears as hard as she could. "I'm fine, you see," she tried to say. "No big deal, that fall." I held her, kissed her, and only then did she give in to them.

She is like this now, telling me about her husband. So many years later, my mouth fills up once more with that taste— Buryana's blood and tears.

"What did I tell you, just now?" she suddenly says. "Are you listening at all?"

"Of course I am. You spoke with your husband. He said he needed time to think."

"To think!" she says. "So I've decided we're staying here to-night. And maybe tomorrow."

I take a moment to think it over. This is such a little room, and even Nora's breathing floods it to the brim with noise at night. And now—two more people breathing, and tossing, and those creaking springs. This means no sleep, I know. Which means remembering the past. But what's an old *dyadka* like me sup-posed to do? And so I call the nurse and after a little fussing she brings two extra cots.

•

Dinner is done, the sun is setting, and while our daughter readies Nora for bed, I grab Pavel by the hand and lead him outside. A few old men are still nesting on the benches and I say, "Pavka, am I like them? Dried up and ugly."

"You *are* like them," he says, "except not ugly."

"I wish I was a kid again. But I don't suppose you understand."

"I wish I was an old man." He takes a silent breath. "I've noticed, *dyadka*, that when old men speak, the young ones listen. And no one listens to a kid. But if I was old, I'd talk to my dad."

We come by a tree whose branches are heavy with sparrows.

"I hate these things," I say. "So loud with their chirping."

We gather some pebbles and throw them, one by one, at the birds. They rise above us black and noisy. But once I'm out of breath, the birds return to their branches.

"Let's throw more stones," I say.

"It's pointless, *dyadka*. They'll come back as soon as we're gone."

I pick up some pebbles and pile them in his palms. "Come on," I say.

●

It's time to sleep and in his cot Pavel starts singing. I'm surprised he hasn't lost this habit of lulling himself to sleep. His voice is soft and thin and clear. I roll over and smile at my wife. She smiles back.

"*Dyado*, I can't sleep. Tell me a story."

Of course you can't, my child. My blood is yours and blood is ageless.

Buryana is trying to hush him, but I sit up in bed and flip the night lamp on. I take out the booklet of letters and say, "This is the story of a *komita*. He died fighting the Turks."

"All right! A rebel story."

Nora doesn't try to stop me. Buryana turns in her cot to hear better. I read and they listen. I can't know what each of them is thinking, but we're connected through the dusty words. "And then?" Pavel says every time I stop to catch some air. "What happens after that? And then?" But halfway through the story, his breathing evens out and he's asleep.

My wife's lover, Mr. Peyo Spasov, has finally made it to Macedonia. Crossing the mountain pass, they have lost another friend to an avalanche. Peyo has barely survived himself, digging his fellows out of the snow. Now, when the *komiti* reach a village, nobody offers them shelter. With knives and guns they persuade the people, for whose sake they have come to die, to take them in. The *komiti* spend the night in a small hut, by the fire. Their goal is to join a larger group of revolutionaries next day and take part in a massive uprising against the Turks which will ignite at once all over Macedonia. The land will be free at last. They don't know if the other *komiti* are waiting, or even alive.

Outside, the dogs begin to bark. The men sneak up to the window, and in the moonlight, they see a peasant pointing in their direction. Soon Turkish soldiers gather outside the hedge. The Turks light up torches, toss them to set the thatched roof aflame. The *komiti* open fire. The Turks return it. While the flames are spreading, with the butts of their guns the men inside hammer their way through the back wall, built from mud, straw and cow dung, and manage to sink into the dark unseen. They run up the slope, then find shelter by a heap of rocks. They're cold and it starts to snow again. Down below them the dogs are barking. Torches flicker and fly one roof to another, and one after the other, the thatched roofs burn. The *komiti* listen to women crying, afraid to make the slightest noise. They find no strength, the cowards, to go down and meet the Turks in battle. When the torches drown in night, like rats the *komiti* flee.

I set the little book aside and flip the lamp to darkness. They are asleep, quietly, softly. It's wrong to envy your own grandchild. But still I do. I envy Nora, too. No one has ever written to me like this. But I no longer envy that other man. Because, like me, he proved himself a coward, and though I know it's wrong, this gives me peace.

I go to check on Pavel. He's pushed the blanket away, and I tuck him in. Then I tuck in my daughter, my wife. I sit by the window. At seventy-one you can't expect to hear a story, any story, and take it as it is. At my age a story stirs up a vortex that sucks into its eye more stories, and spits out still more. I must remember what I must.

•

My brother came back from the war without a scratch. We never spoke of what he'd seen or done. I was ashamed to ask, and he was ashamed to say. We'd lost the war, of course, like all other recent wars, which was regrettable, since we never really lost our battles; we just picked the wrong allies. Or rather, our soldiers never lost their battles. Because what did I know? I herded sheep. So Brother joined me, up on the hills. We'd round the sheep at night and lock them in the pen, boil milk in a cauldron, make hominy and eat in silence while around us the mountain grew restless with barking dogs, with bells ringing from other pens. Sometimes the quiet inside me would weigh me down so much, I'd get up and yell at the top of my lungs. *Eheeeeeee.* And then my brother would yell the shepherd yell. *Eheeeeeee.* And from another hill we'd hear another shepherd and then another, and we would yell, like children, in the night.

It was shearing time, I remember, the spring of 1923. We'd shorn half of the herd and were just laying the fleece under an awning. The dogs barked and down the slope we saw a group of men, tiny at first, and then we saw they carried rifles.

We called the dogs off and waited. The men stood before us, six or seven in shepherd cloaks, hoods over their heads. But these were no shepherds. I could feel it. They held us in their sights and told us to lift our arms. I did, of course. But Brother watched them and chewed a straw. He asked if they were lost. One said, "We've come to take some lambs, some milk and cheese. We have a bunch of hungry comrades in the woods." He waved his rifle at me. "Go choose the lambs."

"We have no lambs for your comrades," Brother said. A man stepped forward and with the stock of his rifle smacked him across the face. But when he spoke it was a woman's voice we heard, and when the hood came down, a woman's face we saw. She spat down on Brother, who lay in blood and straw. She asked him if he reckoned they did all this for pleasure. If they enjoyed living in dugouts, like dogs. She said they fought for the people, for brotherhood, equality and freedom . . . "You're very pretty," Brother said and coughed up some blood. "I'll make you my wife, I think." The woman laughed. "Go get the lambs," she told me. Her comrades tied Brother up. I boiled milk while they slaughtered a lamb and speared it over the fire. They stayed with us that night, talking of how it was the working people who ought to rule. They spoke of change. That September, they said, there would be an uprising. Thousands of comrades would join to overthrow the tsarist regime. The centuries-old wrath of the slave, they called it, would be unleashed at last. I suppose they weren't bad people—just hungry and foolish. The woman sat down beside my brother and gave him milk to drink. I begged them to let him loose, but she said she liked him better, tied so.

It poured that night. I took a brand from the fire, stepped over the sleeping comrades, and went out of the hut to see if the fleece was getting wet under the awning. My brother and that woman lay naked on the heap of wool, smoking. The rain seeped through the thatched roof and in the light from the brand their bodies glistened.

"I'll go with them now," my brother told me in the morning.

And so he did. They gunned him down in August. I was back in our village then. Policemen banged on our gates and rounded up me and Mother, my sisters, the neighbors. The whole village was goaded on to the square.

They'd set up a gallows and on the gallows hung men and women, together.

"These here are partisan rebels," said the police. "Communists we shot in the woods. Some are, no doubt, from your village, your sons and daughters. Give us their names and we might let you bury them in peace."

We formed a line and, one by one, walked by the corpses. It made no sense to hang people already shot. But it made for a terrible display.

"You know this one? And how about this one, you know her?"

And then it was my turn to stand before the gallows. I held my eyes shut as hard as I could and there was nothing in the world then besides the sound of creaking rope.

•

It's Saturday morning and Buryana begins to dress her mother.

"Let me do it," I say. "I can't skip a day."

For lunch we eat chicken with rice, and Buryana tells me to ease up on the salt. For eight years nobody has told me such a thing and it feels strange, but I obey. For dessert we get yogurt with sugar and Pavel eats my cup as well. His mother tells him to ease up on the sugar and we laugh. It's not really funny, but we laugh anyway. A nurse brings Pavel an apple and he thanks her, though I can see he's disappointed.

We let him do his homework in our room and walk a few slow circles in the yard. Buryana keeps quiet, and I, too, have no idea what to say. We find Pavel reading from the book of letters. "Grandma," he's saying, "who did you love more? Grandpa or the *komita*?"

I catch myself waiting for her answer. It seems that Buryana, too, is waiting. Of course she loved the *komita* more—he must have been her sweetheart, her first big love. Most likely, I've come to think, they were engaged. Most likely, they made plans together, imagined a little house, a pair of children. She wouldn't keep his diary for so many years otherwise. And then, with their love peaking, he was killed. I know that much without yet having read the end. At first she felt betrayed. He'd put some strange ideals, brotherhood and freedom, before his love for her. She hated him for that. But then one morning, almost a year after his death, the postman brought a package with foreign stamps. She read the diary, still hating him. She read it every day. She learned each letter by heart, and with the months her hatred thinned, and in the end his death turned their love ideal, doomed not to die. Yes, that's what I've come to think now. Their love was foolish, childish, sugar-sweet, the kind of love that, if you are lucky to lose it, flares up like a thatched roof but burns as long as you live. While our love . . . I am her husband, she is my wife.

But then, as if to pull me out of my own mind, Nora takes my hand and holds it. I kiss her hand. "Let's read," I say. I almost shout it, suddenly with a light and empty head. I take the little book.

The *komiti* reach their meeting destination, the village of Crni Brod. The sun is already setting behind the mountains. The village is very quiet. A man comes forward to meet them. The *komiti* ask him, "Are the Voivodes here?" "Yes, the captains are here, the man answers, they're waiting in my house." "And you're not lying?" the *komiti* ask. "I swear by my children," the man says, and crosses himself three times. He leads them through the village. Black ropes of smoke unwind from the chimneys and the iced roofs blaze with dying sun. The snow crunches under their boots. Nothing stirs.

They arrive at the house. The man pushes the gates open and the Voivode along with two others follow inside. Then suddenly a shell hisses in the snow and Peyo falls, wounded in the thigh. Around him the *komiti* thrash about like fleas on a white sheet. They've been betrayed.

Somehow, without firing a single shot, Peyo limps away. His blood is gushing out. He collapses outside a house, conscious long enough to feel two hands pull him inside.

We sit. It seems that a long time passes without any sound. I go through my drawer until I find an old pack of Arda from the days when I still smoked. I push the window open and light a cigarette and once again no one protests. The taste is awful—stale and damp. When I'm finished I light a second. I watch my wife's reflection in the glass. I wonder if I have brought up things that should be left buried. But I want to read the end. I know she wants to hear it.

The Turks have butchered all the *komiti*, some defiant peasants have sheltered Peyo, but his wound is going septic. I see him clearly now, in my own bed, writing hectically, trying to lock all these events onto paper while he still has some strength. His eyes are black, shiny with fever, and his lips glisten with the fat from the rooster soup the peasants have fed him. But no soup can help. He is kissing death in the mouth.

I turn the final page and read what appears to be a rebel song.

> *I got no father, I got no mother,*
> *Father to scorn me,*
> *Mother to mourn me,*
> *My father—the mountain.*
> *My mother—the shotgun.*

"That's it," I say, "there's no more writing."

Pavel jumps off his cot to grab his apple. He polishes it on his shirt and takes a bite. He offers some to his mother, to Nora, to me. But neither of us speaks.

Then a nurse knocks on the door. "You have a visitor," she says.

•

Quiet, we sit, while out in the yard Buryana is talking to her husband, deciding their life. I can't see them from here—they've moved away from the window, under the trees.

"Why can't I talk to father?" Pavel asks. He sets the half-eaten apple on the ledge and picks up the booklet. "I'll memorize this poem for school, then. I'm bored."

"Pavka, stay with your grandma. I'll be right back."

I limp as fast as I can down the hallway and I'm close to the exit when Buryana walks in. She wipes her cheeks. "It's finished," she says. "He's moved out of the apartment. Which is good news for you, I guess. Four in a room . . ." She fakes a laugh and I hold her in my arms, for the first time in many years. I kiss her forehead, eyes and nose.

"Go back to your child."

Her husband is still sitting on a bench, face in his palms. I startle him, sitting down. I'm old, I think to myself. I'm ancient. When I speak, the young ones listen. But what do you say to a man whose love for a woman is stronger than the love for his own son, for his own blood? Nothing will make this man regret.

I lean back on the bench and cross my legs, regardless of how much pain this brings me. I smooth the creases of my pants.

" 'I got no father,' " I say, " 'I got no mother. Father to scorn me, Mother to mourn me. My father—the mountain. My mother— the shotgun.' " He's puzzled, I can tell, biting his lip. Blood rushes to his face. These words make little sense to him, old rebel words of loyalty and courage, and yet they clasp his windpipe in a fist.

•

Once Buryana and Pavel are gone, I tell Nora all that's happened. I spare her nothing. There should be no secrets between us now.

"She is a strong woman," I say, "our daughter. She'll be all right." I don't know what else to say. I look at the little booklet on my desk, while with effort Nora pushes herself off the bed. Her hip gives a pop, the springs a creak. I rush to help her, but she shakes her head. *No, no,* she wants to say. *I can do this myself. Let me, myself.* She picks the booklet up, and in an instant it is alive. Its dusty body trembles from the touch. A sparrow, which shakes its feathers free of dew. A man's heart, which beats itself to life again. A hand she leads away, ungracious, horrible, horrific. I watch her drag her withered foot across the room and lay the booklet in its box. She lowers the box in a drawer and slides the drawer shut. Her face is calm. Farewell, old boy, it says, old love.

I wonder if the rebel's grave is still there, in that Macedonian village. And if we went there, would we find it? An empty plan starts to take shape. What if I pulled some strings? There are one or two old comrades who can help us out. What if they loaned us a car, stamped our passports? We'll take Buryana and Pavel with us.

I lower the half-eaten apple from the ledge and flip it in my hand. How calm your face, Nora, I want to say, how even your breaths. Teach me to breathe like you. To wave my palm and turn the raging surf to glass.

Instead I call her name. Slowly, she limps over and eases down beside me. "I've never told you this," I say. "We never buried Brother. That was a lie. We never took him off the rope. I'd heard rumors, stories from people in our mountain, of how when mothers recognized their gunned-down children the tsarists pulled them aside and shot them on the spot. And so I told Mother, 'I beseech you in your daughters' blood, keep walking. Don't say a word.' And Mother was so shocked then she stood before my brother and didn't even reach to touch his feet. We walked right past."

I know that this will never be, but still I say, "Let's go to Macedonia. Let's find the grave. I'll borrow a car." I want to say more, but I don't. She watches me. She takes my hand and now my hand, too, trembles with hers. I see in the apple the marks of Pavel's teeth and, in the brown flesh, a tiny tooth. I show it to Nora and it takes her eyes a moment to recognize what it is they see. Or so I think.

But then she nods without surprise, as if this is just what she expected. Isn't it good to be so young, she wants to tell me, that you can lose a tooth and not even notice?

EAST OF THE WEST

It takes me thirty years, and the loss of those I love, to finally arrive in Beograd. Now I'm pacing outside my cousin's apartment, flowers in one hand and a bar of chocolate in the other, rehearsing the simple question I want to ask her. A moment ago, a Serbian cabdriver spat on me and I take time to wipe the spot on my shirt. I count to eleven.

Vera, I repeat once more in my head, *will you marry me?*

•

I first met Vera in the summer of 1970, when I was six. At that time my folks and I lived on the Bulgarian side of the river, in the village of Bulgarsko Selo, while she and her folks made home on the other bank, in Srbsko. A long time ago these two villages had been one—that of Staro Selo—but after the great wars Bulgaria had lost land and that land had been given to the Serbs. The river, splitting the village in two hamlets, had served as a boundary: what lay east of the river stayed in Bulgaria and what lay west belonged to Serbia.

Because of the unusual predicament the two villages were in, our people had managed to secure permission from both countries to hold, once every five years, a major reunion, called the *sbor*. This was done officially so we wouldn't forget our roots. In reality, though, the reunion was just another excuse for everyone to eat lots of grilled meat and drink lots of *rakia*. A man had to eat until he felt sick from eating and he had to drink until he no longer cared if he felt sick from eating. The summer of 1970, the reunion was going to be in Srbsko, which meant we had to cross the river first.

•

This is how we cross:

Booming noise and balls of smoke above the water. Mihalaky is coming down the river on his boat. The boat is glorious. Not a boat really, but a raft with a motor. Mihalaky has taken the seat of an old Moskvich, the Russian car with the engine of a tank, and he has nailed that seat to the floor of the raft and upholstered the seat with goat skin. Hair out. Black and white spots, with brown. He sits on his throne, calm, terrible. He sucks on a pipe with an ebony mouthpiece and his long white hair flows behind him like a flag.

On the banks are our people. Waiting. My father is holding a white lamb under one arm and on his shoulder he is balancing a demijohn of grape *rakia*. His shining eyes are fixed on the boat. He licks his lips. Beside him rests a wooden cask, stuffed with white cheese. My uncle is sitting on the cask, counting Bulgarian money.

"I hope they have deutsche marks to sell," he says.

"They always do," my father tells him.

My mother is behind them, holding two sacks. One is full of *terlitsi*—booties she has been knitting for some months, gifts for our folks on the other side. The second sack is zipped up and I can't see what's inside, but I know. Flasks of rose oil, lipstick and mascara. She will sell them or trade them for other kinds of perfumes or lipsticks or mascara. Next to her is my sister, Elitsa, pressing to her chest a small teddy bear stuffed with money. She's been saving. She wants to buy jeans.

"Levis," she says. "Like the rock star."

My sister knows a lot about the West.

I'm standing between Grandma and Grandpa. Grandma is

wearing her most beautiful costume—a traditional dress she got from her own Grandma that she will one day give to my sister. Motley-patterned apron, white hemp shirt, embroidery. On her ears, her most precious ornament—the silver earrings.

Grandpa is twisting his mustache.

"The little bastard," he's saying, "he better pay now. He better."

He is referring to his cousin, Uncle Radko, who owes him money on account of a football bet. Uncle Radko had taken his sheep by the cliffs, where the river narrowed, and seeing Grandpa herding his animals on the opposite bluff, shouted, "I bet your Bulgars will lose in London!" and Grandpa shouted back, "You wanna put some money on it?" And that's how the bet was made, thirty years ago.

There are nearly a hundred of us on the bank, and it takes Mihalaky a day to get us all across the river. No customs—the men pay some money to the guards and all is good. When the last person sets his foot in Srbsko, the moon is bright in the sky and the air smells of grilled pork and foaming wine.

Eating, drinking, dancing. All night long. In the morning everyone has passed out in the meadow. There are only two souls not drunk or sleeping. One of them is me and the other one, going through the pockets of my folks, is my cousin Vera.

•

Two things I found remarkable about my cousin: her jeans and her sneakers. Aside from that, she was a scrawny girl—a pale, round face and fragile shoulders with skin peeling from the sun. Her hair was long, I think, or was it my sister's hair that grew down to her waist? I forget. But I do recall the first thing that my cousin ever said to me:

"Let go of my hair," she said, "or I'll punch you in the mouth."

I didn't let go because I had to stop her from stealing, so, as promised, she punched me. Only she wasn't very accurate and her fist landed on my nose, crushing it like a Plain Biscuit. I spent the rest of the *sbor* with tape on my face, sneezing blood, and now I am forever marked with an ugly snoot. Which is why everyone, except my mother, calls me Nose.

•

Five summers slipped by. I went to school in the village and in the afternoons I helped Father with the fields. Father drove an MTZ-50, a tractor made in Minsk. He'd put me on his lap and make me hold the steering wheel and the steering wheel would shake and twitch in my hands as the tractor ploughed diagonally, leaving terribly distorted lines behind.

"My arms hurt," I'd say. "This wheel is too hard."

"Nose," Father would say, "quit whining. You're not holding a wheel. You're holding life by the throat. So get your shit together and learn how to choke the bastard, because the bastard already knows how to choke you."

Mother worked as a teacher in the school. This was awkward for me, because I could never call her "Mother" in class and because she always knew if I'd done my homework or not. But I had access to her files and could steal exams and sell them to the kids for cash.

The year of the new *sbor*, 1975, our geography teacher retired and Mother found herself teaching his classes as well. This gave me more exams to sell and I made good money. I had a goal in mind. I went to my sister, Elitsa, having first rubbed my eyes hard so they would appear filled with tears, and with my most humble and vulnerable voice I asked her, "How much for your jeans?"

"Nose," she said, "I love you, but I'll wear these jeans until the day I die."

I tried to look heartbreaking, but she didn't budge. Instead, she advised me:

"Ask cousin Vera for a pair. You'll pay her at the *sbor*." Then from a jar in her night stand Elitsa took out a ten-lev bill and stuffed it in my pocket. "Get some nice ones," she said.

Two months before it was time for the reunion, I went to the river. I yelled until a boy showed up and I asked him to call my cousin. She came an hour later.

"What do you want, Nose?"

"Levis!" I yelled.

"You better have the money!" she yelled back.

•

Mihalaky came in smoke and roar. And with him came the West. My cousin Vera stepped out of the boat and everything on her screamed, *We live better than you, we have more stuff, stuff you can't have and never will.* She wore white leather shoes with little flowers on them, which she explained was called an Adidas. She had jeans. And her shirt said things in English.

"What does it say?"

"The name of a music group. They have this song that goes *'Smooook na dar voooto.'* You heard it?"

"Of course I have." But she knew better.

After lunch, the grown-ups danced around the fire, then played drunk soccer. Elitsa was absent for most of the time, and finally when she returned, her lips were burning red and her eyes shone like I'd never seen them before. She pulled me aside and whispered in my ear:

"Promise not to tell." Then she pointed at a dark-haired boy from Srbsko, skinny and with a long neck, who was just joining the soccer game. "Boban and I kissed in the forest. It was so great," she said, and her voice flickered. She nudged me in the ribs, and stuck a finger at cousin Vera, who sat by the fire, yawning and raking the embers up with a stick.

"Come on, Nose, be a man. Take her to the woods."

And she laughed so loud, even the deaf old grandmas turned to look at us.

I scurried away, disgusted and ashamed, but finally I had to approach Vera. I asked her if she had my jeans, then took out the money and began to count it.

"Not here, you fool," she said, and slapped me on the hand with the smoldering stick.

We walked through the village until we reached the old bridge, which stood solitary in the middle of the road. Yellow grass grew between each stone, and the riverbed was dry and fissured.

We hid under the bridge and completed the swap. Thirty levs for a pair of jeans. Best deal I'd ever made.

"You wanna go for a walk?" Vera said after she had counted the bills twice. She rubbed them on her face, the way our fathers did, and stuffed them in her pocket.

We picked mushrooms in the woods while she told me things about her school and complained about a Serbian boy who always pestered her.

"I can teach him a lesson," I said. "Next time I come there, you just show him to me."

"Yeah, Nose, like you know how to fight."

And then, just like that, she hit me in the nose. Crushed it, once more, like a biscuit.

"Why did you do that?"

She shrugged. I made a fist to smack her back, but how do you hit a girl? Or how, for that matter, will hitting another person in the face stop the blood gushing from your own nose? I tried to suck it up and act like the pain was easy to ignore.

She took me by the hand and dragged me toward the river.

"I like you, Nose," she said. "Let's go wash your face."

•

We lay on the banks and chewed thyme leaves.

"Nose," my cousin said, "you know what they told us in school?"

She rolled over and I did the same to look her in the eyes. They were very dark, shaped like apricot kernels. Her face was all speckled and she had a tiny spot on her upper lip, delicate, hard to notice, that got redder when she was nervous or angry. The spot was red now.

"You look like a mouse," I told her.

She rolled her eyes.

"Our history teacher," she said, "told us we were all Serbs. You know. Like, a hundred percent."

"Well, you talk funny," I said. "I mean you talk Serbianish."

"So, you think I'm a Serb?"

"Where do you live?" I asked her.

"You know where I live."

"But do you live in Serbia or in Bulgaria?"

Her eyes darkened and she held them shut for a long time. I knew she was sad. And I liked it. She had nice shoes, and jeans, and could listen to bands from the West, but I owned something that had been taken away from her forever.

"The only Bulgarian here is me," I told her.

She got up and stared at the river. "Let's swim to the drowned church," she said.

"I don't want to get shot."

"Get shot? Who cares for churches in no-man's-water? Besides, I've swum there before." She stood up, took her shirt off and jumped in. The murky current rippled around her shoulders and they glistened, smooth, round pebbles the river had polished for ages. Yet her skin was soft, I could imagine. I almost reached to touch it.

We swam the river slowly, staying along the bank. I caught a small chub under a rock, but Vera made me let it go. Finally we saw the cross sticking up above the water, massive, with rusty feet and arms that caught the evening sun.

We all knew well the story of the drowned church. Back in the day, before the Balkan Wars, a rich man lived east of the river. He had no offspring and no wife, so when he lay down dying he called his servant with a final wish: to build, with his money, a village church. The church was built, west of the river, and the peasants hired from afar a young *zograf*, a master of icons. The master painted for two years and there he met a girl and fell in love with her and married her and they, too, lived west of the river, near the church.

Then came the Balkan Wars and after that the First World War. All these wars Bulgaria lost, and much Bulgarian land was given to the Serbs. Three officials arrived in the village; one was a Russian, one was French and one was British. East of the river, they said, stays in Bulgaria. West of the river from now on belongs to Serbia. Soldiers guarded the banks and planned to take the bridge down, and when the young master, who had gone away to work on another church, came back, the soldiers refused to let him cross the border and return to his wife.

In his desperation he gathered people and convinced them to divert the river, to push it west until it went around the village. Because according to the orders, what lay east of the river stayed in Bulgaria.

How they carried all those stones, all those logs, how they piled them up, I cannot imagine. Why the soldiers did not stop them, I don't know. The river moved west and it looked like she would serpent around the village. But then she twisted, wiggled and tasted with her tongue a route of lesser resistance; through the lower hamlet she swept, devouring people and houses. Even the church, in which the master had left two years of his life, was lost in her belly.

We stared at the cross for some time, then I got out on the bank and sat in the sun.

"It's pretty deep," I said. "You sure you've been down there?"

She put a hand on my back. "It's okay if you're scared."

But it was not okay. I closed my eyes, took a deep breath and dove off the bank.

"Swim to the cross!" she yelled after me.

I swam like I wore shoes of iron. I held the cross tightly and stepped on the slimy dome underneath. Soon Vera stood by me, in turn gripping the cross so she wouldn't slip and drift away.

"Let's look at the walls," she said.

"What if we get stuck?"

"Then we'll drown."

She laughed and nudged me in the chest.

"Come on, Nose, do it for me."

It was difficult to keep my eyes open at first. The current pushed us away, so we had to work hard to reach the small window below the dome. We grabbed the bars on the window and looked inside. And despite the murky water, my eyes fell on a painting of a bearded man kneeling by a rock, his hands entwined. The man was looking down, and in the distance, approaching, was a little bird. Below the bird, I saw a cup.

"It's a nice church," Vera said after we surfaced.

"Do you want to dive again?"

"No." She moved closer and quickly she kissed me on the lips.

"Why did you do that?" I said, and felt the hairs on my arms and neck stand up, though they were wet.

She shrugged, then pushed herself off the dome and, laughing, swam splashing up the river.

•

The jeans Vera sold me that summer were about two sizes too large, and it seemed like they'd been worn before, but that didn't bother me. I even slept in them. I liked how loose they were around my waist, how much space, how much Western freedom they provided around my legs.

But for my sister, Elitsa, life worsened. The West gave her ideas. She would often go to the river and sit on the bank and stare, quietly, for hours on end. She would sigh and her bony shoulders would drop, like the earth below her was pulling on her arms.

•

As the weeks went by, her face lost its plumpness. Her skin got grayer, her eyes muddier. At dinner she kept her head down, and played with her food. She never spoke, not to Mother, not to me. She was as quiet as a painting on a wall.

A doctor came and left puzzled. "I leave puzzled," he said, "she's healthy. I just don't know what's wrong with her."

But I knew. That longing in my sister's eyes, that disappointment, I'd seen them in Vera's eyes before, on the day she had wished to be Bulgarian. It was the same look of defeat, scary and contagious, and because of that look, I kept my distance.

•

I didn't see Vera for a year. Then, one summer day in 1976 as I was washing my jeans in the river, she yelled from the other side.

"Nose, you're buck naked."

That was supposed to embarrass me, but I didn't even twitch.

"I like to rub my ass in the face of the West!" I yelled back, and raised the jeans, dripping with soap.

"What?" she yelled.

"I like to . . ." I waved. "What do you want?"

"Nose, I got something for you. Wait for—and—to—church. All right?"

"What?"

"Wait for the dark. And swim. You hear me?"

"Yeah, I hear you. Are you gonna be there?"

"What?"

I didn't bother. I waved, bent over and went on washing my jeans.

•

I waited for my folks to go to sleep and then I snuck out the window. The lights in my sister's room were still on and I imagined her in bed, eyes tragically fixed on the ceiling.

I hid my clothes under a bush and stepped into the cool water. On the other side I could see the flashlight of the guard and the tip of his cigarette, red in the dark. I swam slowly, making as little noise as possible. In places the river flowed so narrow, people could stand on both sides and talk and almost hear each other, but around the drowned church the river was broad, a quarter mile between the banks.

I stepped on the algae-slick dome and ran my fingers along a string tied to the base of the cross. A nylon bag was fixed to the other end. I freed the bag and was ready to glide away when someone said, "This is for you."

"Vera?"

"I hope you like them."

She swam closer, and was suddenly locked in a circle of light.

"Who's there?" the guard shouted, and his dog barked.

"Go, go, you stupid," Vera said, and splashed away. The circle of light followed.

I held the cross tight, not making a sound. I knew this was no joke. The guards would shoot trespassers if they had to. But Vera swam unhurriedly.

"Faster!" the guard shouted. "Get out here!"

The beam of light etched her naked body in the night. She had the breasts of a woman.

He asked her something and she spoke back. Then he slapped her. He held her very close and felt her body. She kneed him in the groin. He laughed on the ground long after she'd run away naked.

All through, of course, I watched in silence. I could have yelled something to stop him, but then, he had a gun. And so I held the cross and so the river flowed black with night around me and even out on the bank I felt sticky with dirty water.

Inside the bag were Vera's old Adidas shoes. The laces were in bad shape, and the left shoe was a bit torn at the front, but they were still excellent. And suddenly all shame was gone and my heart pounded so hard with new excitement, I was afraid the guards might hear it. On the banks I put the shoes on and they fit perfectly. Well, they were a bit too small for my feet—actually, they were really quite tight—but they were worth the pain. I didn't walk. I swam across the air.

I was striding back home, when someone giggled in the bush. Grass rustled. I hesitated, but snuck through the dark and I saw two people rolling on the ground, and would have watched them in secret if it weren't for the squelching shoes.

"Nose, is that you?" a girl asked. She flinched, and tried to cover herself with a shirt, but this was the night I saw my second pair of breasts. These belonged to my sister.

•

I lay in my room, head under the blanket, trying to make sense of what I'd seen, when someone walked in.

"Nose? Are you sleeping?"

My sister sat on the bed and put her hand on my chest.

"Come on. I know you're awake."

"What do you want?" I said, and threw the blanket off. I could not see her face for the dark, but I could feel that piercing gaze of hers. The house was quiet. Only Father snored in the other room.

"Are you going to tell them?" she said.

"No. What you do is your own business."

She leaned forward and kissed me on the forehead.

"You smell like cigarettes," I said.

"Good night, Nose."

She got up to leave, but I pulled her down.

"Elitsa, what are you ashamed of? Why don't you tell them?"

"They won't understand. Boban's from Srbsko."

"So what?"

I sat up in my bed and took her cold hand.

"What are you gonna do?" I asked her. She shrugged.

"I want to run away with him," she said, and her voice suddenly became softer, calmer, though what she spoke of scared me deeply. "We're going to go West. Get married, have kids. I want to work as a hairstylist in Munich. Boban has a cousin there. She is a hairstylist, or she washes dogs or something." She ran her fingers through my hair. "Oh, Nose," she said. "Tell me what to do."

•

I couldn't tell her. And so she kept living unhappy, wanting to be with that boy day and night but seeing him rarely and in secret. "I am alive," she told me, "only when I'm with him." And then she spoke of their plans: hitchhiking to Munich, staying with Boban's cousin and helping her cut hair. "It's a sure thing, Nose," she'd say, and I believed her.

It was the spring of 1980 when Josip Tito died and even I knew things were about to change in Yugoslavia. The old men in our village whispered that now, with the Yugoslav president finally planted in a mausoleum, our Western neighbor would fall apart. I pictured in my mind the aberration I'd seen in a film, a monster sewn together from the legs and arms and torso of different people. I pictured someone pulling on the thread that held these body parts, the thread unraveling, until the legs and arms and torso came undone. We could snatch a finger then, the land across the river, and patch it up back to our land. That's what the old folks spoke about, drinking their *rakia* in the tavern. Meanwhile, the young folks escaped to the city, following new jobs. There weren't enough children in the village anymore to justify our own school, and so we had to go to another village and study with other kids. Mother lost her job. Grandpa got sick with pneumonia, but Grandma gave him herbs for a month, and he got better. Mostly. Father worked two jobs, plus he stacked hay on the weekends. He no longer had the time to take me plowing.

But Vera and I saw each other often, sometimes twice a month. I never found the courage to speak of the soldier. At night, we swam to the drowned church and played around the cross, very quiet, like river rats. And there, by the cross we kissed our first real kiss. Was it joy I felt? Or was it sadness? To hold her so close and taste her breath, her lips, to slide a finger down her neck, her shoulder, down her back. To lay my palm upon her breasts and know that someone else had done this, with force, while I had watched, tongue swallowed. Her face was silver with moonlight, her hair dripped dark with dark water.

"Do you love me?" she said.

"Yes. Very much," I said. I said, "I wish we never had to leave the water."

"You fool," she said, and kissed me again. "People can't live in rivers."

●

That June, two months before the new *sbor*, our parents found out about Boban. One evening, when I came home for supper, I discovered the whole family quiet in the yard, under the trellis. The village priest was there. The village doctor. Elitsa was weeping, her face flaming red. The priest made her kiss an iron cross and sprinkled her with holy water from an enormous copper. The doctor buckled his bag and glass rattled inside when he picked it up. He winked at me and made for the gate. On his way out, the priest gave my forehead a thrashing with the boxwood foliage.

"What's the matter?" I said, dripping holy water.

Grandpa shook his head. Mother put her hand on my sister's. "You've had your cry," she said.

"Father," I said, "why was the doctor winking? And why did the priest bring such a large copper?"

Father looked at me, furious. "Because your sister, Nose," he said, "requires an Olympic pool to cleanse her."

"Meaning?" I said.

"Meaning," he said, "your sister is pregnant. Meaning," he said, "we'll have to get her married."

•

My family, all dressed up, went to the river. On the other bank Boban's family already waited for us. Mother had washed the collar of my shirt with sugar water so it would stay stiff, and now I felt like that sugar was running down my back in a sweaty, syrupy stream. It itched and I tried to scratch it, but Grandpa told me to quit fidgeting and act like a man. My back got itchier.

From the other side, Boban's father shouted at us, "We want your daughter's hand!"

Father took out a flask and drank *rakia*, then passed it around. The drink tasted bad and set my throat on fire. I coughed and Grandpa smacked my back and shook his head. Father took the flask from me and spilled some liquor on the ground for the departed. The family on the other side did the same.

"I give you my daughter's hand!" Father yelled. "We'll wed them at the *sbor*."

Elitsa's wedding was going to be the culmination of the *sbor*, so everyone prepared. Vera told me that with special permission Mihalaky had transported seven calves across the river, and two had already been slain for jerky. The two of us met often, secretly, by the drowned church.

One evening, after dinner, my family gathered under the trellised vine. The grown-ups smoked and talked of the wedding. My sister and I listened and smiled at each other every time our eyes met.

"Elitsa," Grandma said, and lay a thick bundle on the table. "This is yours now."

My sister untied the bundle and her eyes teared up when she recognized Grandma's best costume readied for the wedding. They lay each part of the dress on its own: the white hemp shirt, the motley apron, the linen gown, festoons of coins, the intricately worked silver earrings. Elitsa lifted the gown, and felt the linen between her fingers, and then began to put it on.

"My God, child," Mother said, "take your jeans off."

Without shame, for we are all blood, Elitsa folded her jeans aside and carefully slipped inside the glowing gown. Mother helped her with the shirt. Grandpa strapped on the apron, and Father, with his fingers shaking, gently put on her ears the silver earrings.

•

I woke up in the middle of the night, because I'd heard a dog howl in my sleep. I turned the lights on and sat up, sweaty in the silence. I went to the kitchen to get a drink of water and I saw Elitsa, ready to sneak out.

"What are you doing?" I said.

"Quiet, *dechko*. I'll be back in no time."

"Are you going out to see him?"

"I want to show him these." She dangled the earrings in her hand.

"And if they catch you?"

She put a finger to her lips, then spun on her heel. Her jeans rasped softly and she sank into the dark. I was this close to waking up Father, but how can you judge others when love is involved? I trusted she knew what she was doing.

For a very long time I could not fall asleep, remembering the howling dog in my dream. And then from the river, a machine gun rattled. The guard dogs started barking and the village dogs answered. I lay in bed petrified, and did not move even when someone banged on the gates.

My sister never used to swim to the Serbian side. Boban always came to meet her on our bank. But that night, strangely, they had decided to meet in Srbsko one last time before the wedding. A soldier in training had seen her climb out of the river. He'd told them both to stop. Two bullets had gone through Elitsa's back as she tried to run.

•

This moment in my life I do not want to remember again:

Mihalaky in smoke and roar is coming up the river, and on his boat lies my sister.

•

There was no *sbor* that year. There were, instead, two funerals. We dressed Elitsa in her wedding costume and lay her beautiful body in a terrible coffin. The silver earrings were not beside her.

The village gathered on our side of the river. On the other side was the other village, burying their boy. I could see the grave they had dug, and the earth was the same, and the depth was the same.

There were three priests on our side, because Grandma would not accept any Communist godlessness. Each of us held a candle, and the people across from us also held candles, and the banks came alive with fire, two hands of fire that could not come together. Between those hands was the river.

The first priest began to sing, and both sides listened. My eyes were on Elitsa. I couldn't let her go and things misted in my head.

"One generation passes away," I thought the priest was singing, "and another comes; but the earth remains forever. The sun rises and the sun goes down, and hastens to the place where it rises. The wind goes toward the West, toward Serbia, and all the rivers run away, East of the West. What has been is what will be, and what has been done is what will be done. Nothing is new under the sun."

The voice of the priest died down, and then a priest on the other side sang. The words piled on my heart like stones and

I thought how much I wanted to be like the river, which had no memory, and how little like the earth, which could never forget.

•

Mother quit the factory and locked herself home. She said her hands burned with her daughter's blood. Father began to frequent the cooperative distillery at the end of the village. At first he claimed that assisting people with loading their plums, peaches, grapes into the cauldrons kept his mind blank; then that he was simply sampling the first *rakia* which trickled out the spout, so he could advise the folk how to boil better drink.

He lost both his jobs soon, and so it was up to me to feed the family. I started working in the coal mine, because the money was good, and because I wanted, with my pick, to gut the land we walked on.

The control across the borders tightened. Both countries put nets along the banks and blocked buffer zones at the narrow waist of the river where the villagers used to call to one another. The *sbor*s were canceled. Vera and I no longer met, though we found two small hills we could sort of see each other from, like dots in the distance. But these hills were too far away and we did not go there often.

Almost every night, I dreamed of Elitsa.

"I saw her just before she left," I would tell my mother. "I could have stopped her."

"Then why didn't you?" Mother would ask.

Sometimes I went to the river and threw stones over the fence, into the water, and imagined those two silver earrings, settling into the silty bottom.

"Give back the earrings," I'd scream, "you spineless, muddy thief!"

•

I worked double shifts in the mine and was able to put something aside. I took care of Mother, who never left her bed, and occasionally brought bread and cheese to Father at the distillers. "Mother is sick," I'd tell him, but he pretended not to hear. "More heat," he'd call, and kneel by the trickle to sample some *parvak*.

Vera and I wrote letters for a while, but after each letter there was a longer period of silence before the new one arrived. One day, in the summer of 1990, I received a brief note:

Dear Nose. I'm getting married. I want you at my wedding. I live in Beograd now. I'm sending you money. Please come.

There was, of course, no money in the envelope. Someone had stolen it on the way.

Each day I reread the letter, and thought of the way Vera had written those words, in her elegant, thin writing, and I thought of this man she had fallen in love with, and I wondered if she loved him as much as she had loved me, by the cross, in the river. I made plans to get a passport.

•

Two weeks before the wedding, Mother died. The doctor couldn't tell us of what. Of grief, the wailers said, and threw their black kerchiefs over their heads like ash. Father brought his drinking guiltily to the empty house. One day he poured me a glass of *rakia* and made me gulp it down. We killed the bottle. Then he looked me in the eye and grabbed my hand. Poor soul, he thought he was squeezing it hard.

"My son," he said, "I want to see the fields."

We staggered out of the village, finishing a second bottle. When we reached the fields, we sat down and watched in silence. After the fall of communism, organized agriculture had died in many areas, and now everything was overgrown with thornbush and nettles.

"What happened, Nose?" Father said. "I thought we held him

good, this bastard, in both hands. Remember what I taught you? Hold tight, choke the bastard and things will be all right? Well, shit, Nose. I was wrong."

And he spat against the wind, in his own face.

•

Three years passed before Vera wrote again. *Nose, I have a son. I'm sending you a picture. His name is Vladislav. Guess who we named him after? Come and visit us. We have money now, so don't worry. Goran just got back from a mission in Kosovo. Can you come?*

My father wanted to see the picture. He stared at it for a long time, and his eyes watered.

"My God, Nose," he said. "I can't see anything. I think I've finally gone blind."

"You want me to call the doctor?"

"Yes," he said, "but for yourself. Quit the mine, or that cough will take you."

"And what do we do for money?"

"You'll find some for my funeral. Then you'll go away."

I sat by his side and lay a hand on his forehead. "You're burning. I'll call the doctor."

"Nose," he said, "I've finally figured it out. Here is my paternal advice: Go away. You can't have a life here. You must forget about your sister, about your mother, about me. Go west. Get a job in Spain, or in Germany, or anywhere; start from scratch. Break each chain. This land is a bitch and you can't expect anything good from a bitch."

He took my hand and he kissed it.

"Go get the priest," he said.

•

I worked the mine until, in the spring of 1995, my boss, who'd come from some big, important city to the east, asked me, three times in a row, to repeat my request for an extra shift. Three times I repeated before he threw his arms up in despair. "I can't understand your dialect, *mayna*," he said. "Too Serbian for me." So I beat him up and was fired.

After that, I spent my days in the village tavern, every now and then lifting my hand before my eyes to check if I hadn't finally gone blind. It's a tough lot to be last in your bloodline. I thought of my father's advice, which seemed foolish, of my sister making plans to go west and of how I had done nothing to stop her from swimming to her death.

Almost every night I had the same dream. I was diving at the drowned church, looking through its window, at walls no longer covered with the murals of saints and martyrs. Instead, I could see my sister and my mother, my father, Grandpa, Grandma, Vera, people from our village and from the village across the border, painted motionless on the walls, with their eyes on my face. And every time, as I tried to push up to the surface, I discovered that my hands were locked together on the other side of the bars.

I would wake up with a yell, the voice of my sister echoing in the room.

I have some doubts, she would say, *some suspicions, that these earrings aren't really silver.*

.

In the spring of 1999 the United States attacked Serbia. Kosovo, the field where the Serb had once, many centuries ago, surrendered to the Turk, had once again become the ground of battle. Three or four times I saw American planes swoop over our village with a boom. Serbia, it seemed, was a land not large enough for their maneuvers at ultrasonic speed. They cut corners from our sky and went back to drop their bombs on our neighbors. The news that Vera's husband had been killed came as no surprise. Her letter ended like this: *Nose, I have my son and you. Please come. There is no one else.*

The day I received the letter, I swam to the drowned church without taking my shoes or my clothes off. I held the cross and shivered for a long time, and finally I dove down and down to the rocky bottom. I gripped the bars on the church gates tightly and listened to the screaming of my lungs while they squeezed out every molecule of oxygen. I wish I could say that I saw my life unwinding thread by thread before my eyes: happy moments alternating with sad, or that my sister, bathed in glorious light, came out of the church to take my drowning hand. But there was only darkness, the booming of water, of blood.

Yes, I am a coward. I have an ugly nose, and the heart of a mouse, and the only drowning I can do is in a bottle of *rakia*. I swam out and lay on the bank. And as I breathed with new thirst, a boom shook the air, and I saw a silver plane storm out of Serbia. The plane thundered over my head and, chasing it, I saw a missile, quickly losing height. Hissing, the missile stabbed the river, the rusty cross, the drowned church underneath. A large, muddy finger shook at the sky.

I wrote Vera right away. *When Sister died,* I wrote, *I thought half of my world ended. With my parents, the other half. I thought these deaths were meant to punish me for something. I was chained to this village, and the pull of all the bones below me was impossible to escape. But now I see that these deaths were meant to set me free, to get me moving. Like links in a chain snapping, one after the other. If the church can sever its brick roots, so can I. I'm free at last, so wait for me. I'm coming as soon as I save up some cash.*

•

Not long after, a Greek company opened a chicken factory in the village. My job was to make sure no bad eggs made it in the cartons. I saved some money, tried to drink less. I even cleaned the house. In the basement, in a dusty chestnut box, I found the leather shoes, the old forgotten flowers. I cut off the toe caps and put them on, and felt so good, so quick and light. Unlucky, wretched brothers. No laces, worn-out soles from walking in circles. Where will you take me?

I dug up the two jars of money I had kept hidden in the yard and caught a bus to town. It wasn't hard to buy American dollars. I returned to the village and lay carnations on the graves and asked the dead for forgiveness. Then I went to the river. I put most of the money and Vladislav's picture in a plastic bag, tucked the bag in my pocket along with some cash for bribes and, with my eyes closed, swam toward Srbsko.

Cool water, the pull of current, brown old leaves whirlpooling in clumps. A thick branch flows by, bark gone, smooth and rotten. What binds a man to land or water?

When I stepped on the Serbian bank, two guards already held me in the aim of their guns.

"Two hundred," I said, and took out the soaking wad.

"We could kill you instead."

"Or give me a kiss. A pat on the ass?"

They started laughing. The good thing about our countries, the reassuring thing that keeps us falling harder, is that if you can't buy something with money, you can buy it with a lot of money. I counted off two hundred more.

They escorted me up the road, to a frontier post where I paid the last hundred I'd prepared. A Turkish TIR driver agreed to take me to Beograd. There I caught a cab and showed an envelope Vera had sent me.

"I need to get there," I said.

"You Bulgarian?" the cabdriver asked.

"Does it matter?"

"Well, shit, it matters. If you're Serbian, that's fine. But if you're a *Bugar*, it isn't. It's also not fine if you are Albanian, or if you are a Croat. And if you are Muslim, well, shit, then it also isn't fine."

"Just take me to this address."

The cabdriver turned around and fixed me with his blue eyes.

"I'm only gonna ask you once," he said. "Are you Bulgarian or are you a Serb?"

"I don't know."

"Oh, well, then," he said, "get the fuck out of my cab and think it over. You ugly-nosed Bulgarian bastard. Letting Americans bomb us, handing over your bases. Slavic brothers!"

Then, as I was getting out, he spat on me.

•

And now we are back at the beginning. I'm standing outside Vera's apartment, with flowers in one hand and a bar of Milka chocolate in the other. I'm rehearsing the question. I think of how I'm going to greet her, of what I'm going to say. Will the little boy like me? Will she? Will she let me help her raise him? Can we get married, have children of our own? Because I'm finally ready.

An iron safety grid protects the door. I ring the bell and little feet run on the other side.

"Who's there?" a thin voice asks.

"It's Nose," I say.

"Step closer to the spy hole."

I lean forward.

"No, to the lower one." I kneel down so the boy can peep through the hole drilled at his height.

"Put your face closer," he says. He's quiet for a moment. "Did Mama do that?"

"It's no big deal."

He unlocks the door, but keeps the iron grid between us.

"Sorry to say it, but it looks like a big deal," he says in all seriousness.

"Can I come in?"

"I'm alone. But you can sit outside and wait until they return. I'll keep you company."

We sit on both sides of the grid. He is a tiny boy and looks like Vera. Her eyes, her chin, her bright, white face. All that will change with time.

"I haven't had Milka in forever," he says as I pass him the chocolate through the grid. "Thanks, Uncle."

"Don't eat things a stranger gives you."

"You are no stranger. You're Nose."

He tells me about kindergarten. About a boy who beats him up. His face is grave. Oh, little friend, those troubles now seem big.

"But I'm a soldier," he says, "like Daddy. I won't give up. I'll fight."

Then he is quiet. He munches on the chocolate. He offers me a block, which I refuse.

"You miss your dad?" I say.

He nods. "But now we have Dadan and Mama is happy."

"Who's Dadan?" My throat gets dry.

"Dadan," the boy says. "My second father."

"Your second father," I say, and rest my head against the cold iron.

"He's very nice to me," the boy says. "Yes, very nice."

He talks, sweet voice, and I struggle to resist the venom of my thoughts.

The elevator arrives with a rattle. Its door slides open, bright light out of the cell. Dadan, tall, handsome in his face, walks out with a string bag of groceries: potatoes, yogurt, green onions, white bread. He looks at me and nods, confused.

Then out comes Vera. Bright, speckled face, firm sappy lips.

"My God," she says. The old spot grows red above her lip and she hangs on my neck.

I lose my grip, the earth below my feet. It feels then like everything is over. She's found someone else to care for her, she's built a new life in which there is no room for me. In a moment, I'll smile politely and follow them inside their place, I'll eat the dinner they feed me—*musaka* with *tarator*. I'll listen to Vladislav sing songs and recite poems. Then afterward, while Vera tucks him in, I'll talk to Dadan—or, rather, he'll talk to me: about how much he loves her, about *their* plans—and I will listen and agree. At last he'll go to bed, and under the dim kitchen light Vera and I will wade deep into the night. She'll finish the wine Dadan shared with her for dinner, she'll put her hand on mine. "My dear Nose," she'll say, or something to that effect. But even then I won't find courage to speak. Broken, not having slept all night, I'll rise up early and, cowardly again, I'll slip out and hitchhike home.

"My dear Nose," Vera says now, and really leads me inside the apartment, "you look beaten from the road." *Beaten* is the word she uses. And then it hits me, the way a hoe hits a snake over the skull. This is the last link of the chain falling. Vera and Dadan will set me free. With them, the last connection to the past is gone.

Who binds a man to land or water, I wonder, if not that man himself?

"I've never felt so good before," I say, and mean it, and watch her lead the way through the dark hallway. I am no river, but I'm not made of clay.

BUYING LENIN

When Grandpa learned I was leaving for America to study, he wrote me a goodbye note. "You rotten capitalist pig," the note read, "have a safe flight. Love, Grandpa." It was written on a creased red ballot from the 1991 elections, which was a cornerstone in Grandpa's Communist ballot collection, and it bore the signatures of everybody in the village of Leningrad. I was touched to receive such an honor, so I sat down, took out a one-dollar bill, and wrote Grandpa the following reply: "You communist dupe, thanks for the letter. I'm leaving tomorrow, and when I get there I'll try to marry an American woman ASAP. I'll be sure to have lots of American children. Love, your grandson."

•

There was no good reason for me to be in America. Back home I wasn't starving, at least not in the corporeal sense. No war had driven me away or stranded me on foreign shores. I left because I could, because I carried in my blood the rabies of the West. In high school, while most of my peers were busy drinking, smoking, having sex, playing dice, lying to their parents, hitchhiking to the sea, counterfeiting money or making bombs for soccer games, I studied English. I memorized words and grammar rules and practiced tongue twisters, specifically designed for Eastern Europeans. *Remember the money*, I repeated over and over again down the street, under the shower, even in my sleep. *Remember the money, remember the money, remember the money.* Phrases like this, I'd heard, helped you break your tongue.

My parents must have been proud to have such a studious son. But no matter how good my grades, Grandpa never brought himself to share their sentiments. He despised the West, its moral degradation and lack of values. As a child, I could read only those books he deemed appropriate. *Party Secret* was appropriate. *Treasure Island* was not. The English language, Grandpa insisted, was a rabid dog, and sometimes a single bite was all it took for its poison to reach your brain and turn it to crabapple mash. "Do you know, *sinko,*" Grandpa asked me once, "what it is like to have crabapple mash for brains?" I shook my head, mortified. "Read English books, my son, and find out for yourself."

The first few years after my grandmother's death, he stayed in his native village, close to her grave. But after Grandpa had a minor stroke, my father convinced him to come back to Sofia. He arrived at our threshold with two bags—one full of socks, pants and drawers, the other of dusty books. "An educational gift," he said, and hung the bag over my shoulder and tousled my hair, as though I were still a child.

Every week, for a few months, he fed me a different book. Partisans, plots against the tsarist regime. "Grandpa, please," I'd say. "I have to study."

"What you have to do is acquire a taste." He'd leave me to read but then would barge into my room a minute later with some weak excuse. Had I called him? Did I need help with a difficult passage?

"Grandpa, these are children's books."

"First children's books, then Lenin's." He'd sit at the foot of my bed, and motion me to keep on reading.

If I came home from school frightened because a stray dog had chased me down the street, Grandpa would only sigh. Could I imagine Kalitko the shepherd scared of a little dog? If I complained of bullies Grandpa would shake his head. "Imagine Mitko Palauzov whining."

"Mitko Palauzov was killed in a dugout."

"A brave and daring boy indeed," Grandpa would say, and pinch his nose to stop the inevitable tears.

And so one day I packed up the books and left them in his room with a note. *Recycle for toilet paper.* Next time he saw me, I was reading *The Call of the Wild*.

From then on Grandpa listened to the radio a lot, read the Communist newspaper *Duma* and the collected volumes of his beloved Lenin. He smoked unfiltered cigarettes on the balcony and recited passages from volume twelve to the sparrows along the TV antenna. My parents were concerned. I was truly amused. "Did you hear, Grandpa," I asked him once, "about the giraffe who could fly?"

"Giraffes can't fly," he said. I told him I'd just read so in *Duma*, on the front page at that, and he rubbed his chin. He pulled on his mustache. "Perhaps a meter or two?" he said.

"Did you hear, Grandpa," I kept going, "that last night in Moscow Yeltsin fed vodka to Lenin's corpse? They killed the bottle together and, hand in hand, zigzagged along the square."

There was something exhilarating about teasing Grandpa. On the one hand, I was ashamed, but on the other . . . Sometimes, of course, I went too far and he tried to smack me with his cane. "Why aren't you five again?" he'd say. "I'd make your ears like a donkey's."

It was not the teasing but rather the sight of me hunched over an abridged edition of the *Oxford English Dictionary* that finally drove Grandpa back to his native village. When my father asked for an explanation, he could not let himself admit the real reason. "I'm tired of looking at walls," he said instead. "I'm tired of watching the sparrows shit. I need my Balkan slopes, my river. I need to tidy your mother's grave." We said nothing on parting. He shook my hand.

Without Grandpa to distract me, I focused on my studies. It had become popular at that time for kids to take the SAT and try their luck abroad. Early in the spring of 1999 I got admitted to the University of Arkansas, and my scores were good enough to earn me a full scholarship, room and board, even a plane ticket.

My parents drove me to Grandpa's village house so I could share the news with him in person. They did not believe that phones could handle important news.

"America," Grandpa said when I told him. I could see the word dislodge itself from his acid stomach, stick in his throat and be expelled at last onto the courtyard tiles. He watched me and pulled on his mustache.

"My grandson, a capitalist," he said. "After all I've been through."

•

What Grandpa had been through was basically this:

The year was 1944. Grandpa was in his mid-twenties. His face was tough but fair. His nose was sharp. His dark eyes glowed with the spark of something new, great and profoundly world-changing. He was poor. "I," he often told me, "would eat bread with crabapples for breakfast. Bread with crabapples for lunch. And crabapples for dinner, because by dinnertime, the bread would be gone."

That's why when the Communists came to his village to steal food, Grandpa joined them. They had all run to the woods where they dug out underground bunkers, and lived in them for weeks on end—day and night, down there in the dugouts. Outside, the Fascists sniffed for them, trying to hunt them down with their Alsatians, with their guns and bombs and missiles. "If you think a grave is too narrow," Grandpa told me on one occasion, "make yourself a dugout. No, no, make yourself a dugout and get fifteen people to join you in it for a week. And get a couple pregnant women, too. And a hungry goat. Then go around telling everybody a grave is the narrowest thing on earth."

"Old man, I never said a grave was the narrowest thing."

"But you were thinking it."

So finally Grandpa got too hungry to stay in the dugout and decided to strap on a shotgun and go down to the village for food. When he arrived, he found everything changed. A red flag was flapping from the church tower. The church had been shut down and turned into a meeting hall. There had been an uprising, the peasants told him, a revolution that overthrew the old regime. While Grandpa was hiding in the dugout, communism sprouted fragrant blooms. All people now walked free, and their dark eyes glowed with the spark of something new, great and profoundly world-changing. Grandpa fell to his knees and wept and kissed the soil of the motherland. Immediately, he was assimilated by the Party. Immediately, as a heroic partisan who'd suffered in a dugout, he was given a high position in the Fatherland Front. Immediately, he climbed further up the ladder and moved to the city, where he became something-something of the something-something department. He got an apartment, married Grandma; a year later my father was born.

.

I arrived in Arkansas on August 11, 1999. At the airport I was picked up by two young men and a girl, all in suits. They were from some sort of an organization that cared a whole lot for international students.

"Welcome to America," they said in one warm, friendly voice, and their honest faces beamed. In the car they gave me a Bible.

"Do you know what this is?" the girl bellowed slowly.

"No," I said. She seemed genuinely pleased.

"These are the deeds of our Savior. The word of our Lord."

"Oh, Lenin's collected works," I said. "Which volume?"

•

My first week in America unfolded under the banner of International Orientation. I made acquaintances from countries smaller than my own. I shook hands with black people. Those of us for whom English was a second language were instructed what to expect when it was fixin' to rain. What "yonder" meant, and how it was "a bummer" to be there "yonder" with no umbrella and it "fixin' to rain."

Every English word I knew, I had once written at least ten times in notebooks Grandpa brought from the Fatherland Front. Each page in these notebooks was a cliff face against which I shouted. The words flew back at me, smashed into the rock again, rushed back. By the end of high school I had filled with echoes so many notebooks they towered on each side of my desk.

But now in America, I was exposed to words I didn't know. And sometimes words I knew on their own made no sense collected together. What was a hotpocket? I wondered. Why was my roommate so excited to see two girls across the hallway making out? What were they making out? I felt estranged, often confused, until gradually, with time, the world around me seeped in through my eyes, ears, tongue. At last the words rose liberated. I was ecstatic, lexicon drunk. I talked so much my roommate eventually quit spending time in our room and returned only after I'd gone to bed. I cornered random professors during their office hours and asked them questions that required long-winded answers. I spoke with strangers on the street, knowing I was being a creep. Such knowledge couldn't stop me. My ears rang, my tongue swelled up. I went on for months, until one day I understood that nothing I said mattered to those around me. No one knew where I was from, or cared to know. I had nothing to say to this world.

I barricaded myself in the dorm—a narrow cell-like room cluttered with my roommate's microwave, refrigerator, computer, speakers and subwoofer, TV, Nintendo. I watched *Married with Children* and *Howard Stern*. I spoke with my parents, rarely, briefly, because the calling rates were high. I cradled the receiver, fondled the thin umbilical cord of the phone that stretched ten thousand miles across the sea. I listened to my mother and felt almost connected. But when the line was cut, I was alone.

•

When he was thirty and holding the position something-of-the-something, Grandpa met the woman of his heart. It was the classic Communist love story: They met at an evening gathering of the Party. Grandma came in late, wet from the rain, took the only free seat, which was next to Grandpa, and fell asleep on his shoulder. He disapproved of her lack of interest in Party matters, and right there on the spot he fell in love with her scent, with her breath on his neck. After she woke up, they talked about pure ideals and the bright future, about the capitalist evil of the West, about the nurturing embrace of the Soviet Union and, most important, about Lenin. Grandpa found out that they both shared the same passion for following his shining example, and so he took Grandma to the Civil Office where they got married.

Grandma died of breast cancer in 1989, only a month after communism was abolished in Bulgaria. I was eight and I remember it all very clearly. We buried her in the village. We put the open coffin in a cart and tied the cart to a tractor, and the tractor pulled the cart and the coffin and we walked behind it all. Grandpa sat by the coffin, and held Grandma's dead hand. I don't think it actually rained that day, but in my memories I see wind and clouds and rain; the quiet, cold rain that falls when you lose someone close to your heart. Grandpa shed no tears. He sat in the cart, the rain from my memory falling on him, on his bald head, on the coffin, on Grandma's closed eyes; the music flowing around them—deep, sad music of the oboe, the trumpet, the drum. There is no priest at a Communist funeral. Grandpa read from a book, volume twelve of Lenin's collected works. His words rose to the sky, and the rain knocked them down to the ground.

"It's a good grave," Grandpa was saying when it was all over. "It's not as narrow as a dugout, which makes it good. Right? It's not too narrow, right? She'll be all right in it. Certainly, she'll be all right."

It was this funeral, with Grandpa's words rising and falling broken in the mud, that I started to dream about during my sophomore year of college. I no longer went to class regularly because the professors' words now tormented me like a rash, but I read a great deal in my room. I had chosen psychology as my major, mostly on a whim, so I devoured Freud and Jung in industrial quantities. "Their words are the yeast that brings my brain to life," I'd tell Grandpa a few months later, and he would say, "You got that right. Your brain is dough. Or better yet—crabapple mash."

I was fascinated to learn that our dreams reflected not only our personal unconscious but also the collective. My God, was there such a thing? A collective unconscious? If so, I wanted in. I longed to be a part of it; connected, to dream the dreams of other people, others to dream my dreams. I went to sleep hoping to dream vivid, transcendental symbols.

Today, I wrote in a little journal, *I dreamed of Father on the sofa, peeling sunflower seeds, his socks pulled off halfway like donkey ears.*

I dreamed of Mother spooning yogurt from a jar.

I dreamed of Grandpa, waiting in the hallway to trip me up with his cane.

It was after this particular dream and after two years without Grandpa's voice that I finally picked up the phone, on the eve of Fourth of July, and dialed.

I tried to imagine him, out in the yard, straining his eyes to read in the dusk. He would hear the ringing phone, and slowly, with pain, make his way into the house. I tried to see his face, so old and terrifying that I graced it with an imaginary beard to hide its age. The beard must be white, I thought. No, yellow from nicotine. A lion's mane, angry and wild, which had consumed the face. Two fiery eyes peered out from the mane, burning with Lenin's words. *Electrification plus Soviet power equals Communism. Give us the child for eight years and it will be a Bolshevik forever.* I waited, petrified, for his incinerating voice to turn me to ash, for his brimstone breath to scatter me like wind.

"Grandpa," I said.

"Sinko."

I shivered so bad the cord between us crackled. I was afraid he'd hung up already.

"Grandpa, are you there?"

"I'm here."

"You're there," I said. I said, "Grandpa, there is so much water between us. We are so far apart."

"We are," he said. "But blood, I hope, is thicker than the ocean."

•

After Grandma's funeral, Grandpa had refused to leave the village. In one year he'd lost everything a man could lose: the woman of his heart, and the love of his life—the Party.

"There is no place for me in the city," I remember him telling my Dad. "I have no desire to serve these traitors. Let capitalism corrupt them all, these bastards, these murderers of innocent women."

Grandpa was convinced that it had been the fall of communism that had killed Grandma. "Her cancer was a consequence of the grave disappointments of her pure and idealistic heart," Grandpa would explain. "She could not watch her dreams being trampled on so she did the only possible thing an honest woman could do—she died."

Grandpa bought a village house so he could be close to Grandma, and every day at three o'clock in the afternoon he went to her grave, sat by the tombstone, opened volume twelve of Lenin's collected works and read aloud. Summer or winter, he was there, reading. He never skipped a day, and it was there, at Grandma's grave, that the idea hit him.

"Nothing is lost," he told me and my parents on one Saturday visit. "Communism may be dead all over this country, but ideals never die. I will bring it all here, to the village. I will build it all from scratch."

On October 25, 1993, the great October village revolution took place, quietly, underground, without much ado. At that time, everybody who was sixty or younger had already left the village to live in the city, and so those who remained were people pure and strong of heart, in whom the idea was still alive and whose dark eyes glowed with the spark of something new, great and profoundly world-changing. Officially, the village was still part of Bulgaria, and it had a mayor who answered to the national government and so on and so forth; but secretly, underground, it was the new Communist village party that decided its fate. The name of the village was changed from Valchidol to Leningrad. Grandpa was unanimously elected secretary general.

Every evening there was a Party meeting in the old village hall, where the seat next to Grandpa was always left vacant, and water was sprinkled from a hose outside on the windows to create the illusion of rain.

"Communism blossoms better with moisture," Grandpa explained, when the other Party members questioned his decision; in fact, he was thinking of Grandma and the rain on their first meeting. And indeed, communism in Leningrad blossomed.

Grandpa and the villagers decided to salvage every Communist artifact remaining in Bulgaria and bring them all to

Leningrad: to the living museum of the Communist doctrine. Monuments chiseled under the red ideal were being demolished all over the country. Statues, erected decades ago, proudly reminding, glorifying, promising, were now pulled down and melted for scrap. Poets once extolled now lay forgotten. Their paper bodies gathered dust. Their ink blood washed away by rainwater.

Once the two years of silence was broken by our call, Grandpa began to write me letters. I was amazed, but not surprised, to learn that, now back in Leningrad, he'd still not given up on his ideas. In one of his letters, Grandpa told me that the villagers had convinced a bunch of Gypsies to do the salvaging for them. "Comrade Hassan, his wife and their thirteen Gypsy children," Grandpa wrote, "doubtlessly inspired by the bright Communist ideal, and only mildly stimulated by the money and the two pigs we gave them, have promised to supply our village with the best of the best 'red' artifacts that could be found across our pitiful country. Today the comrade Gypsies brought us their first gift: a monument of the Nameless Russian Soldier, liberator from the Turks, slightly deformed from the waist down, and with a missing shotgun, but otherwise in excellent condition. The monument now stands proud next to the statues of Alyosha, Seryoja and the Nameless Maiden of Minsk."

•

I made a point of talking to Grandpa twice a month. At first we spoke of little things. He told me of rearranging his collection of Communist artifacts, of reading *The Modern Woman* at Grandma's grave. For thirty years, he said, she had received this magazine once a month and he didn't want to break the cycle.

"Although," he told me once, "I'm slightly tired of weight loss diets and relationship advice. Three rules for dating, three steps to getting slim. Nowadays, Grandson, there are three easy steps for everything under the sun."

I asked him if this meant he no longer read Lenin.

"I thought you'd never ask," he said. "Listen," he said, "I have been thinking. Why don't I recommend a book for you?"

I begged him not to start again.

"I've failed you," he said. "Sometimes I think you went away just to spite me."

I told him that, contrary to what he thought, he was not the center of the world. I got along with my American friends handsomely, I felt at home.

"Bullshit," he said. "You hate it there."

My loneliness rose up in me like steam over a barren field. I choked with rage. Surely he had no way of knowing that these friends I spoke of did not exist? That I hadn't left my room in days?

"You are a stubborn mule, Grandpa," I declared. "Give up already. Burn your collection of artifacts, your books. The past is dead."

"Ideals never die," he said.

"But people do. Or what, you think you'll live forever?"

I knew it was wrong of me to say such things, but I wanted to hurt him. And when he laughed, I knew I had.

"I think you're jealous," he said. "As jealous as a one-legged maiden before the village dance. You can't stand the thought that your grandpa is happy and you are not."

"I can't stand the thought that my grandpa is crazy. That he has filled his life with chaff."

"A steady job? A loving wife? A son I managed to send to college? Is all this chaff to you?"

I must have kept silent for quite some time. At last he spoke. "My boy, do you remember the parades? I think about them often. You were so I little, I'd let you sit on my shoulders and we'd march together with the crowd. I'd buy you a red balloon, a paper flag. You'd chant for the Party and sing the songs. You knew them all by heart."

"I remember," I said. But it was not the parades I thought about.

•

When I was still a boy, I spent my summers at the village, with my grandparents. In the winter they lived in Sofia, two blocks away from our apartment; but when the weather warmed, they always packed and left.

At least once a summer, when the moon was full, Grandpa would take me crawfish hunting. We spent most of the day in the yard, reinforcing the bottoms of big bags with tape, patching the holes from previous hunts. Finally, when we were done, we sat on the porch and watched the sun dive behind the Balkan peaks. Grandpa lit a cigarette, took out his pocket knife and etched patterns along the bark of the chestnut sticks we had prepared for catching the crawfish. We waited for the moon to rise, and sometimes Grandma sat by us and sang, or Grandpa told stories of the days he had been out in the woods, hiding in the dugouts with his Communist comrades.

When the moon was finally up, shining brightly, Grandpa would get to his feet and stretch. "They are out on pasture," he would say. "Let's get them."

Grandma made paté sandwiches for the road and wrapped them in paper napkins that were always difficult to peel off completely. She wished us luck, and we left the house and walked out of the village and then on the muddy path through the woods. Grandpa carried the bags and sticks, and I followed. The moon was bright above us, lighting our way; the wind soft on our faces. Somewhere close by the river was booming.

We would step out of the woods, into the meadow, and with the night sky unfolding above us, we would see them. The river and the crawfish. The river always dark and roaring, the crawfish on the grass, moving slowly, pinching blades of crowfoot.

We would sit on the grass, take out the sandwiches and eat. In the sharp moonlight the wet bodies of the crawfish glistened like live coal, and the banks seemed covered with burning embers and the hundreds of little eyes that watched us through the dark. When we were done eating, the hunt began.

Grandpa would give me a stick and a bag. Hundreds of twitching crawfish at our feet: poke their pincers with the stick, and they pinch as hard as they can. I learned to lift them, then shake them off in the bag. One by one you collect.

"They are easy prey," Grandpa would say. "You catch one, but the others don't run away. The others don't even know you are there until you pick them up, and even then they still have no idea."

One, two, three hours. The moon, tiring, swims toward the horizon. The east blazes red. And then the crawfish in perfect synchrony turn around and slowly, quietly, make for the river. She takes their bodies back, and lulls them to their sleep as a new day ripens. We sit on the grass, our bags heavy with prey. I fall asleep on Grandpa's shoulder. He carries me home to the village. But first, he lets the crawfish go.

•

The possibility that I was jealous of my grandfather's life gave me no rest. At night, hugging the pillow, I tried to picture him my age, remembering vaguely a portrait Grandma had kept on her night stand—handsome face, eyes burning with Communist ideals, lips curved in a smile, a sickle readied for revolutionary harvests, sharp enough to change the world. And what could be said of my eyes and lips?

I wondered if I had made a mistake resisting him all these years. But then, when I would finally begin to drowse off, Grandma would come to my bed and caress my forehead the way she'd done when I had been sick with fever. "Your grandpa's dying," she'd say. "We are expecting him soon. But please, my dear, next time you talk to him, ask him to stop reading Lenin at my grave."

•

"I'm writing my senior thesis on you," I told him one day in my final year of college.

On the other end of the line something fell with a deafening bang. Grandpa's voice seemed to come from a distance across the room, and then, much closer.

"I dropped the receiver," he said apologetically. "You bored me so much I fell asleep."

"What you call boredom," I corrected him, "psychology refers to as denial. I talk about this in my paper and also I explain why you believe the things you do. Care to hear?"

"Categorically not."

I cleared my throat. *"The Lenin Complex is the representation of a person's overwhelming need to organize his life around the blind following of an ideology, without regard for the validity of its ideals; of a person's consuming need to participate in a group. Both the need and the necessity are motivated by irrational fears of loneliness and/or rejection."*

I let the silence between us accentuate my words.

"I never knew," Grandpa said, "that my grandson was so damned crazy, and/or such an ass."

•

I finished my undergraduate studies summa cum laude, which was something, I'd noticed, Americans liked to mention if they'd done. Still, I had no idea what to do next. I applied and was accepted to graduate school. I tried to save up money for a ticket home, but the graduate program was in another state and all my savings were wasted on the move. I hoped that a change of scenery would lift my spirits. Instead, I found it increasingly difficult to talk to people. Mostly I stayed home, missed Bulgaria as much as I ever had, and for some strange reason, now missed Arkansas as well.

"Grandpa," I sometimes asked over the phone, "what are you eating?"

"Watermelon with cheese."

"Is it good?"

"It was good for Lenin, his favorite snack."

"I wish I had a plateful."

"You always hated fruits with cheese."

"Grandpa, what are you drinking?"

"Yogurt."

"Is it good?"

"The best there ever was."

"Grandpa, what are you looking at, right now, this very moment?"

"The slopes above the house. The linden trees are white. The wind has turned their leaves before the coming rain."

I knew he was teasing me, sowing my wounds with salt, and still I kept asking. If only I could borrow his eyes for an instant, if only I could steal his tongue—I would eat my fill of bread and cheese, drain six gourds of water from our well, fill my gaze with slopes, fields, rivers.

"Grandpa," I said once, squeezing the receiver. "I have been thinking. How about you recommend a book?"

"A book?" he said. "I thought you hated my books."

I told him to forget it.

"Is the prodigal son doing an about-face?"

"I'm hanging up."

But I didn't. We were quiet for a while. I could tell he was choosing his words carefully. "I'll give you something better than a book," he said at last. "I'll give you three easy steps."

•

"First," Grandpa told me, "you need to learn who Lenin really was. Obtain volume thirty-seven of his collected works."

"*Letters to Relatives,*" I repeated the subtitle after I had obtained the tome.

"The best kind of letters. Read those to his sister. No," he corrected himself, "read *to his mother* first."

Mother dearest, Lenin wrote, *send me some money because I've spent mine.* In one letter he was in Munich, in another he was in Prague. In one he crossed a half-constructed bridge in a horse sleigh, and in another he wanted to see a doctor for his catarrh. Like me, he'd spent his youth abroad, in exile. He sounded permanently hungry and cold. He dreamed of sheepskin coats, felt boots, fur caps. *Mother dearest*, he complained from an Austrian train station, *I don't understand the Germans at all. I kept asking the conductor the same question, unable to understand his answer, until at last he stormed angrily away.*

Mother dearest, I am miserable without letters from home. You must write without waiting for an address.

My life goes on as usual. I stroll to the library outside town, I stroll in the neighborhood, and sleep enough for two . . .

The letters weren't half bad. That's what I told Grandpa. "Grandpa dearest, Lenin and I are so much alike."

He snickered.

"What's that supposed to mean?"

He said he didn't know. He said he had his doubts.

"Your grandson's finally doing what you want him and *now* you sulk?"

"I'm not sulking," he said. "But I've been thinking. When I was young I hid in dugouts. I didn't read books."

"Should I dig a hole in the ground, then? Is this step two?"

"My boy," he said. "Don't be an ass."

He'd pestered me with this ideological crap all my life, and now, when I was finally getting interested, he had his doubts. "Are you afraid I'll take your Lenin away from you?"

"I'm hanging up," he said.

"Don't bother," I told him, and slammed down the phone.

•

I kept reading. Notebooks on Imperialism, on the Agrarian Question. But with every page, whatever connection I'd felt through the letters weakened irretrievably. Grandpa was right—these texts would get me nowhere.

"You're twenty-five," he'd told me once. "Your blood should be champagne, not yogurt. Go out. Mix with the living, forget the dead."

I felt low for hanging up on him like that. As penance, I decided to buy him something little from eBay—a badge, a pin, a set of cheap stamps he could add to his collection. I did not expect to stumble upon an auction for Lenin's corpse. *CCCP Creator Lenin. Mint Condition*, it said. *You are bidding for the body of Vladimir Ilyich Lenin. The body is in excellent condition and comes with a refrigerated coffin that works on both American and European current.* The Buy It Now button indicated a price of five dollars flat. And five more for worldwide shipping. The seller's location was marked as Moscow.

This was a scam, of course. But what wasn't? I clicked Buy It Now, completed the transaction. *Congratulations, Communist-Dupe_1944*, the confirmation read. *You bought Lenin.*

•

The following day I called Grandpa and told him what I'd done. I told him to consider the purchase as step two of his three-step plan. I'm not sure he understood me.

"I'm getting old," he said. "I feel pinching in my arm and leg. Surely a new stroke waits for me around the corner. So I've been thinking. You are a good boy, my son, but I failed you. You have all the right to mock me."

I had relished mocking him once, I said, but not any longer. "Tell me the third step. I need to know."

"Step three," he said after some thought. "Come home."

•

I did not sleep that night. Nor did I sleep well for two weeks after. My thoughts were murky, sunk to their chins in the crab-apple mash that was my brain.

I phoned and told him just enough. How unhappy I was in America. How I'd come here, not as a reaction against him, but because I'd wanted to try something new. I said, "It's payback time, old man. Go on, it's now your turn to tease me."

"*Sinko,*" Grandpa said instead. He spoke to me the way he'd done so often when as a child I'd thrown a fit or bloodied my knees. "Stop for a minute. Hear me out. Today, not one hour before you called, a large red truck arrived at our house. Inside the truck was an enormous crate. Inside the crate lay Lenin. The leader of nations now lies in your room, glorious, refrigerated, as peaceful as a lamb."

Silly, hollow words that I knew were chaff, and still I listened, eyes dreamily closed. "Do you remember, Grandson," he was saying, "the story I used to tell you, of how I lived in a dugout, with fifteen other men, two pregnant women and a hungry goat, and how, desperate and starving, I finally found the courage to go down to the village? Well, I wasn't desperate or starving. At least not in the corporeal sense. I simply couldn't stand it any longer. The men cheated at cards. The women gossiped. The goat shat in my galoshes. Three years later I went back to that same place in the forest. I wanted to see the dugout again, now with my free eyes. I counted twenty steps from a crooked oak we'd used as a marker, found the entrance and climbed down the ladder. They were still there, all of them, mummified. No one had told them the war was over. No one had told them they could go. They hadn't had the courage to walk out themselves, and so they'd starved to death. I felt like shit. I dug and I dug and I buried them all. I told myself, what kind of a world is this where people and goats die in dugouts for nothing at all? And so I lived my life as though ideals really mattered. And in the end they did."

I held the receiver and thought of Lenin lying refrigerated in my childhood room, and an awful feeling swept me up, a terrible fright. I wanted the old man to promise he'd wait for me out in the yard, under the black grapes of the trellised vine. Instead, I started laughing. My belly twisted, my temples split. I couldn't help it. I laughed until my laughter took hold of Grandpa, until our voices mixed along the wire and echoed like one.

THE LETTER

It's not like Grandmoms is urging me to steal from the British. But she knows I can't help it. So when I walk under the trellis, she looks up from her newspaper and says, "Maria, today Missis was seen at the store with new earrings. Real pearls."

She tells me to tie the end of a loose vine string, and while I tie it Grandmoms says, "I'm not saying, you know. But we could split it down the middle."

I throw her this look. She says, "Sixty-forty?" and then she's back to her paper. Turning one page and licking her fingers to turn the next, like the ink on her fingers is honey.

I know what she needs the money for. She'll fold the bills neatly and wrap them in some old article about hog farming and seal the envelope with two strips of tape. Then she'll mail the envelope to my mother so she won't call for a couple of months.

I go to feed the chickens, to unthink the earrings, but it's all pearls before my eyes. I collect four eggs. Two of them are big enough and I polish them in my apron, then I put them in a basket. I pick some dahlias, white, that's how Missis likes them, and put them in the basket. Then from the basement I pour Missis a hundred grams of Grandpa's *rakia* in a small bottle and that, too, goes in the basket.

Missis is sunbathing in her yard and her long, smooth legs are reflecting sun like they are tin-plated with the best tin a Gypsy can sell you. "*Hello, Mary*, dura-bura-dura-bura," Missis says in English. She looks bored and depressed as always, but when she takes off her sunglasses her eyes glisten. She's a Russian dog, salivating at the sight of me. She knows I always bring baskets.

First she takes a tiny gulp, elegant, but then it's Grandpa's *rakia*, that good grape, that dark oak cask, so she kills half the bottle. Thirty-three years old and a woman, drinks more than uncle Pesho. And Uncle Pesho drives the village bus.

"Is Mister home?" I ask her. She shakes her head. The earrings make this expensive sound. The pearls beam with sun and I'm suffocating.

"Drink up, Missis," I say, and sit at the edge of the lounge chair.

Missis is the single most unhappy woman I have ever robbed. For starters, she makes us call her "Missis," but she isn't British. Her Bulgarian is native, soft, a northern accent, yet when she speaks her sentences are littered with foreign sounds, with words that hold no meaning up here in our village. She strolls the dirt roads with a parasol that never opens, she powders her nose while waiting for the bread truck to arrive from town. She asks the bartender for drinks with English names and rolls her eyes when he pours her mint with *mastika*. But she drinks it all the same. When Missis leaves the pub, with the loaf in a netted sack and her high heels clunking, all the village drunks drool after her calves, and all the peasant women after her sophisticated nature. Missis is very pretty, no doubt in that, though I think her neck's a bit too long (bred to showcase jewels, Grandmoms says). But I think Missis would be prettier still if she didn't pretend to be some other woman. I've seen her around the corner, thinking she can't be seen, sink her teeth into the bread ear and take a sloppy bite. I've seen her step into a buffalo splash on the road and curse a saucy curse. I like her much better that way. Sometimes I wonder if her depressed look too isn't just a pretense. Especially since last she went to town and back her sighs have tripled in duration. But then again, I've seen the hide buyer drive down our

road yelling, "I'm buying hides, I'm buying leather," and sometimes, when Mister is away, I've seen him sneak inside Missis's
house. He comes back out in thirty minutes. Always. I've timed
him. And I know no pretense will ever justify your lying down
with hide buyers; her sadness at least seems genuine enough.

"Hey, *Missis*," I say and move up the lounge chair slightly,
"who sunbathes with jewelry on, eh?"

She fakes a smile and smacks her lips together. She is a nice
woman, but right now I'm thinking how easy it is to steal a pair
of pearl earrings off a pair of drunk ears.

•

The British, as we like to call them, came to our village two years
ago, when I was fourteen. First we heard that someone bought the
house across from ours. Then these workers arrived and gutted
the house. Threw the entrails on the dump, chairs, tables, book-
shelves. Whitened the façade with lime, fixed new window frames,
aluminum, put new doors, new gates. Raked the yard. Planted
seeds. Transplanted boxwood shrubs and cherry trees. When the
cherries blossomed the British arrived. Missis and Mister.

Mister is a century older than Missis and he speaks decent
Bulgarian. His face is wrinkled, but his eyes are blue. He wears
white suits and white hats made of puppies. I *thought* they were
made of puppies because when he let me touch the brim once, it
felt just as smooth. Some folks say he was a spy and it is rumored
that Mister lived in Sofia for many years, working the embassy.
Most folks call him zero-zero-seven and he laughs, a set of perfect teeth, but I call him "Mister." Zero-zero is like toilet language, unaristocratic.

"What do you know about aristocrats?" Grandmoms tells
me, but she knows I'm not a peasant, she knows I was born in
the city. I was born the winter after the Soviets fell. I don't really
give two shits about the Soviets falling, but Grandmoms makes

me learn these things because she says I ought to know my history. I think that's pretty daft of her to say, because of all the
things she's kept secret from me. Personal histories, mostly. But
Grandmoms teaches me like there will be no tomorrow if I
didn't know when the Berlin wall was knocked down, or why it
was put up in the first place.

The winter I was born, Grandmoms says, wolves roamed the
streets and snatched away babies. She says money was toilet
paper and coupons were the new money and you had to stand in
line for coupons days in a row. Three hundred coupons bought
you a loaf of bread. Five hundred bought you cheese. She says a
wolf snatched my father and chewed his dick off. And then, she
says, your father came home a man without a dick.

My pops works in England now. I haven't really met him, but
I would like to meet him. I would like to send him a letter and
tell him how things are here, in our village. I suppose he has forgotten our language, but sometimes I go to Missis and I almost
tell her, listen, Missis, how about . . .

Then I know better. I am my mother's daughter, which is to
say I'm a bitch. I lie and steal. I can't help it. It's like if I don't
steal, my lungs get filled up with magic glue. C-200. And I can't
breathe. Also, I'm mean to people for no reason. Not always,
of course. Only when it counts. "Maria, for God's sake," Grandmoms says. "I gave you this name so you could be like Jesus's
mother." But she always plays me. Look at those earrings, check
out that wallet. Then she sends the money to my mother. So I say,
"Grandmoms, don't be stupid. You gave me this name because
you lack imagination. Because you gave that same name to our
mother and look at her now, gone three hundred and sixty days
a year and begging for money the other five." And I say, "Grandmoms, would Jesus's mother have left him in the manger? Would
his grandmother have picked him up to raise him a savior? And,
Grandmoms, how come you picked *me* up and left my sister an
orphan?"

•

In the summer, Tuesdays and Saturdays. That's when we have buses running, one in the morning and one in the p.m. When we have school, Saturdays only. Sometimes I skip school just to go, but rarely since Grandmoms sets all over me for turning down the knowledge. She says only men can afford to be uneducated. "Women," she says, "need to develop their brains." "Oh, yeah?" I say. "And how about Magda? Her brain is the opposite of developed, but she is always well fed, wears nice clothes and sleeps in nice sheets. Watches a plasma TV." "Now, now," Grandmoms says, "don't be a bitch."

At the bus station I pay the driver, Uncle Pesho, and he says, "Mariyke, did you rob a bank?" I shove the money in my pocket. Thirty levs. The other twenty were for Grandmoms, after she sold the earrings. And two are gone for the ticket, there and back. The bus is empty and I'm cold so early in the morning. "Can't you turn the heat on, Uncle?" He turns and looks at me, then at my shirt. "I *see* that you're cold. I like it." And, laughing, he starts the bus and off we go.

He is a good man, Uncle Pesho, he's known me for ten years now. And he's been driving me for seven. That's when I started seeing Magda. Before that, I didn't know about her. Nine years. Days, nights, summers, winters. I'd go to bed and wake up in the morning, I'd swim in the river, work the fields, go to school, clueless. Then, when Grandmoms told me, it was, like, yes, I knew it all along. Like I didn't know it, but like I've *known* it. Like when old people say their kneecaps hurt so it must rain soon. Only my kneecaps hurt *after* the rain. I might have shown it because one day Grandmoms said, "Okay, okay, I'll take you there. Just stop."

Magda was this tiny thing. A whole head shorter than me, and her face was like this, distorted. Her tongue was swollen in her mouth. I couldn't look past her rolling tongue, and the spit trickling down her chin. Grandmoms wiped it with a kerchief as if she'd wiped it time and time before. Later I asked her, "How long?" and she said, "On and off, once a month for three years."

"Why three?"

She said, "I couldn't go on forever without sleep. I thought I could. But I couldn't."

When we first met, Magda put her hands all over my face. Sticky hands on my cheeks, on my ears. She poked inside my nose. "Quit it!"

"Now, now," Grandmoms said, "that's how she's getting to know you."

You can't get to know someone by shoving a finger up their nose. But if someone shoves their finger up your nose, you learn some things about them. It's called a one-way implication. We studied it in Math.

I try to teach Magda some things. Since we're not men and can't afford. I take my books to her and sit her in a corner in a nice room that smells of rice with milk and cinnamon and teach her things. She does okay in math. She knows multiplication. At first it was, like, 1×1, 1×2, and it was never past the two, everything equaled two. 5×7, 9×8, everything was 2. But now she gets it. She gets history. She likes simpler things, made up stories, poems, but she is awful with language. And she can't spell to save her life. There is one letter in particular she just can't write. Ж.

Ж is the gallows upon which Magda will hang. I tell her, "Girl, you are sixteen and your Ж looks like a dead frog." And she laughs. At least she laughs. Her words might be all mumbly and downright stupid sometimes, but her laughter is snowdrops and there is nothing stupid about her laughter.

Now, on the bus, Uncle Pesho calls me over. "Mariyke, you want to sit in my lap? Drive the machine?" That's what we used to do when I was little. I'd sit in his lap and hold the wheel and drive. So I say, "Okay, why not." Because the way my thoughts were going, I'd rather change their course.

I sit in his lap and the bus goes and then he moves his hand up. He pinches my nipple and laughs and I say, "*Pederas*, let me out." He's laughing, laughing, and I stand up and slam my foot onto his knee and he veers the bus off the road. I pull the hand brake and then it's all nuts and bolts thrashing underneath us, and smoke. The bus halts. I hit the button, out the door, and I'm two hills away.

Then I cry a little. Shut up, I say, and slap my own face. Slapping your own face is very effective in case of tears. I saw a woman do it in this American movie. Grandmoms and I watch every movie on TV. So the tears are almost gone when a car comes toward me up the road. The car stops, window comes down. "*Mary*, is that you?"

Mister opens the door and I jump in without a word.

"Are you going to the orphans?" he says. He sounds just like Magda. The right words, but every word a touch off, crippled.

"Yes," I say, and Mister says, "Let me take you."

Grandmoms is secretly in love with Mister. And she hates Missis in the guts. We watched this one movie *Zorba the Greek* and Grandmoms said, "I hope Missis dies like that old whore so we can rob her house, vases and jewels and even her nightgown, still warm with her heat. I hope the peasants catch her with the hide buyer, naked on his furs, and, like in the movie, slice her throat side to side for the infidelity." Then there will be no more Missis, and it will be all Mister. White skin and blue eyes. Soft hair. Mister looks just like the gentleman in the movie, the writer. Older of course, but more handsome, because of his age. Because of his white suits and smooth hats. Because of his eyes.

I put my hand on his as he shifts gears. "Dear girl," he goes, and adds something about how cold my hand is, but I'm not listening.

"This is a nice car, Mister." His hand is warm and I can feel his knuckles moving and his muscles.

"How is your sister?" Mister asks me. He knows all about

her. He's been pouring money into the orphanage, dumping money with a shovel. Out of pure kindness, I think, though Grandmoms once told me it had to do with taxes and things along those lines. "That poor girl," he says.

"She's not so poor, now, is she?" I say. I mean you bought them new cribs, new curtains. You bought them a microwave! But I don't say this of course. I just keep my hand on his and I'm glad the hills are hills and the road snakes the way it snakes, so the stick would shift as much as it shifts. So his knuckles would move.

"Do you know that she pisses her bed?" I say, just to say something. "She's sixteen."

"You're twins, right?"

"No one can tell. I wonder if she even knows it. Her face is all like that and mine is all . . ." I look at my face in the mirror. Jesus! I hide to the side and search my pockets for a tissue.

"Here," Mister says, and passes me his kerchief.

"Why didn't you tell me?" I wipe off the mascara and he says, "It's only a little bit."

My face is flaming and I almost say, Stop the car, please let me go. But he takes out a cigarette and lights it with the car lighter, then returns the lighter in its slot. Davidoff. And the lighter is so shiny, I tussle for air.

"I'm sorry," I say, and Mister says, "It's okay. Of course you'll get emotional when you speak of your sister."

Then we arrive and he reaches over to open the door. He smells like pinecones.

"The door sticks," he says, and pushes it open.

"Thanks." While he ashes the cigarette out his window, I palm the lighter and hide it in my pocket. "Can I keep the kerchief?" I say, and he says, "Keep it. And say hi to your Granny." And out of nowhere there is this big smile on his face.

•

Today I quiz her over old lessons. We sit in the corner and she is restless as always, rocking back and forth in her chair, eyes out the window. "Magda, when was Bulgaria founded?" "Six eighty-one," she says. She smacks her lips, the swollen tongue rolls. Spit trickles. I tell her, "Two thousand and seven is when Bulgaria ends; Grandmoms said that. Once we join the EU, Bulgaria ends. Do you know what the EU is?" "EU, EU," she repeats, and I say, "Stop saying it. It makes you sound inarticulate." "EU." She laughs. "Come here." I wipe the spit off her chin and then I'm, like, Oh, crap, Magda, this is Mister's kerchief. You ruined Mister's kerchief.

We do some dictation. She's biting her tongue and writing, diligently, and around us children are running and playing so I tell them to turn that TV down. All these children are normal, though they are orphans. But Magda is here because there is no other place she could be. Not close to our village, anyway.

Mother left both of us here. Back then the building was a mess and they didn't have TVs and curtains. It was wolves on the streets, so Mother was scared we would get snatched and she brought us here to safety. Grandmoms says that and tears up and I always think, Grandmoms you have got to be shitting me. And now I watch Magda chew on her tongue and write tiny letters and I think to myself, What if that teacher had beaten *me*? We were the same then, two years old. Would Magda come to see me, teach me things? Nice room, cinnamon, soft pillows. Just today they were eating sandwiches with ham and cheese when I walked in. And when Mister made that big donation, Magda sat in his lap and he petted her hair and brushed her cheeks. In a parallel world, it might not be so bad.

We are done writing and Magda looks up. She giggles and motions me closer and when she talks she spits on my face.

"I got something alive in my belly," she says.

•

I am told our father's name is Hristo. I don't blame him for running away at all. I should probably blame him, but I don't—it's nature, really—spread the seed and run, move on for more seed spreading. But a mother betraying her own? Blood betraying blood? Now, that's low. So all my hate goes toward Mother and there just isn't any left for anyone else. At least Pops never calls. He never says, How is my beautiful girl? To which I always respond, Chewing her own tongue. And the saddest thing is Mother doesn't even understand what I'm saying. She's never seen Magda—not after she left her, anyway. So if she calls she keeps me on the phone for a minute, I've timed it. "How's life treating you?" she says exactly in those words. Life treating you . . . A stupider question was never asked. Life doesn't treat you. People do.

And then the phone is off to Grandmoms. Five minutes. Done. And after that, Grandmoms searches for an old article to wrap whatever my mother asked for.

But it can't be just any old article. Grandmoms never throws a newspaper away. And she reads old newspapers. Mostly the stuff Grandpa wrote. She reads them in the yard over and over again. Calls me sometimes and says, "Listen to this: *The General Secretary spent ten minutes tying up red balloons for the Day of the Child.* See how nicely your grandpa put it?" I guess Grandpa could put it nicely. But why does she have to keep those papers everywhere, always?

When I first told Mister my father worked in England, Mister asked me what city and I said, "Why, of course London." Like I was offended by him asking, like my Pops wouldn't be working just anyplace. I told him my Pops was a construction supervisor and had supervised the building of that big Ferris wheel, the one on the Thames. Mister's eyes nearly flew out. "Why, your Pops is really someone," he said, and then I was, like, offended again: "You think?"

Mister said I should write Pops a letter. I said, "That's okay,

Mister. Pops must have other children now, his own missis."
"And that doesn't make you sad?" Mister said, and I said, "No,
it's all good." But on the inside I was, like, You think?

I think about my Pops sometimes. And I can't get that stupid
wheel out of my head, now that I lied about it. I see Pops by the
wheel with his new kids and his new missis. It's always dark and
the wheel is always lit and spinning. The Thames smells like watermelon. My sister is with me, naturally, and we are hiding by a
stand where they sell ham and cheese. Pops picks one kid up on
his shoulder and lifts the other, like a demijohn of *rakia*, and
carries them both to a basket on the wheel. His missis laughs,
authentic, long-necked, pearl-eared. *Dura-bura*, Pops says in
English, meaning, Now we're going to have some good times.
And then my sister turns to me and says, "God damn it, Maria,
why does it have to be like this? This is your daydream. Make it
better." And when she says it, suddenly we are transported to the
wheel, a hundred meters above the ground, and we walk across
its metal frame, unscrewing one bulb after the other. There is no
danger of falling. Gravity does not exist. Only the gravity between us. And the bulbs keep glowing even after we put them in
our pockets and our pockets are full with one million stolen,
glowing bulbs, burning fireflies so strong, they take us upon their
wings. Then we fly, my sister and I, illuminated, hand in hand
above the Thames. "Now, that's a dream," she says.

•

Violation of policy number, paragraph number, point number . . .
that's what the principal of the orphanage is droning about. I'm
sitting in her office, waiting for a good moment to snatch a pen
from the desk. An orange Bic with a blue tooth-marked cap.
Long story short, they're kicking Magda out on the street.

"She has no place to go," I say, and the principal smiles at me,
"Of course she does."

On the bus home I can't think of anything else. What if the

baby turns out like Magda? Swollen tongue, inarticulate mumbling. I know that's not how she got to be the way she is, but what if somehow with her blood or milk that swollenness gets passed on to the baby? It won't be fair. And how would Grandmoms take the news? A stroke? A heart attack? A baby needs food to keep it quiet, clothes, a crib. A baby needs something better than Magda, Grandmoms and me.

Back in the village, I look for Mister. A spy of his caliber, with his connections in Sofia, will surely know what to do. But Mister isn't home again, and Missis is bathing in the sun. *"Hello, Mary,"* she fakes.

"Dear God, Missis, you have to help me."

I blurt this out before I know it. And I just don't know what to do with my hands, my hair, my nails. Missis sits me on a large oak table inside and I can see my own face distorted in the table, with the sun slipping across the wood. I recognize that face and run my hands over its cheeks as if to smooth them. With light steps, Missis floats to the countertop. *"Cocktail?"* she says.

To save us time, I tell her I've seen the hide buyer come in and out of her house and promise not to tell Mister if she would help me. She sobers up. Her lips pursed, she holds the shaker like it's a neck to choke. She dumps the drink in two tall cups, then adds some extra olives to my drink. "You are a little nosy snake," she says. "I like that in a girl."

We down the drinks.

"Nothing a drink can't solve," says Missis as I fight to breathe the fire away. "So, Marche, what do you want?"

I tell her all there is to tell.

She ticks her tongue, runs a finger over the glass rim, and suddenly she is alive. Her drowsiness evaporated, cheeks rosy, sparkling eyes. "Tell me more. Who is the father? When and where? I want to know it all . . ."

"The father doesn't matter, and I don't know about the rest."

Missis sticks her bottom lip out. "You are no fun. All day I

listen to these walls and now, at last, some excitement. And you
don't know . . . you must find out . . ."

"I'd rather talk to Mister."

"Now, wouldn't you!" she says. She licks the glass. Then
something strikes her. "You think the baby will be like her? You
know . . . That will be very sad. We mustn't let such sad things
happen."

"How can we not?"

For some time she plays with the pearls on her necklace and I
can hear the click they make. "Get rid of it," she says. "That
ought to do the trick."

She goes back to the counter. "I did it once or twice," she
says. "It helped *me* very much." She gulps down the drink she's
fixed and brings another to the table. "I know a great doctor.
Very handsome. And you don't have to go to Sofia to see him.
Just go to town. But it'll cost you a thousand green."

"We'll never have a thousand green," I say. But then a possibility reveals itself as clear as Magda's laugh. "Unless we write
to Pops."

Missis considers something for a moment. She claps her hands.
"Of course. A letter to your Pops." And goes to get good, fancy
paper so Pops would know we mean business. I take out the orange Bic.

"We'll write this in English in case your Pops has forgotten
our language."

"And to the side in Bulgarian," I say, "in case he is dumb
enough to have never learned theirs."

The letter goes like so: *Татко, Магда забременя. Гонят я от
пансиона. Молим те за помощ. Абортът струва скъпо. Прати
пари в плик до баба. Желаем ти много здраве. Мария и Магда.*
Missis translates it. She tells me to copy the writing myself, as
would be proper form.

I can't write English, though we studied it in school, but it's
not so hard to copy. At least on paper words are words. *Pops,*

*Magda is pregnant. They are kicking her out of the Home. We
ask for your help. The abortion costs a lot of money. Send it in an
envelope to Grandma. We wish you health. Maria and Magda.*

After I'm finished, Missis inspects the writing. "Mistake,"
she says, and shows me where I've butchered one letter. "Again."

I copy it again and she says, "Mistake," and brings more sheets
and over and over again it's mistake, mistake, mistake. Missis is
drinking her fifth cocktail when she starts to cry. "Oh, my," she
says, and tries laughing instead.

Then she is quiet, but I can tell she wants to speak.

"Missis," I go. She goes, "I knew this girl, very pretty. A neat
student at the language school. She served cocktails to foreigners
in the Balkan Tourist hotel for cash. Her father was a drunk who
wasted all their money. One night, an old English bastard asked
the girl to make him a Corpse Reviver. The girl had no idea what
that was."

She shakes her glass. "It's not that bad. It's just a simple operation really. You never feel a thing." And then, like that, as if
she's slapped her own face, Missis is once more collected. "Go
on, now, finish the letter."

I copy a few more times and must be making little mistakes,
which is strange, because I can't really see how what I've written
is wrong. But Missis says it's wrong. Finally she says, "Give me
the pen and stretch out your hand." She smacks the pen on my
fingers again and again. "This is how you learn your English.
This is how you marry Mister and live rich. What? You don't
think I know you've been stealing my things? My shoes, my earrings, my necklaces. You are a little thieving bitch, aren't you?"

It hurts. But I'll be damned if I pull my fingers back. Let her
hit. Let her hit *me* for once. Bring it on, Missis. It isn't even a
thing.

When she's had her hitting, Missis calms down. She seems to
think of something for a time. Her back stiff and straight, she
leaves the room and then returns with a wad of money. "Forget

the letter," she says, and places the wad before her on the table. "Do one thing for me and this is yours."

I don't like now the way her eyes have blurred.

"Kiss me," she says.

One thousand dollars for a single kiss. I say, "You got it," and lean forward ready to get this done. Then Missis giggles and she, too, leans forward, eyes closed, whole body swaying slightly, her face streaked from the crying, her upper lip beaded with sweat. She smells of perfume and *rakia*. We touch lips, my eyes tightly shut, because I am afraid to look, when Missis squeals. "Oh, garlic. Gross!" and pushes me away. She bursts out laughing. "I can't do this!" She shakes her hands like little wings. "Take it, it's yours . . ." she manages at last, and keeps on laughing.

•

From there I run to the bus, as hard as I can, fighting to keep an empty head. "You want me to sit in your lap again, Uncle? You want to pinch me some more?"

"Mariyke," he says, "I didn't mean nothing by it. Please, my soul. Forgive."

"I'll forgive if you do me a favor," I say, and he goes, "For you, always."

He drives and I sob in the back. The wad is like mud in my hand. The more I squeeze it, the more it runs in dirty trickles down my sleeve.

In the orphanage Magda is sitting on her bed, rocking slightly. The bedsprings squeak beneath her like the village wailers at their last funeral for the day. Her hair is cut short and there are tiny hairs all over her forehead, cheeks and neck. She wears a blue dress, a soft fresh color. No doubt a dress they bought with Mister's money.

"Well, Magdichka," I say, "there are no dresses like this with Grandmoms." I wrap all her clothes in a blanket: a pair of jeans, three blouses, six underpants, six bras, six pairs of socks that don't really match. With the bundle in one hand, and holding Magda with the other, I walk out of the home.

I tell her it's okay. "We're going on a trip," I say.

"All right," she manages to say.

We sit back and Uncle drives. He wants to know exactly where in town.

"Just drop us at the station and wait," I say. I count the money. A thousand green. Dr. Rangelov is the name. A yellow co-op, on the second floor. I'll know it by the linden tree outside, struck by lightning, all charred. I'll tell him Missis sends us and let him count the money. And then it's a simple operation. And then we won't feel a thing.

It's early afternoon, but out the window the sky is dark. The road black, the clouds black and the hills round like Ferris wheels. "They look like Ferris wheels," I say, and Magda smears her hands all over the window, pulls on the curtains, chews on the strings.

Gently, I brush the cut hairs one by one off her neck and sweaty forehead. It won't be fair, I think. To have a baby with a swollen brain, with Grandmoms for mother. With me for aunt. "Stay still," I say.

At last we are in town. The driver is nagging me about the bus. By six o'clock, he says, we must be back in the depot. I tell him I have to think. "Go smoke a cigarette outside. Get coffee," and keep at the tiny hairs. "It's just not fair, Magda, you know?"

"All right," she says.

"No wonder you're where you are. That's all you say."

"All right."

We burst out laughing. And then I picture her, spread like a Ж, the baby gone. Or else, I see the baby crying, all day, all night, hungry, and then I see it grown up, choking for air, because like me it feels the need to steal. And I am always by its side, filling its little head with tricks. I teach it how to pocket pens, necklaces, lighters . . . *Quickly, like so, and no one will see.*

One thousand green in my hand. And if I left now, no one would see. One thousand green would get me so far away from all this mess, so quickly, even my thoughts would fall behind. I say, "Wait here, Magda. I'll be back before you know it. Just hold on to the blanket, hold tight like so, and I'll be back." She holds. I kiss her swiftly on the lips, a spit-wet little peck.

I am my mother's daughter. And so I run as fast as you can run through rain—and even out of breath I keep on running. I fear that if I stop, my feet might take me back.

At last I find myself at the other end of town, muddy and soaked, outside some beauty parlor. Beyond the parlor glass I see women nesting in rows of chairs, long-necked and elegant, aristocratic, some with blow-drying helmets on their heads and others with cotton balls between their toes. I also see my own reflection in the glass, as thin as a ghost and just as lively. All through my life it has been Grandmoms cutting my hair with the same pair of scissors her grandma used on hers. To hell with it, I think.

And twenty dollars later I'm in a chair.

"I want it short," I say, and watch in the mirror, one wet rope falling after the other. By now they must be home. Uncle Pesho would have taken Magda to Grandmoms, who would be worried sick. At last the mirror girl is someone else—a lighter, more beautiful version of me. A stranger really.

After the cut, I need dry clothes. A dress. Green, red, yellow, blue. It doesn't matter as long as it's expensive and new. I need new shoes, high heels that splash clink-clanking through the puddles. From there, of course, I'm off to the hotel. Balkan Tourist.

The waiter calls me "Mademoiselle" and walks me to a table. The dress rustles against my thighs, the heels peck the polished floor. He lights a candle. White cloth and forks of different sizes. I order sandwiches with ham and cheese and eat them, while to the side some grandpa plays the piano, his bald head twinkling, itself a candle top. I order chicken fricassee and fish, flan for dessert, and crème brûlée, and rice with cinnamon and milk, and barely touch them, but still I order more.

From there I fly up to the hotel bar. Tonight as every night, a poster says, it's a variety show. I sit in the corner and call for almonds, for orange and pineapple juice. The bar is half empty, here and there older men in pairs sip on their drinks—they're all nicely dressed, most of them foreign it seems. And on the stage, under the glow of a million tiny colorful lights, dance glittering girls, long-legged, short-skirted, with haircuts like mine, with big and stupid smiles. *Variété.* It seems more like a circus to me. I bet they make some decent cash. I bet I could be such a girl. I'll rent a room in town, I'll work the nights and sleep the days, a dreamless sleep, until one day a British man, with hats made from puppies and snow-white suits, will offer me a drink.

Pops, Magda is pregnant. They are kicking her out of the Home.

I read the letter again. I can barely make out the words, with all the flashing lights onstage, but words are words. I think of Grandmoms, then of Magda, by now most likely sleeping in my bed.

I know all this is not a dream, but even so—why does it have to be like this?

I feel the suffocating need to stuff my pockets with all those shiny lights onstage. If I don't, I'll positively drown. I sit and watch the bulbs explode, a thick fiery swarm, but I'll be damned if I move.

Some petty change. That's all that's left when the program ends. I phone from the lobby and Grandmoms picks up right away. I don't wait to hear her speak.

"How's life treating you?" I say. "Listen," I say, "I need some money for a ticket home."

A PICTURE WITH YUKI

Yuki and I arrived in Bulgaria three weeks before our hospital appointment, mostly so we'd have enough time to get over jet lag, but also so we would get there before the big summer heat, and not buy plane tickets at peak season prices. We spent the first week in Sofia, with my parents, and got along with them surprisingly smoothly, considering the circumstances. But my hometown did not sit well with my wife. When they'd first heard we were coming, my parents had equipped my old room with a new bed and an AC. But the AC had arrived defective, and it would take a month before the new part was delivered. At night Yuki complained of the heat and when I opened the window it was the boulevard that annoyed her, the barking stray dogs, the drunks who had turned the bus stop into their drinking spot.

For a few nights straight Yuki did not sleep. She would sit in bed and press the AC remote repeatedly and the AC would rattle but not cool.

"It's all nerves," I told her. I reminded her that just the other day she had smoked her last cigarette outside O'Hare. She reminded me that just the other day her suitcase had not landed with us in Sofia. That when it had finally arrived, her toothbrush had been missing, her blue Starter sneakers, the box of Nicorette gum.

"These things happen," I assured her. "Besides, I bought you Bulgarian gum. Just as good, and probably better."

She popped a piece and chewed it vehemently for a while. She dug her thumb, with the nail peeled ragged by her other nails, into the remote. "Bulgarian crap," she said, "it doesn't work. Nothing here works."

She started to cry. I told her she was wrong. Some things, yes, but not all things. Some things, I told her, were bound to work. We deserved a break, I told her, because we were good people and good things happened to good people, sooner or later. I blabbered like that for a while and she said, "You're blabbering. Stop it." She said I didn't know anything. If I'd known something, she said, I wouldn't have married her in the first place.

That's when my mom knocked on the door. I was glad she had it in her, the audacity, to knock on our door at four in the morning.

"Tell Yuki I bring linden tea," my mother commanded, and found her way in the semidarkness to set the tray on the night stand. *"Lipov chay, Yuki,"* she said in Bulgarian. "It'll help her sleep. Tell her that. With acacia honey. Why aren't you telling her that?"

I told her that and Yuki, who'd hidden under the blanket, peeked up to nod thankfully.

"Did I . . ." my mother said and raised an eyebrow. "Were you—"

I said we weren't—

"I didn't think you were," she said, waiting for Yuki to drink the tea. "After all, in your condition, what's the point?"

The following morning I asked my father for the old Moskvich and by sunset, Yuki and I were two hundred kilometers north, in my grandparents' old village house.

·

We'd learned about the in vitro program in Sofia last year, from a friend of my mom's—a forty-something schoolteacher who, after many barren years, was now, finally, the mother of twins— Lazar and Leopold, or some similar-sounding madness.

By that time Yuki and I had been married and had tried to conceive for eighteen months. We consulted a doctor in Chicago, a Bulgarian my friends at O'Hare had recommended. It turned out there was something the matter with Yuki's fallopian tubes. It would be very hard, the doctor said, to get pregnant as nature designed it, though by all means, he said, keep trying. It would be easier to try other means, but these, of course, required hefty sums. I am a luggage loader at O'Hare. Yuki waits tables at a low-level sushi restaurant, imaginatively named Tokyo Sushi, and on the side babysits youngster Americans, whose parents have deemed her speaking Japanese to their children somehow beneficial. We cannot produce hefty sums.

A phone call to Japan revealed even grimmer prospects, and I found myself forced to get my parents involved. At that time my mother still did not speak to me, so when she picked up the phone I had to wait for my father to take the receiver. That wasted almost a minute of my expensive calling card. "What time is it in Chicago?" my father asking, and "What's the weather like?" wasted another. Seven years in the States and their questions were the same; so were my answers. Eight hours behind. Windy.

"I need to speak to you about Yuki," I told him. I could hear my mother's voice from the other end of the room, like a ghost's from another dimension, instructing him what to say and waiting for him to relate the things I was saying.

"Tell Mom to come to the phone," I said.

"Tell him to invite me to his wedding next time," I heard her saying.

"There will be no next time," I said, and watched the phone tick away more pricey seconds.

"There might be," my father said. He asked my mother to repeat something and then related it.

I told them about the problems at hand.

"I expected this," my mother said, and I hung up before Father could speak.

The thing about Yuki—at least, that which infuriates my parents even more than the fact that she is not a good Bulgarian girl—is her age. The fact that she is four years my senior seems to have a cataclysmic effect on them.

"You cannot blame her for this," I told them once I dialed again.

"We blame you," I heard my mother. "And your poor choices," my father added.

I hung up again. More cents were wasted from my card. We repeated this charade several times before finally I heard my mother promise she would look into things.

"We're also considering adoption," I said. This time my father didn't wait for instructions. "Nonsense," he said. "Our seed must not be lost. Do you hear me?"

A week later Mother called me herself with the news of Lazar and Leopold.

"It will cost three thousand dollars," she said.

"We can make three thousand," I told her.

"It's on us," she said. "A wedding gift."

·

My grandparents were dead now, but even before we arrived in Bulgaria I knew I would take Yuki to see their vacation house. I had spent every summer since the age of five in there: two rooms, a kitchen, an attic with an inclined ceiling that was too low to stand straight under, an acre of orchard for a yard. There was a river in the village, and above the village there was the mountain. You could ask for nothing more.

We carried our bags to the front door, and while I fought with the lock, Yuki chewed nicotine gum and took pictures of the yard and the outdoor toilet. She took a picture of me fighting the lock and then carrying the bags into the dark hallway.

"Please stop with the pictures," I told her.

She put the camera back in its case. "Are you all right?" she said.

I walked from room to room and opened the windows. I climbed into the attic and opened the window and I opened the window in the basement. Back in the living room I sat on Grandma's bed, and Yuki sat on Grandpa's. For a very long time we said nothing at all. I watched the cherry trees, and the peaches, the apples, the plums in the yard, which all looked dead now, completely dried. The sun was slipping behind the giant walnut, and I watched it, orange in the bare branches. It was starting to smell better inside.

"My parents were here last week," I said. They had stopped by to clean the house and bring clean blankets. My father had mowed a path to the toilet in the yard.

"It looks nice," Yuki said. "The house looks really nice."

I lay my palm on the bedcover and ran it up and down and in circles.

"This is Grandma's bed," I said. "This is where I slept."

Then I showed Yuki a hanger in the corner, a wooden stand, with a wool jacket on it and a pair of blue trousers. "These are Grandpa's trousers."

•

We didn't have anything to eat, so we went down the road to a neighbor, an old woman who'd been friends with my grandma. The woman cried and kissed me on both cheeks. I was afraid she would want to kiss Yuki. Japanese people, especially strangers, don't kiss each other nearly as much as we do.

"My God," the woman said, and clapped her hands. "She is so tiny." Then she studied Yuki, head to toes. Yuki stood, flaming red, smiling.

"They aren't that yellow," the woman told me at last.

"What did she say?" Yuki asked.

"What did she say?" asked the woman. Inevitably, she plunged herself forward with unexpected agility and took Yuki's hands. She kissed them and then she kissed Yuki on the cheeks. Yuki obeyed, but wiped her face when the woman wasn't looking.

Then everyone came out to see Yuki. There were many faces I didn't recognize, many children and young women. They sat us down on a table in the yard, under the trellised vine, which was just budding green.

"Your family has grown, Grandma," I told the woman. They were all watching Yuki, all beaming with excitement. One little girl edged herself closer, touched Yuki on the knee and ran away giggling.

"I feel awful," Yuki said.

"What did she say?" someone asked. They asked if this was Japanese.

I didn't tell them it was English we spoke. They brought dinner and we ate under the vine, with the sky almost dark and the moon big and still red, low above the hills.

"Is this a camera, Yuki?" a little boy asked. He pronounced her name perfectly. She showed him the tiny device and then she took his picture. Everyone gathered to see the picture on the back screen.

"Can we take a picture with you, Yuki?" someone said. Someone said, "Yuki, have you ever tried Bulgarian *rakia*? Grandma," someone said, "bring *rakia* for Yuki."

•

Yuki and I first met by baggage claim number eight. Her bag from Tokyo hadn't arrived and she looked on the verge of tears.

"These things happen," I assured her. I had just finished my shift, but I took her to her airline office so she could file a claim and helped her to the front of the line. My Bulgarian friends whistled after us as her high heels clicked down the hall. I asked her if she wouldn't want to grab some coffee and she said all she wanted was a cigarette and to go home and maybe have a bath.

I pictured her in the bath, her shoulders shiny above the foamy water and her long hair tied in a ball.

I talked to her while she lit up outside and I also lit up when she offered. She had first come to the States four years ago, she said, to study art. She wanted to be an animator but was sick of Japan, of how you had to know people to get good jobs. There was a problem of course: the kind of animation she wanted to do was best done in Japan, not in the States. Now that she was finishing her degree, she had to decide . . .

I started coughing. Distracted by her closeness, I had inhaled by mistake. I dropped the cigarette at my feet. She laughed. She bowed over and clapped a hand on her knee, that's how hard she was laughing.

"Have you never smoked before?"

I shook my head.

"Really? Never?"

"Never," I said.

"Why did you do it, then?" she asked, though I'm sure she knew why. She kept laughing at me and I didn't mind it one bit. I asked her to finish her story but no longer listened to the things she said. I was afraid that at the end she'd simply bid me farewell and walk away, that once her story ended she would dissolve like smoke. "You look awfully pale," she said, and searched for a place to throw the stub away. "Tell me about yourself," she asked. "What are *you* doing in the States?"

So I told her. I was loading other people's bags in the States. I was unloading other people's bags. I lived in a small apartment with two other Bulgarians and was saving money to go to college. I had arrived in the U.S. five years before, winner of a green card.

The day I won my green card it stormed in Sofia, ravaging wind, deluging summer rain. I had come back home from work, soaking wet, to find the thick envelope stuck in the mailbox like a heart too big for its chest. *Dear winner*, the letter began.

I sprinted up eight flights of stairs to find my parents watching the rain out the living room window. My mother wept when I told them.

"When did you do this?" she asked. "Why didn't you tell us?"

"I didn't think I'd win the lottery."

"Now, let's all calm down now," Father said. "No need for tears. Have a seat. Let's talk it over. What are your reasons? What are you missing here? Are you unhappy? You're not hungry. You have a good room, a computer with Internet. You have a job. Let's talk it over. What are your reasons here?"

"I'm twenty-seven. I can't still live with my parents. My job . . ."

"You're absolutely right," my father agreed. He nodded and rubbed his chin. "We'll get you your own place. One of my colleagues is leasing."

"*Taté,*" I said. "I don't want *you* to get it for me. I want to try my own luck in America. Do you understand?"

He said nothing. He put his arm around my mother and said nothing.

•

After we ate what our neighbors brought for breakfast, I decided to show the village to Yuki. We took turns with the camera. She posed by a house where I'd often played as a child. The house was in ruins now. There were many obituaries on the gates and Yuki asked me what these were. I told her that in Bulgaria when someone died the family made a *nekrolog*, a sheet with the deceased's name and picture, a brief, sorrowful poem underneath. People pasted this necrology on their gates, on light poles, and all around their villages or towns so others who might have known the dead would learn the news.

"We do something similar in Japan," Yuki said, staring closely at the face of an old man, almost inkless from rain. "But no pictures. We post a notice on the entrance to the house of the dead. So and so died, the funeral will be at this time, this place.

People often rob those houses," she said, and took the camera from my hand. She made me pose under an old linden tree. "They lurk outside, wait for the procession to leave, then rob the house. When my uncle died my aunt asked their neighbor to stay in and guard while everyone was away for the service."

I made the typical peace sign Yuki made on every picture, to mock her. "What if the neighbor wanted to come to the funeral as well?"

"No one wants to go to funerals," Yuki said. We took more pictures. We followed the road down to the square. An old Lada loaded with Gypsies whizzed by us in a cloud of dust. They blew their horn. "Be very careful here," I told Yuki. "If you hear a car coming, always step to the side. Always, do you understand?"

She nodded.

"I didn't know there were Gypsies in the village," I said.

"Gypsies? Were these Gypsies?" She grew excited. She had always wanted to see real Gypsies, beautiful dark-eyed enchantresses dancing barefooted around tall fires, and violin players whose fingers flew up and down the fingerboards so fast only a deal with the devil could explain their mad skill.

"But that's in the fairy tales, Yuki."

She was unbending. I had to, she said, at all cost, take her to see the Gypsies, let her photograph them. I had no intention of doing such a thing.

"Okay," I said. "Maybe later."

It was a little after noon and people were coming home from their fields. Yuki greeted everyone with a smile and everyone smiled back at her and watched us long after we'd passed.

"I don't get it," Yuki said. "Why am I so interesting to them?"

We took pictures of the square, of the bridge and the river, barely a trickle underneath, then of the fountain with the five spouts—one for each partisan from our village who had been killed in 1944.

"What happened in 1944?" Yuki asked me. "In Bulgaria I mean."

She stood by the fountain, whose pool was overflowing, its bottom clogged with rotten leaves. Water barely oozed out of two of the spouts that had been bashed in with something. Yuki made the peace sign as I took a picture.

"In '44 the Communist partisans seized power," I said. "But not without a fight. Many of them were killed."

"Why are these spouts bashed in?" Yuki asked me.

"I don't know," I said. "When communism fell, people got braver. I guess that's how someone must have shown their dislike for the Party."

With two fingers Yuki held a ladle tethered to the fountain with a rusty chain. The ladle was green except for the rim where thirsty lips had kissed it for over sixty years: the metal there shone, as pure as the day it had been forged. Yuki brought the ladle to her nose, sniffed it and let it dangle on the chain.

"They look like they were bashed in with a rock," she said.

I took the ladle and drank the cold mountain water. "Well," I said, "how would *you* bash them, Yuki?"

We bought groceries from the shop on the square; then, as we walked up the road, people called us over to their gates and gave us bags of tomatoes as gifts, an early greenhouse sort, slightly rosy, which though not as good as the summer tomatoes was still a million times sweeter than what we bought in the States. The neighbors gave us cheese and bread, a bottle of red wine. We ate a good lunch in our yard. We drank some of the wine.

"I really like it here," Yuki said.

"Good," I said. I hugged her and kissed the top of her head. She put her arms around my waist and we held each other in the yard. "Remember," I said, "good things happen to good people. All right? Look at me," I said, and she looked up. "All right?"

•

Yuki and I had gotten married quickly, cheaply, and without much fuss. That's not to say we didn't fantasize about a proper wedding. And then another in Tokyo. And a third in Sofia. But we had to hurry things up not just for the lack of money. After graduating from college, Yuki would lose her student visa. My green card would allow her to stay in Chicago without hiding.

I called my parents to let them know we were about to get married. I told them who Yuki was, how good she was to me—for me—how much we loved each other.

"I can't believe you're telling us now," my father said.

"I didn't want to jinx it," I told him, which was the truth. "You know my luck."

"Where is she from, again?" my mother asked, and I told her.

"At least she isn't black," my mother said.

•

In the afternoon I took Yuki to the river. We waded in the water, which was still cold, then sat on the rocks and watched some village children splash in a shallow pool below us. There were a good twenty of them, and their bicycles, parked side by side up where the road was, shone with the sun. Another car whizzed madly by and blew its horn and down below the children yelled and waved as if the car could see them.

"I'll jump in with them," I said.

"No you won't."

I took my shirt and pants off and walked down to the pool and jumped in. The water was cold and I screamed and up above Yuki laughed and made her beloved peace sign.

"That's some cold water," I told the children.

"No it's not. Just keep moving," they said. We splashed around. They climbed on my shoulders, muddy feet, and held me by the neck and hair and by my ears. "My ears!" I cried, and up above Yuki laughed again. I could see she was getting ready for a picture. She stood up on the cliff and leaned forward.

"Stop!" I yelled. I rushed out of the pool and scrambled up the rocks.

"What's the matter with you?" she said.

"You scared me. Don't lean forward like that."

"Psycho," she said. She kissed me. I kissed her on the belly. We watched the footsteps I'd left on the rocks dry up, then I got dressed and we walked back to the house. I asked her if she wanted to see something historic. I led her to the barn and I shoveled very dry hay away from a corner. There was an old wooden gate under the hay, with big runny letters painted on the wood.

"What does it say?" Yuki asked me.

I knew the gate from my father because Grandpa never spoke of such things. On the morning of September 9, 1944, a bunch of beardless boys, fresh out of the woods after months of hiding in dugouts, knocked on my great-grandfather's gate. They informed him that all his stock, fifty cows, one hundred sheep, and his land—three hundred decares—were now property of the Communist Party and would be added to a collective farm. It was the Communist Party, they said, that had taken over and now governed Bulgaria.

My great-grandfather asked to be excused for a moment and returned with his shotgun. How things unfolded exactly I don't know in detail, but he ended up shooting one of the boys dead. Three days later the comrades returned, summoned an improvised people's court, declared my great-grandfather an enemy of the people and hanged him on the lower branch of the walnut tree. They made Grandpa, then in his twenties, watch and draw conclusions about his own future. The comrades wrote KULAK on the gates in big tarry letters so everyone who passed by would know our family was a class enemy.

When I was twelve Father brought me to the barn and showed me the gates, which Grandpa had taken off the hinges and preserved hidden under the hay. I remember I didn't feel anything special reading the letters, with the tar running at their base like green onions that had sprouted roots. But now, with Yuki by my side, I felt something I could not explain, something that, suddenly, I did not want to be passed on to her.

"I don't know what it says," I told her.

"You *are* a psycho," she said.

•

I was all out of ideas for the rest of the afternoon, so Yuki asked if she could drive the Moskvich. I saw no reason against it. I took her photo by the car, then one of her inside as she waved out a window eternally doomed to open only halfway.

"Maybe we could drive to the Gypsies," she said.

Instead, I told her to drive up the road, out of the village. She shifted the gears clumsily at first, the teeth grinding as she shifted, but she got into a rhythm soon.

"This isn't nearly as bad as I expected," she said, and I told her the engine of the Moskvich was a copy of a BMW engine, so it was, in reality, a BMW we drove.

"It feels more like the Flintstones' car."

"The Flintstones? Really, Yuki? That's your best joke?"

The road wound around the mountain, with a thick pine forest on one side and down below us the gorge where the river flowed. When we passed by the children's bicycles, Yuki blew the horn. We drove for about four kilometers and I told her to pull over where the road broadened, where a huge concrete pipe stuck out and, when it rained, dumped water from the hills down into the gorge.

We leaned on the hood and watched the pine trees on all sides, the mountain hills on fire with the setting sun. I remembered how Grandma would take me mushroom hunting after every major rain, how once we filled two sacks so large we barely managed to haul them home, fueled, I suppose, only by the exhilarating prospects of all the jars we'd can for the winter. But at home we discovered the mushrooms had drowned in their own blue milk, poisonous doubles of edible mushrooms not even the neighbors' goats would eat.

I wanted to share this memory with Yuki, but I did not know the names of the edible mushrooms in English, nor of their poisonous doubles.

"Why do we live in America?" I asked her instead. "Can you tell me that? If it's for the money, we make no money. We have other places to go. We could move back here."

"I don't know," Yuki said. "I don't see myself living here. There is nothing for me to do here."

"This is a good place to raise a child," I said.

"Maybe."

I looked at her. I said, "Don't say such things unless you mean them."

"Let's see how things go next month," she said. "Let's not talk about it now. Let's not jinx it." She popped a piece of nicotine gum and chewed it quietly. "It's like I don't really need this stuff anymore. I'm fine without it."

"Good things, Yuki," I reminded her. We got in the car and she drove back to the village, the gears grating as she shifted.

"Go neutral down the hill. It's the Bulgarian way. Save gas."

She flicked the stick in neutral and we moved faster, without the rattle. I held her hand. I felt really good about our situation. "I feel good about our situation," I said.

"Me too," she said, and turned to look at me.

The boy, too, must have been riding his bike without looking. But Yuki saw him when we were still a good distance away. She jerked the steering wheel and slammed on the brakes. The tires locked and we slid with a screech, off the road and into the ditch. We hit a rock, but it wasn't a bad hit. Yuki was okay, and I was okay. We looked at each other to make sure. She turned off the engine and we got out.

The boy lay on one side of the road with his bicycle a few feet away in the grass. He was a tiny boy, dark-haired, dark-skinned. He couldn't have been older than ten.

"Oh, my God," Yuki said, and started crying. But the boy sat up and rubbed his head.

"I'm all right," he said, and looked at me and then at Yuki. She kneeled down and kissed him on the cheeks, on the forehead, she smothered him with kisses.

"Get away from him," I said, "don't touch him."

"You're very pretty," the boy told her. He rubbed his head.

I told him to stay as he was, then I told Yuki to go back to the car. She had stopped kissing him but refused to go. She no longer cried. She watched the boy.

"Are you really all right?" I said.

"Yes, baté, I'm fine."

"Did you hit your head?"

"Maybe. But it doesn't hurt."

"How are your arms? Anything broken?"

"No," the boy said. He shook his arms. He touched his legs to check them. He smiled at Yuki.

"We need to take him to a hospital," she said.

"What's your name?" I asked him.

"Assencho."

"We'll take you to the hospital, Assencho. We'll have a doctor look at your head."

The boy sprung up to his feet. He seemed really okay. He didn't wobble or limp. We had not hit him. He had just fallen off his bike, an orange Balkanche, like the one I'd ridden as a kid. In the grass, the boy tried to readjust the chain, which had come off the cog.

"Let me help you," I said. I kneeled beside him and turned the bike on its side. I held one end of the chain and the boy the other and we stretched it and fought to line it up against the gear. By the time we were done, my fingers and the boy's were black with grease.

"Come on," I said, and wiped my fingers in the grass. "We'll put the bike in the trunk and take you home."

The boy pulled up his bike. "If Father learns I was here, he'll tan my hide. I'm supposed to be helping Brother with the wood. But if I come early to the river, other kids won't let me swim with them. I wait for all the kids to leave. Then I have the pool to myself. And it's warmer in the evening. The water's warmer."

The boy chattered excitedly like this for a while.

"What's he saying?" Yuki said. She was sitting in the middle of the road, so I told her to get up and go back to our car. The boy mounted his bike.

"Listen, Assencho," I said.

"Goodbye, *baté*," the boy said. He waved at Yuki, rang the bell on his bike and set off down the road.

We sat in the grass and said nothing for a long time. I tried to wipe my fingers. Yuki took out some gum. "But we didn't hit him?" she asked, and I told her that no, we hadn't hit him.

"How do you know? How can you be sure?"

"We were going too fast. It would be different if we'd hit him."

"We should have taken him to the hospital. Why did you let him go?"

"He jumped on his bike and was gone. You saw that. He was all right. He didn't wobble."

"No, he didn't wobble," she said. She wiped her cheeks. I got in the car and started it and the car started without a problem. I pulled out of the ditch. The fender was bent where we'd hit the rock and some of the paint had come off.

"Was the boy a Gypsy?" Yuki said as I drove down the mountain, but I'm not really sure that's what she said.

•

We didn't sleep that night. We lay in bed and listened to the mice in the attic, to the wind in the walnut branches, to the pines up the slope. We lay stiff and did not hold hands.

"Let's talk about something," Yuki said. She sat up in bed. We talked about some things. How sweet the tomatoes had been. What our friends might be doing at this time in Chicago.

"It's no good," she said. She got dressed and went outside. I didn't follow her right away. I watched the walnut out the window and for some reason, maybe because the moon was behind clouds, maybe because of the shadows, I thought of my great-grandfather. I'd never thought of him before, but now it was him I thought about. Then I brought my fingers to my nose and sniffed that faint smell of grease from the bike chain still lingering unwashable. I remembered how the boy had smiled at Yuki, how he'd called her pretty. No one had called her pretty so far. But I thought she was. Very. I thought of how the boy had mounted his bike. How he didn't wobble at all and how his head had not hurt.

"I'm sure he's all right," I told Yuki, who sat on the threshold to the yard and chewed gum. "We can ask about him tomorrow."

"I'm dying for a cigarette," she said.

I sat beside her. I wanted to, but I did not touch her.

•

There was no need to ask the neighbor at breakfast. He came to bring us some *buhti* and milk and sat down while we ate. "Let me tell you what happened," he said. "This Gypsy kid came home last night and his father beat him. I mean with a stick, tanned his hide, battered him real good. And after that the boy just went to his bed, lay down and closed his eyes. They haven't been able to wake him up since. The doctor visited and said it was a coma. That's how hard his father had thrashed him."

I'm not really sure what we did that afternoon. We didn't leave the house and we didn't speak. "Please, go find me some cigarettes," was all Yuki managed to say, and at one point I walked down to the square and was glad to finally leave the house. I bought her a few packs.

"Did you hear about the boy?" the cashier asked me. "Awful

story," she said. "And the father . . ." She shook her head. "Wanted to drown himself in the river."

On my way back, outside our house, I saw a neighbor inspecting the Moskvich.

"*Zdrasti, amerikanets,*" the neighbor said. He was holding a large pan in his hands. "Where did you hit the car?"

I mumbled something. It was like this already, I said, my father had done it.

"I heard Yuki wasn't feeling too well," the neighbor said. "I heard she didn't look good at breakfast. Hardly ate a thing. So my wife made her one of her *banitsas*. With extra eggs and butter."

I thanked him and took the pan.

"You all right, *amerikanets*?" he said.

"I'm fine," I said. "Thank you, we'll be fine."

•

After three days in which Yuki and I barely ate, slept, or talked, the boy died. We heard about it from another neighbor. There wasn't much more to it really. The boy had died.

"Is she saying something about the boy?" Yuki asked while the neighbor was speaking.

"Yes," I said.

"What is she saying?"

"He's dead. He died this morning."

Yuki didn't cry. She stood very still and I stood still until the neighbor left us.

"What are we going to do?" she said.

"There is nothing we can do. The boy is dead."

"I know that. Stop saying it. I know that already. But we have to tell them. Don't we have to tell them?"

We didn't know what to do. We were in limbo, weightless, floating in empty space. We were really scared. I'd never felt scared like that before.

Then, early that afternoon, someone knocked on the gates and out the window we saw a cart with a donkey, and a Gypsy man by the cart. Yuki gave out a cry. She dug her peeled nails into my arm. For a minute we watched the man crumple his cap in his big hands. He wore no shoes, I could see that; blue working trousers, a sailor T-shirt with white and blue stripes. His skin was very dark from the sun and his bald head glistened with sweat. For a minute we just watched him and I thought we should hide until he left.

"Open the gates," Yuki said, and sent me out on my own.

I opened the gates.

"Are you . . ." the man said. He came closer.

"Yes, yes," I said. "I'm the American, yes."

The man apologized. "I apologize," he said. "I'm sorry to bother you." He spoke fast, as though he were afraid he might never speak again if he stopped. "My boy just died," he said. "We'll bury him tomorrow and we don't have a picture of him. We never took his picture. My wife won't look at me now, but I know she would have liked me to come here. We heard, someone told us—Tenyo, was it, or someone else?—someone told us you were taking pictures. Your wife was taking pictures. You had a camera, someone told us. Tenyo, was it? It wasn't Tenyo, I don't think." Then the man held his cap and watched me in silence.

I told him to wait there. I told him I'd be back right away. I rounded the corner and bowed, fell to the ground. I wanted to vomit but couldn't. It was that bad. Back in the house, I told Yuki what the man had come to ask for.

"We can't say no," she said. "We have no right to say no. But I can't come with you. I can't stomach this."

"You're coming," I said. "You're not leaving me alone. Do you hear me, Yuki? We're going together." We turned on the camera. We made sure the batteries were charged. We made sure there was room on the memory card. We made sure the strap wasn't tangled.

The Gypsy was looking at the Moskvich outside. He nodded at my wife. He kissed her hand. He thanked us. He apologized again. "Mighty good car," he said at the Moskvich. He ran his hand over the bump in the fender. "I can fix this for you. Bring it to my place. I could use some work."

He invited us to his cart. I was relieved we wouldn't have to drive. He helped Yuki get in. We sat in the back and he lashed the donkey. "*Diy,*" he called. "*Diy,* Marko. Git."

The cart rattled. We went through the village and I could see people watching us as we passed. The sun was still high and there was no wind and the air felt stuffy, unbearably hot. I touched Yuki's elbow, but she wiggled away. She was pale and her lips were chapped. She looked thirsty. She held the camera in her lap with both hands the way she had held a live chicken at the neighbors, afraid it would flap its wings or scratch her.

"We have to tell him," she said. She whispered.

"He can't understand you."

"We have to tell him."

The Gypsies lived on the other end of the village. They'd made a little hamlet for themselves. The man's house wasn't nearly as bad as I thought it would be. They had a satellite dish, a garden with flowers in it. There were many people in the yard, and cars all up the street, with license plates from other places. More people were arriving and the air smelled of boiled cabbage and car exhaust.

The Gypsy spoke only once, just before we got out, and I didn't know if he spoke at us at all. "I don't know how it happened," he said. "How did it happen?"

We walked in the yard and all the people there stood up to meet us. They all wore black, even the children. Some of the women were sobbing behind black shawls. One by one the men came to us and shook our hand.

"Why are they doing this?" Yuki asked.

"I don't know," I said. I wanted to run. I wanted to turn

around and run and never look back. They took us inside the house. We walked through a curtain of bamboo beads—with flies perched along the strings, waiting for someone's hand to grant them passage.

"The flies," I heard a voice say as we stepped inside and saw a few shoot in. The whole house smelled of the cabbage I'd noticed before. In the hallway we walked by a large round mirror that was covered with a white sheet, so the boy's bodiless soul wouldn't catch a glimpse of itself. There were women in the kitchen making salads and stirring pots. Someone was cleaning fish and I smelled that too. The women looked at us when we passed and nodded. Yuki sought my hand. We held hands as they led us in the room with the boy.

The boy lay on a small bed and looked the way we remembered him. His mother sat on a chair by his side and fended the flies off his face with a newspaper. She didn't look at us. She flapped the paper. For a moment she adjusted his collar with her free hand. The boy was dressed in black pants, a brown sweater, a white shirt underneath. He had black shoes on, which they had tried to polish. His hair was combed neatly to one side. He looked as though any moment now he'd sit up, rub his head and smile. I searched his face for bruises, but saw none. His fingers were entwined, and I recognized the shadows of the grease his mother had tried to wash off, but couldn't.

I retracted my own fingers into the shell of my fist. Yuki started to cry. It seemed like that's what the women were waiting for. They tore their head scarves and tossed them up in the air, and wailed like bagpipes in the head-scarf rain. But the mother hushed them. "A curse on you, furies. You're scaring him. He's watching us now and you're scaring him with your wailing."

"Yuki," the father said. He knew her name. He said it beautifully. "Is this a good place for the picture? Or is it too dark?"

My wife was in no shape to answer. It was very difficult for me to speak, but I said it was too dark here. Our camera was cheap, I said, and made poor pictures indoors. The flash was bad. I had to shut myself up. I had to force myself to be quiet.

I led Yuki outside by the hand. I told her to breathe deeply. Someone brought water and she drank. She asked for more. She sprinkled some on her face. Finally they carried the boy out.

Everyone huddled to the sides as though the boy and the people were magnets facing each other with the same pole. They brought a chair and sat the boy in it.

I could see what they were trying to do.

"Oh, no," I said. I had not expected them to do such a thing.

"They can't," Yuki said. "He's not . . ."

But they brought pillows to steady his body. His brothers and sisters stood around him and held him upright. Then the mother joined her children on one side and the father stood on the other, but she said something to him in their language I couldn't understand. He said something back. He begged her, but she said no, no, no. She chased him away from the picture.

Careful not to expose my grease-stained fingers, I held them locked inside the LCD screen—a box in which their two-dimensional images would remain linked forever, in which time did not exist, nor did the need to breathe. There were no living in this box, no dead. Just perfect stillness.

"We are ready," the mother said at last. "Take the picture."

·

The Gypsies insisted we stay for dinner. They fixed a long table in the yard and started to bring food. They put bricks on the ground and long planks on the bricks for sitting.

"No," I said.

"Né, né, né," said Yuki. She waved about.

"You can't say no," the father said. "Sit down. You can't say no."

We sat almost in the middle of the table. We held hands. People crowded on the planks, like fat swallows along a wire.

"Eat as much as you like," the mother told us. "This is fresh cabbage. This is lamb soup. This is river fish, so watch out for the bones. It's all very good."

No one spoke. We heard only spoons against the metal plates, the licking of fingers. Someone sucked marrow from a bone, and outside, on the road, a bicycle bell rang.

"Is it nice in America?" a man asked us.

"Not really," I said.

"Is it nice in Japan?"

"I haven't been yet. I would like to go."

"You'll go," another man said. "You're still young. There is a whole world at your feet."

"We're trying to have a baby," I said. I don't know why I said it. I shouldn't have. This was not the place, not the time. But I couldn't help it. Yuki was looking at me. *Stop*, her eyes were telling me. "We can't conceive," I kept on going. "We've tried for a long time, but we can't. We're going to the hospital next week. We'll try in vitro. Do you know what that is?"

"Sure," the Gypsy said.

Some woman said, "I can give you a few herbs. Raspberry leaf, nettle, damiana. Those should help. Those are always good."

"Really?" I said. "Would you really?"

The woman stood up. "I'll be back," she said.

"What are you doing?" Yuki asked me. "I beg you, let's go. I can't take this any more."

I held her down. "Wait," I said. "In a minute. Wait."

The woman came back with a small bag of herbs. "Boil them like tea. Let her drink it. Then let the doctors do what they do."

I thanked her. I took the bag and explained to Yuki what this was about.

The woman smiled at her. "Are you having trouble, my child?" she said. "Do you mind?" I scooted over and she sat between us. "You don't mind, do you?" she said, and put her palm on Yuki's belly. Yuki didn't protest. She closed her eyes. Her face became very still. The woman ran her palm in circles over Yuki's stomach and her calluses caught on Yuki's dress and moved it slightly. Then the woman held her palm still. "There you go," the woman said. "There you have it."

•

It was dark when we stood up to leave.

"You can't leave yet," the father said, but didn't stop us. "Are you coming tomorrow?"

"Yes," I said. "We'll be at the graveyard at ten. And we'll go to town right after that and get the picture printed."

"Thank you," the father said. He caught me by the elbow. "Please come with me inside," he said. "Leave your wife for a moment. She'll be all right. But take the camera." I looked at Yuki. I knew she didn't want to be left alone.

"It's okay," she said. She sat down at the table again and someone filled her glass half with lemonade and half with red wine.

The father took me to his boy's room. Two older girls were sitting by the bed, in the glow of a small oil lamp whose reflecting mirror, too, was clothed over with a kerchief. The girls fled and their shadows scattered long across the wall, like tall grass cut down and blown away by a gust. The father kneeled beside the boy and lay a hand on his shoulder.

"A quick picture before my wife sees us, will you?" he said.

I fixed the camera on them and watched their grainy image in the back screen. The half of the boy's face that was close to the light looked bright yellow, almost glowing. The Gypsies had put two coins on his eyes to keep them from opening, so one coin, closer to the light, shone like a cat's pupil. The other coin was dark and that whole side of the boy's face was darker and then his chest, his hands stiffly tied together with stained fingers were darker still, and finally his shoes were almost invisible in the dark, so far away from the oil lamp.

I pressed the button and the flash came on and in the picture both the father and the boy were flushed with flooding light. Everything shone.

The father looked at the little screen. "Is this a scratch?" he said. "Why is there a scratch here?" He had seen something on the boy's photographed face I couldn't see. "His face isn't scratched," the father said. "No scratches at all on his face."

I looked closer at the screen and then at the boy.

"It's an eyelash," I said.

The father went to see for himself. He licked his finger and picked up the eyelash from the boy's face. He didn't know what to do with it right away. Then with his free hand he took a kerchief from his pocket, lay the lash in it and bundled it up.

I watched him do this and I knew if I didn't tell him now, I'd never tell him. And if I didn't tell him now, I'd never forgive myself, not in a thousand years.

He came to me and leaned down to kiss my hands. He did not notice the grease.

•

Back in our yard, Yuki pulled out a cigarette. But she didn't light it. We sat at the threshold, and she played with her lighter. She flipped it open and stared at the flame in silence, until the flame burned her finger and she let the light expire.

"We have to get the picture printed out tonight," she said, and dropped the unlit cigarette at her feet. "We'll make a *nekrolog* and paste it around the village."

I told her it was already after nine. It would be difficult to find a printer in town.

"We'll find something," she said. "An Internet café. There must be something that's open."

"Okay," I said. "We can do that."

"But we're not going to the funeral tomorrow. We'll print the picture out and we'll take it to them tonight. We're not going tomorrow."

I agreed. I told her we should get going, then; we had a long way to go. But she didn't move.

"Just a little longer," she said. I could see she was waiting for me to put my arm around her shoulder, to kiss her forehead. Good things, Yuki, she wanted me to tell her, happened to good people.

But I couldn't tell her such a thing now. I couldn't pull out the camera, the way I would have at the end of a pleasant vacation, and prop it on the hood of the busted car for one final, memorable picture. I couldn't ask her, while I played with the self-timer, to stand just a little to the right, yes, right there, Yuki, so there'd be room for me by your side, so the house, and the orchard, and the barn would be visible behind us.

I had kept quiet before the Gypsy, quiet before the gates in the barn. And now at the threshold, I kept quiet still. After a minute, I went in for the car keys, and while Yuki packed our bags, I folded Grandpa's trousers and, so they wouldn't get dusty, lay them out in a drawer. I made sure all the windows were shut, all the doors. Yuki waited in the car while I struggled with the lock. I stood outside the gate and allowed myself one final look at the yard, at the walnut tree. But I did not allow myself to think of the child, our child, nor of the summers that would have to pass before we could return to the village.

In the car I checked the backseat to make sure we hadn't forgotten anything.

"Did we get everything?" I said. "All the bags? Your cigarettes?"

"I don't need cigarettes," she said. "I threw them away." She was chewing nicotine gum.

I started the engine.

"Wait," she said. She turned around and rummaged through the luggage. She pulled things out and put them back again. At last she held out the bag of herbs the Gypsy woman had given us. She cradled it in her lap. "It's all here," she said, "now we can go."

CROSS THIEVES

A girl with no breasts storms inside the café to tell us the government has fallen and there will be no school today. Someone throws a beer bottle at her so she will shut the door. It's minus five outside but in the schoolyard café it's just right. We've stayed up all night, drinking clouds and playing *svarka*. Very early on, Gogo managed to flap a thirty-three against this rich kid who bet his watch and pager on a pair of aces, so for the rest of the night we keep getting pages from the kid's parents. *Dechko, where are you? Dechko, come home!*

"You imagine my parents paging me?" Gogo asks me.

"What's so hard to imagine? You owning a pager or them calling you '*dechko*'?"

It's not that Gogo's parents don't give a shit about him. But then there's his big brother who always keeps their hair on fire. As for my parents, let's say I haven't seen them in four days, blame Father for it and leave it at that.

The girl shuts the door and goes to the bar to get a ViK. She is an all right girl, maybe too short in the legs. She downs her vodka and wipes her mouth with her sleeve. Then she drinks her kola in tiny sips.

"*Kopche*, look at that dog," Gogo says, and yells at her, "Woof-woof." Right now that's what we call each other. *Kopche*, which means *button*. Before that it was, What's up, *shnur*. Cable. Before that, what's up *shprangel*, which isn't even a word. Why? I don't know, it's nonsense. We've renounced our names. No more Radoslav, no more Georgi. I was named after my Grandpa who was named after his, but so what?

"*Kopche*, watch my chips," I say, and leave the café to take a piss. Glass shatters behind me and Bay Petko, the owner, curses at whoever threw it. It's a chilly, bitter morning and already the streets beyond the school fence are teeming with people, a dirty flood. I watch it whirl, a mishmash of faces, arms and legs, and the chants, loud and angry, blow fuses in my skull. *Down with the Reds!* Cherveni boklutsi. *Communist trash!*

It's January 1997 and once again the government has fallen. That's hardly a surprise. The first time it fell I was seven. November 1989. It was a spectacular collapse—the end of communism. At home we were glued to the TV while in a droning voice some big-shot Party member declared that the head of the Party, Todor Zhivkov, was stepping down from power. Zhivkov himself sat left of the podium, his eyes fixed dully on something only he could see, unblinking, like a cow's, his mouth half open and glistening with spit. "My God, these bastards have drugged him," my father said, and bit into the dried tail of a tiny salted fish. "I thought he'd rule forever," said my mother.

"No, thank you very much," Father said, and pointed the fish at me like a mummified finger. "Are you watching this, Rado? This is important. Make sure you remember this." As if I ever forgot a thing.

Then people choked the streets in mass protests and walls crumbled all over Eastern Europe. Bulgaria held its first democratic elections and since then the governments have dropped like rotten pears. 1990, 1992, 1994. Hyperinflation, devaluation. My father now makes 15,000 levs a month and a loaf of bread costs 600. And the zeros keep piling up.

Sometimes it seems to me things can't get worse than they already are. Surely we've sunk as deep as you can sink. Surely we should be pushing off the bottom, kicking, up and out of the swamp.

Last week, Gogo says, his brother beat their mom. She wouldn't tell him where she hid the money, so he splintered a chair and thrashed her with the leg. When their dad came home Gogo's brother was in the corner, shaking and chewing on his fingers. Gogo's father dragged him out on the street and found the dealer and bought him his dose. He bought him a clean syringe, then left him on a bench and went home to take care of his wife.

Awful story, right? And what did Gogo do to help? A few days later he found the money his mother had buried in the ficus pot and blamed the theft on his brother, who, naturally, was in no shape to deny a thing. But, you'd say, that's what friends are for, right? A few reproachful words, some sensible advice on my behalf and goodness will be restored once again. The money returned, we will be pushing off the muddy bottom, if only momentarily.

We spent the money on two bottles of vodka, three loaves of bread, we played the lotto and gambled the rest on cards. Playing the lotto was my idea. "Sometimes, I have this feeling," I told Gogo as I was scratching crosses inside the tiny number boxes on the ticket, "that things can't get any worse than this. We'll get a break, *kopche*. Just wait and see."

•

So now I'm pissing on the school wall, with the protestors chanting beyond the fence, when the guard sees me. He's just put a lock on the school to show it's closed and runs toward me, grunting.

"Chill there, Gramps," I say. "Can't you see I'm drawing a star?"

I've been known to go out of my way on several occasions just to piss on the school wall. Once I took the trolley from the Palace of Culture all the way to school, holding it back so long my dick was on fire for an hour. My father said I had passed a grain and probably had stones in my kidneys. That I should drink more water.

"I'll cut your dick off, Rado!" the guard yells at me.

"Want to bite it off?"

He leans on his knees to catch some air. "The Amazing Rado," he says, though I've told him a million times not to call me this. His breaths escape in sharp clouds against the cold like souls of words he is about to speak. "Can't even piss a straight spurt, zigzagging drugged."

"I don't do drugs, Gramps," I tell him. "I drink Doctor's vodka, the one that comes with vitamin C in it."

I zip up and he offers me a ciggy. We smoke as the morning mist unfolds around us, as kids arrive to find the school locked. Gramps is all right for an old guy. Used to be in the army, a UAZ driver, but during the hungry years they caught him stealing provisions from the tank brigade, beat him and threw him out on the street. He told me he had been stealing cans of buffalo meat for six months before they caught him. The cans were thirty years old but the meat, he said, was juicier than chicken. A thirty-year-old can, that's twice my age.

"Any new gigs this month?" Gramps says, and nudges me in the ribs. "Will the Amazing Rado grace us old farts at the retiree club with his gift again?"

"Knock it off, Gramps, will you?"

"Just making small talk, Rado," he says. "Just being friendly." He pulls a stone out of his pocket and lets me hold it. "You feel how much freedom is packed inside?" he asks.

Then he tells me his nephew, a TIR driver who often travels to Germany on rounds, brought it the other day. "A piece of the wall," he says. "Do you believe it? I'll get at least ten thousand levs for this."

"No, Gramps," I say, "I don't. This here is slate. A metamorphic rock. The wall was made of concrete, like our apartment blocks. Haven't you seen those pictures of Russian soldiers lining up the panels side by side?"

"I have no time for pictures," Gramps says and pockets the

rock. "You're a smart devil. But someone stupid might pay," and leaning over he whispers in my ear, "Speaking of devils, do you have something to sell? A coin? A silver spoon?"

I brush him off. "I heard the government has fallen."

That's all it takes for Gramps to bite. He starts his rant about how much he hates the government, how one day he wants to sneak back into the barracks, steal a BTR—a tank, even—and drive into the parliament head-on. "I think I'll look good smashed in a tank," he says. "A glorious, heroic death becomes me. Fuck it, Rado, let's get a tank." And then he pesters me to go with him to the protests. There will be one million people out on the streets today. All of Sofia. "I got no one else," he says.

"You're an ill man, Gramps," I say, and tell him how all politics is kitsch.

"Your dick is kitsch," he says.

Back in the café I look for Gogo. But Gogo is gone and I lie in the corner, on a pile of jackets and school bags, and close my eyes for just a moment.

•

I am the smartest kid you'll ever meet. So in this context, I suppose I *am* amazing. But I'm not really science-smart, or street-smart, even. It's just that I never forget a thing. They wrote about me in the paper once. "WUNDERKIND: Phenomenal Memory Turns Kid into a Walking Encyclopedia." I was six. The reporter came to our apartment in the small town where we lived before we moved to Sofia. He started off with questions right away.

"How many meters in a mile? How many feet in a meter? My daughter was born on March 21, 1980. What day was that? What does traffic sign B1 signify? How many elements in the periodic table? Which element is number 32?"

I didn't like his questions. For one thing, I was sad he didn't know what day his daughter was born. *Rado is an alert little boy*, the article read, *interested in everything that is unified in a system. He was only two when he memorized all 110 traffic signs as well as the Cyrillic and Latin alphabets. Once he turned three, his father says, he was given a world atlas and he memorized all countries, all capitals, all flags. In front of this reporter Rado draws the flag of Cameroon with a pencil and then explains which stripe is green, which red, which yellow. The star in the middle, he explains, is also yellow. Then he draws a diagram of the human hand and labels each bone. To the question of what he wants to become when he grows up Rado answers: a cosmonaut, like Georgi Ivanov, the first Bulgarian in space. Soyuz 33 from Baikonur, April 10, 1979, at 17:34 . . . Little comrade, bright future awaits you . . .*

The following year my parents moved to Sofia in hopes of placing me in a school for gifted children. But I didn't pass the entrance exam, and so they signed me up in the neighborhood school instead. Two months into first grade, our rent jumped so high we had to move to a cheaper neighborhood. I've changed schools eleven times because of high rent. Finally my father took me to the city council. "This boy," he said, "has a phenomenal memory but no place to live." He made me do a trick: I read from a book some clerk had left behind, *Accounting Principles for Non-Accountants*, and recited the page backward word by word. Then he showed everyone the newspaper clipping and everyone laughed. "If you had ten children," an official told him, "maybe then we could give you a flat. But at this point it's the Gypsies, with their countless offspring, that take precedence."

"Ten children like this one?" my father said outraged. "No, thank you very much."

We walked out, homeless still. About a week later a friend of my father's took him to some apartment in the outskirts he'd noticed nobody lived in. And we moved in. Just like that, without permission. There are thirteen Gypsies below us in a two-bedroom. Great-grandparents and a girl at fourteen breast-feeding her second, but at least now we don't have to move. Not until they catch us and kick us out.

Little comrade, bright future awaits you . . . I've never had a teacher come to me and say this. But I had a teacher say to me once, "Big deal, Rado, you can calculate pi to fifty decimal places. We got calculators for that, and now," he said, "we got the Internet."

•

Someone kicks my boots. "Wake up, *kopche*."

"I'm awake."

I take Gogo's hand and he helps me up. Every muscle hurts and I'm still a little drunk from the mint and mastic brandy. We smoke in the school yard and watch the streets boiling and the sky white above us, readying for snow.

"Gramps told me a million people will be out today."

"I don't give a shit about the people," Gogo says. "*Kopche*, my brother is in some serious trouble. He's fucked us all up. He pawned everything. My sweet Sony TV, the fridge, the oven. He pawned my fucking bed. I gotta sleep on the floor."

I laugh and then apologize. One thing I've learned from our politicians is you can say or do close to anything provided that you apologize afterward. Or beforehand, as is often the case.

"I need cash quick, right now," Gogo says. "The shithead at the pawnshop won't give us the furniture back. Brother's throwing a fit and we don't have the money to buy his stuff. We're keeping him chained to the radiator, which is stupid. He only needs to pull on the pipe once and then the whole place will be flooded."

"Let me stop you right there, *kopche*," I say. "I've had enough of your brother. It's too much."

"I'm serious. We need to help him. The other day," he keeps going, "my mother dragged me to that church, Sveti Sedmochislenitsi. She brought bread and wine for the priest to bless. She paid him to sprinkle some of Brother's shirts and pants with holy water. I bet she would have dragged Brother himself if she could. To get exorcised, you know, like in the movie. She bought candles for five thousand levs and left another five in a wooden box. She gave me a bunch of coins to place on the icons. She said, if the coin sticks to the glass, your prayer might come true. She didn't even say *will*. She said *might*. She told me to pray for Brother and wish for good things."

"What did you wish for?"

"Not to be in the fucking church."

He lights another cigarette off the one he's just finished and looks at me, a mirror. His eyes are red from the smoke, his face yellow from the cold, lips chapped.

Up the street, someone yells that all Communists are faggots.

"Tell me something I don't know," I say, and Gogo says, "Okay, here it is. In that church, above the wooden throne, there is a cross. The cross is made of gold and you, *kopche*, will help me steal it."

•

Gogo and I have turned stealing into a humanitarian mission of sorts. We steal magnanimously, with great unwillingness, with repulsion. We don't do it for ourselves, of course, because that would be low. We steal for Gogo's brother. We buy him heroin, we bail him out of jail, we purchase tickets for football games so Gogo's brother, too, will feel like a normal person and have some healthy fun. Half of the time, it just so happens, we forget to pass the money on to him. For instance, we didn't really bail him out of jail. We figured some discipline would do him good. How could we know the hooks in uniform would beat him so bad they'd break his nose?

Gogo and I steal things and sell them, mostly to Gramps. We snuck into the biology classroom and took the skull our teacher used for an ashtray. Later Gramps claimed he resold it on the black market as an authentic skull from the 1944 Communist uprising. He was not impressed when I told him the skull had actually belonged to Toshko Afrikanski, a chimp at the Sofia Zoo. "That wouldn't sell so well, now, would it?" he said. "Listen, Rado, a shoe, without the proper history to back it up, is nothing, less than shit. But say it's the shoe that Khrushchev smashed against that table and then the price jumps to at least ten thousand. I've sold five of those, and two were sneakers. Even the shit, with proper history, becomes important." And then he shoves stolen objects in my hands and asks me to endow them with history and meaning.

Gogo and I have stolen flasks and pipettes from the chemistry classroom that later Gramps resold as Nazi flasks and pipettes brought to Bulgaria after the fall of Berlin (the reason for their smuggling into our country as mysterious as the acid that erased their swastika stamps). We've stolen coils of copper wire from the physics lab (a Soviet leftover from the '68 Prague spring), a map of the Balkan Wars (vintage, first edition!), a globe (with the USSR still whole and strong). In Bulgaria today there is a black market for everything, it seems.

But Gogo and I are no thieves. Appropriators, maybe. Mythmakers. But thieves would be too low. You ought to draw the line some place, and drawing lines, I've come to realize, is just like offering apologies. Sometimes you are allowed to draw a line after the fact.

•

"Communist trash!" Gogo chants, and we flow with the torrential crowd. It's exhilarating, like on the way to a good football match. Funny I should think of that, because some of the chants, it strikes me now, are really football chants. Only we've substituted the rival team's name with that of the Party, the referee's with the premier's. It's mostly young people around us. Right in front a little girl in a pink anorak is nagging her father. "I can't breathe," she whines. He picks her up on his shoulders and I watch her ponytail jerk up and down like a flag from the olden days of khans—a horse tail on a spear. "I can't hear you," her father says and the girl shouts, "Red trash! Red shit!" and everyone around her laughs. She basks in this attention. "Say 'Red cunts!'" Gogo tells her, and she yells it, *"Cherveni putki."* More people laugh. The wind bangs on the balconies above us, flaps frozen laundry on the lines, and then the girl complains she's cold. Her father brings her down and I can hear her little voice cursing long after the torrent has taken them away.

We are by the Levski memorial when Gogo tells me he has to eat, something, anything, or he'll die. My stomach, too, is churning. I'm getting dizzy with the heat from all the bodies around us, so we elbow out.

There is a bakery around the corner. The smell of bread scratches purple shavings across my eyes.

"We're closed," the saleswoman tells us, and fastens her coat with safety pins. Behind her I can see whole tins of hot bread, steaming golden.

"Gospozho, we need just a loaf," I say. I'm hoping that *gospozho*—"missis"—will warm her Communist-despising heart. But secretly I wish she was our comrade—*drugarka*—so we might eat for free, the way we used to when we were kids, when bakeries belonged to the state and cashiers would give you bread and not care one bit about losing money.

"I got some protesting to do," she says. "But fine. One thousand levs." And then she nooses a scarf around her neck.

"Gospozho," Gogo says, "we're short on cash. But this boy here's a wunderkind. He can do a trick for a loaf."

"I've seen tricks to last me six lifetimes," Missis says. She sizes me up with greedy eyes. "Who'll win the parliament elections? No, wait. What are the winning numbers to the lotto?"

I shrug. "I'm not that kind of wunderkind," I say. Missis rounds the counter and prepares to lock the door. "But of course. You are some other kind. In Bulgaria today, everyone's a wunderkind," she says, and shoos us out.

"Why the hell didn't we just take a loaf and run?" I ask Gogo, and he says, "We aren't like that. Our ancestors died for bread. We can't steal bread."

That's rare talk from Gogo. But when you're hungry, all your history reveals itself clearly before you, if only in a flash. Though I suppose Gogo has a point. Some things are bigger than we are. "The essential" being one of them. *Nasashtniyat*, "the essential," that's what we call bread here in Bulgaria. No one is bigger than bread. *Proverbs and Sayings*, volume 35, page 124.

"Gogo," I say now to add a proverb of my own, "no one gives you bread for free."

•

When I was still very young, Father would often call me over to the table, where he and his friends worked on the nth bottle of vodka and the always-present string of dried, salted little fish. They'd pick up the daily paper and read in hoarse, drunk voices whole passages, pages sometimes, which I'd repeat from memory in the same sluggish, drunken manner word for word. I imagine it was in such a moment of intoxicated clarity one of them suggested that my father should send me to study in Sofia, in the school for gifted children.

There is such a school in Sofia, where, in theory at least, children with gifts are handpicked through rigorous examination and then their gifts—scientific, humanitarian, artistic—are allowed to bloom and bear sweet, juicy fruit.

"If they find out your kid is in fact a genius—" the friend must have explained, and my father must have interrupted on the spot: "What do you mean, *if*? What do you mean, *in fact*? Look at him! It's a sure thing."

"Anyway, *when* they establish that he has a gift, they'll move your whole family to Sofia. They'll buy you an apartment, give you and your wife good jobs. They'll take good care of him."

"We'll do it," Father must have said, and slammed a determined

fist on the table, "but not for our benefit. No, comrade, thank
you very much. We're not like this. We'll do it for his own good
sake."

But I was still too young to apply for school, and Father decided to use the remaining time to make my name heard through-
out the Motherland. He dug up some archaic textbooks, history,
chemistry, physics, visited every school in town and convinced a
few teachers to let us interrupt their classes. He'd sit me down in
a chair before the gaze of bored tenth graders and pass around
the books we'd brought. It was always I who carried the heavy
tomes, because Father insisted such physical effort would develop
my endurance for knowledge. "Open to any page," he'd tell the
students, "and read aloud. Then my son will repeat back to you
like a miraculous echo!" The students read, one after the other.
We'd let some time pass and then I'd repeat, words whose meaning I did not understand, but whose sounds had imprinted themselves eternally upon my ear. "The square of the orbital period
of a planet is directly proportional to the cube of the semi-major
axis of its orbit. Valence is a measure of the number of chemical
bonds formed by the atoms of a given element. Pi is the sixteenth
letter of the Greek alphabet."

The students would produce a mangy clap. The teacher
would pet me on the head. "Look at you bums," she'd say to the
class, "a five-year-old made you look foolish," as if everyone's
memory were supposed to be an all-retaining sponge. After that,
Father and I would eat lunch at the school cafeteria and fill up
with *musaka* or *gyuvech* the jars we'd hidden under our coats
and call this dinner.

"When you get into that school in Sofia, we'll never have to
eat the same food twice. We'll never have loud, drunken neighbors, either, because the government will give us a flat in an expensive complex. Things will get stellar when we move to Sofia.
You wait and see."

When the town newspaper wrote about me, Father bought

dozens of copies to hand out to friends. He even mailed one to his pen pal, someone in Yekaterinburg he hadn't exchanged letters with in thirty years.

I took the exams at the school for gifted children in the spring of '89. I was denied admission two months later. I remember waiting in the car with my mother while Father took the newspaper article to the principal's office to demand an explanation. A spiky metal fence separated the school's campus from the rest of the world, and I walked to it and glued my face to the posts. I could see a football field, a tennis court on the other side. "It would be nice to study here," I told my mother, and she started to cry.

Father said nothing on the way back from the school. He smoked one cigarette after the other, but wouldn't open the window because it rained and he didn't want the orthopedic sheet of stringed bamboo beads on his seat to get wet.

"They said he wasn't special enough," he told my mother at last. We were waiting for a traffic light to change and he turned around and looked at me through the smoke, with more smoke coming from his nose as he spoke. "Is this true?" he asked me.

Years later we found out that admission to this school was really a scam. That to get in, you needed connections; it was a place where all high-profile Party members sent their children to study. But we didn't know this at the time.

"We can't leave Sofia now," Father said, and turned to look at me again, though this time the car was in motion. "You'll retake the tests next year. You'll prove yourself special."

I nodded, absolutely ashamed.

That November, after thirty-five years as the first secretary of the Bulgarian Communist Party, Todor Zhivkov stepped down from power. Many saw this as a crack in the wall and great masses were unleashed upon the streets. It was a cold and dark winter that followed, but Father recognized much promise in our situation. We would sit in the evenings by the candle, waiting for electricity to come back, and Father would smoke and speak of the bright future that awaited us. "Things will turn out stellar for us," he'd say. "This kid has a gift. He's bound to get some recognition."

But on the following spring I was not even admitted to the school entrance exam. "You cannot apply again if you've been rejected once," an official told Father. "But we were told we could," Father protested to no avail.

I was very happy with the situation. I hated Sofia. I dreamed of going back to our little town, to our apartment and the acres of woods above it, with the deer and the bunnies, with the snowdrops Mother and I picked once the snow began to melt in March.

"We cannot surrender," Father said one night, and slammed a fist on the table. "No, thank you very much. We need to regroup, that's all. There is opportunity that must be seized here. There is finally free market. People would pay to see your gift." He held a cigarette to the candle and smoked for some time in silence. "Why couldn't you be some other kind of genius?" he said at last. Then he said, "Go tell your mother to stop crying and fix some dinner. Then come back and help me figure out a way to introduce you to the crowd. I'm thinking something simple: 'Ladies and Gentlemen, please welcome the Amazing Rado to the stage . . .'"

•

The flood drags us to the parliament building, the one Gramps wanted to kamikaze into with a tank. A double helix of policemen entwines around its base, but most of them look half asleep, tenth graders propped on their shields with apathetic weariness. They've been out here so long, four days now, it seems they've lost all interest. Gogo greets them accordingly. "Pigs, hooks, fucking Ushevs," but even then they don't react. One of them asks me if I got the time. His watch, he says, has stopped.

"Do I look like someone who cares?" I tell him, and then I ask Gogo the same.

"No, *kopche*, you just don't give a shit."

The crowd splits in two streams, because right in front of the parliament there stands a huge pile of stones. A huge pile. Someone has stuck a flag on top, white-green-red, but the flag has frozen like a pair of boxers on the laundry line.

I recognize now that everyone in the crowd is carrying a stone. As they pass by, the people dump their stones and the pile grows immense, ugly, like a pile of broken bodies. I know that's not the freshest way to paint it, but that's what it looks like to me: hands and feet on top of skulls and torsos.

I ask Gogo if he knows what this is all about. "The Amazing Rado doesn't know?" he says, and I say, "Yeah, yeah, very funny." I tell him I haven't been home for a few days, remember? I haven't watched TV the way he has, on a nice, big Sony Trinitron set.

"Oh, fuck you, *kopche*. That TV is the first thing I'm buying back." He tells me then that all this masonry charade is part of the civilized protest. It was decided that people ought to lay stones this way instead of throw them like savage beasts. It's all a message to the politicians inside.

"*Kopche*, we don't have any stones," I say.

A woman right beside opens her bag. "I have some extras," she says. Her bag is a quarry. We each dump a stone on the pile and I'm thinking, some message this is. Dear madams, dear sirs, parliament members, we are displeased. Our pockets are full of stones, not money. Fix this injustice. We're civil still, but we're also hungry. Here are some of the stones we carry, in a pile.

We have become so meek, much worse than sheep. But I suppose five hundred years of Ottoman rule will do that to a people. And then forty-five years of the Communist yoke. That's what's eating me as we walk away from the pile. We didn't used to be this way. We were once fierce horsemen. We stormed blazing from the east, shot arrows riding backward, made treaties with the Byzantines, conquered the Slavs. Man, would I have liked to live back then. When the treaties were broken we went to war. Khan Krum the Terrible slew Nikephoros, one of only a handful of Greek emperors to ever die in battle, and turned his perfectly human skull into a cup from which he sipped his wine. Tsar Simeon the Great defeated Leo the Wise and chopped off the noses of five thousand of his men, just because—just to insult him. And we weren't simply a brute force: when Great Moravia imprisoned the first apostles who worked on creating our alphabet, we rescued them and let them transcribe books in the safety of our land. The seven apostles of the Cyrillic alphabet. *Sedmochislenitsi.* Those were some amazing men. And now what? A pile of stones. Stones are created to break skulls and we lay them down like flowers.

"*Kopche,*" Gogo says. "You look like a pelargonium someone's pissed on."

That's a pretty common expression, but still I laugh. We keep on walking and I remember how in our block of flats some neighbors would keep their pots of ficus, of pelargoniums, out on the stairway and how Gogo and I sometimes pissed in those pots. Eventually the neighbors took their burned plants in, never daring to put them on the stairs again. And then it strikes me that it wasn't Gogo but some other boy whose name I can't remember, in some other block of flats a long, long time ago.

"We should do that again, *kopche,*" I say.

"Do what again?" asks Gogo.

•

Here is my all-time favorite joke. No one ever laughs when I tell it. A circus. Almost end of the show. The announcer says, "And now, ladies and gents, please welcome the boy with phenomenal memory." Drumroll. A little boy walks into the ring and for ten seconds stares bluntly into the front rows. Complete silence. Then the announcer says, "And now the boy with phenomenal memory will piss on the front two rows." People start running and the announcer says, "No point in running, ladies and gents. There is no escape. The boy with phenomenal memory already has all of you memorized."

•

"*Drugarki i drugari,* dear comrades, please welcome the Amazing Rado!"

This is how my father introduces me to the crowd. For the past seven years, at least once a week. Nursing homes, neighborhood retiree clubs—of the retired engineer, retired welder, retired crane operator. There I am, in a room that smells of lavender spirit, in front of two rows of wheelchairs, trembling chins, dangling tubes, bags of urine, doing my mnemonic tricks to weak, Parkinsonian applause. And after that, my father begins his rounds among the rows, an empty three-liter jar in his hands. The label on the jar is peeled off almost completely and on the white space Father has scribbled boldly: *Amazing Rado's Scholarship Fund.* But if you look closely, you'll see a corner of the original label still standing and then you'll know: this jar was once full of pickled cauliflower. On with his rounds Father goes, courting the poor old women, sweet-talking the poor old men. And sometimes, this week or the other, he manages to half fill the jar with wrinkled bills.

For seven years we've toured retiree clubs like these. We've read from the same old textbooks Father once found in the basement, beside the strings of dried, salted fish—history, chemistry, physics. I told him all of this once. I said, "In seven years a monkey will learn to recite the periodic table."

"There is enough change in this country as it is," Father said. "We have a good thing going. Why mess it up?"

And on he strolls between the rows, the jar in hand. He always goes for seconds, because sometimes people are too senile to remember whether they've dropped their share or not. I watch him from the side and wonder, is this the bright future he spoke of in the light of the candle? Is this the stellar potential he prophesized? And sometimes, this week or the other, I am convinced that in his mind we're simply playing the cards we were once dealt, as best as we can. "Life has given us medlars," Father sometimes says, "heaps, and heaps of tough, unripe medlars. We could sulk. We could cry. Or we could wait for the fruit to rot and turn it into marmalade."

I wonder if you know what medlars are? If you've ever snuck into a cooperative orchard with rows and rows of the short trees, their branches heavy with fruit, filled your pockets, the bosom of your shirt, and then been chased by the orchard guard and shot at with pellets of salt, dropping brown medlars behind you as you ran, like a little scared goat? I wonder if you've eaten the fruit, sucked out the tart juice and munched on the pits, and then regretted it, because your gums feel swollen, your throat hurts, because the kid whose name you can't remember got shot in the butt and then back home his father beat him for ruining his only good pair of pants? *Kopche*, I'm tired of waiting for the medlars to rot.

"I swear, *kopche*," Gogo says, and holds me by the shoulder, "I have no idea what you're talking about."

•

We keep on marching, chanting. At one point someone gives me a blue balloon to hold. Its end is tied in a knot and frozen with the spit of whoever blew it up. Blue is now the democratic color. Gogo is waving a little paper flag. The sky above us has gone whiter, and any minute now there will be snow.

I see a black cross above the frozen branches of pussy willows, branches with yellow lashes still hanging like golden hair. I see a dome, a bloated belly with ashen skin. I see a bell tower. I see the Church of the Seven Apostles. The church with the cross we are about to steal. And on the square before that church and in the branches are people waving large blue flags. It seems that Gramps was right, that everyone is out, that there are more of us than the land can bear.

The democratic leaders are standing on the church steps and one of them is shouting something in a megaphone. I can't make out his words, except when he yells, "Whoever doesn't jump is Red!" Around us everyone begins to hop.

"Are you red, *kopche*?" Gogo grunts. "Don't be a Commie. Jump!"

I, too, start hopping, mostly to warm up. And suddenly it strikes me that Gogo's grunting, this hungry, foreign sound is just the way he laughs.

I'm faint with jumping hunger. We elbow our way to one side of the church and stand by a window. The windows are on our level, which is good, but they're fenced off with black gratings. I hold my face against the bars and try to peek inside. The glass is smoked and I see nothing except my own faint reflection.

We pull on the metal grating, there for decoration only, and it comes undone. Then Gogo retreats his fist into his sleeve and breaks the glass. Around us people watch, but no one cares enough to stop us. And soon the megaphone entices them to keep on jumping and jump they do.

"All right, *kopche*," Gogo says. He crosses himself like someone who's never really done it, from left to right. He sinks into the church and I follow.

It's dark and cold and somehow very still inside. It's like all voices from the square are only wind in a well. There is the howl of words, but not their gist. Words lose their meaning inside this church, and for a moment Gogo and I stand in the middle, stunned. The air is thick with the smell of candles, but there are none in the candelabra, none in the sand trays for the deceased; there is just wax, frozen down the brass holders, just frozen sand.

"It's so quiet," I say, and watch my breath float away in the gloom.

"Listen," Gogo says. "Shhhhh, *kopche*, listen!" and then he belches out a ravenous burp.

"You slob," I laugh.

Martyrs and virgins, cherubs and doves, watch us with pious boredom. To the side I see the archbishop's throne—its intricate wood carvings, the four beasts of the revelation, the calf, the lion, the whole shebang—and above that throne, high up, expensive in the dark, two elbows long, the golden cross.

"HiBlack Trinitron, here I come," Gogo says, and hops upon the armrests. He grabs the cross by the arms. He pulls and pushes. The cross gives out a tortured creak as Gogo lets his whole weight snap its base. It's like when in school we got new hoops and didn't rest until we snapped them all clean off the boards—for no good reason, really, just because we could, just out of spite.

They fall together to the ground. Gogo stands up, turns his head from side to side and cracks his neck. He blows the dust from the cross and the dust hangs around him momentarily in a halo, which the air draft scatters away. Holding the cross, Gogo is like a midwife who knows exactly how much the newborn weighs. "Well, I'll be fucked," he says. "This shit is made of wood."

We examine the cross in the light of a window: the yellow paint, not even gold leaf, is flaking off and the wood underneath is black and porous like a femur sick with osteoporosis. There are woodworms here and there in the little pores, curled up to pass the winter cold.

"Now what?" I start to say, but Gogo has already flung the cross aside and is working to prop the box with donations open. But the box is empty. Even the petty change along some of the icons has been wiped clean.

"Fuck, *kopche*, this is the wrong church to rob," Gogo says. He tries to wrap his arms around an icon of Bogoroditsa and her infant son. "You think we can carry this out?"

No, the icon is too big. We need something expensive, yet small enough to hide in our coats and carry through the crowd unnoticed. I say, "Right there, behind that wooden wall," and lead him to the iconostasis. I run my hand along the painted faces, along the wooden gates. There is a padlock on the gates but, like the cross, this wood too is brittle. One kick is all it needs.

The sanctuary is darker, colder still. I recognize an altar covered in a thick, red cloth, and on it a golden candelabra, a golden cup, a golden tray. They weigh just right.

"*Bog si, kopche,*" Gogo says, and kisses me on the head. "You're a god!"

"Keep off, you fag," I say. I'm starting to feel really good. My blood gets going. I tuck my shirt in, tighten my belt and stuff the cavity with the loot. The gold is so nicely cold against my skin, then warm.

"Look here," Gogo says, and picks up a real golden cross. He kisses it. He rubs it in his sleeve and stows it in his jacket.

My eyes adjusted to the dark, I recognize a table in the corner, and on the table something long and bulky, wrapped in the same altar cloth.

I know immediately what this is. I call for Gogo and we stand by the bundled corpse, the mummy of a saint, a holy relic. Its face seems almost alive, unnaturally well preserved. "It's considered a blessing to kiss the relic," I say. "Come on, *kopche.* Give it some tongue."

"You're sick, you know that?" Gogo says. He looks disgustedly at the corpse, and then peers around. He finds two large nylon bags at the bottom of the table and rummages through what's inside.

I wonder what this old man did to deserve such high esteem: sainthood and a cloak upon a table in a church. I lean forward and sniff his cheeks. A saint should smell like frankincense and myrrh. This saint smells nothing like that. But what the hell? We sure could use some luck.

"Wait, *kopche,* this isn't right," Gogo says, still going through the bags.

I kiss the wrinkled cheek, dry, very cold.

And then a sigh escapes the saint, a low, long moan, and with his opened mouth the stench of rotten meat.

We stumble back. The things we've stolen rattle in our coats. "My fucking heart will stop," I say. I try to shake this off; a horde of woodworms, wet and wriggly, roll down my back. I wipe my lips on my sleeve and keep on wiping.

"This is no saint, you all-knowing shit," Gogo says, and takes some clothes out of one bag: a T-shirt, long white underpants, a wool sweater. "Look at this," he says, and goes through the other. A round loaf of bread, a demijohn of wine, a jar of boiled wheat. "This is just like the stuff my mom brought the priest to bless for Brother."

We sneak up closer to the groaning saint. His mouth closes and opens, his eyes turn to us. Tarry, bulging eyes. That's all he is, this old cocoon, a pair of eyes that watch first Gogo, then me.

I say, "Old man . . ." but I don't know what else to say.

"Hey, Grandpa," Gogo calls and snaps his fingers. "Shhh, *alo*. Look at me. What's your name? You been here long?"

The eyes blink, the mouth opens, closes, opens again. The stench is too much.

"How did you like your kiss?" Gogo says, and looks at me. "Lover boy," he says.

I take the demijohn and gulp up a few strong gulps of wine. I rinse, wipe my lips, repeat.

I say, "They brought him here so the priest would bless him. So would be cured. Then they ran away. Isn't that right, Grandpa? They left you behind?"

Gogo takes the demijohn and drinks. We watch the cocooned man.

If that was me, I think, I'd lose my mind. Just lying like a grub in that cloak, and only my eyes moving, and my mouth. I wonder if this old man knows he was left behind to die? Does he begrudge those who left him? Does he remember anything at all?

I hope, for his sake, he has no memory left—of who he is, of where he lies. I hope he is the opposite of me.

Gogo lights up and tells me to watch this shit. He holds the cigarette to the old man's lips and lets him take a drag. Smoke gushes out of the old man's nose, his eyes fill up, he coughs.

"You were a smoker, weren't you, Grandpa?" Gogo says. "That's what did you in." He takes the round loaf from the towel and tries to break off a chunk against his knee. "Is this a loaf or a stone? Jesus Christ." He bites off a morsel and spits it in his hand. He holds it to the old man's lips and the old man sucks on it until the morsel turns to mash. Then the old man sucks on Gogo's fingers. "This is so vile, *kopche*," Gogo says, and wipes his fingers in his coat.

"That's enough," I say. "You hear me, Gogo. Enough of that."

But Gogo breaks off another piece. "Who is my hungry saint?" he says. "Are you my hungry little saint?" Then he brings the demijohn to the old man's lips but doesn't touch them. He pours wine from a distance. The old man drinks; the wine runs red down the creases of his wrinkled neck.

"Look at yourself, Grandpa," Gogo says at last, happy with himself. "Some saint you are," and starts with his grunting laugh.

I don't know what to make of this.

I touch the cloak. "God damn it, *kopche*, he's soaking wet."

"He'll be all right."

"The hell he will."

"Well, change him up, then, wunderkind."

And then it strikes me: this is exactly what I need to do. I peel back the edge of the cloak to unwrap the man. "Oh, Christ."

"Sweet Jesus, cover him up. That is some pungent shit."

I take a few more gulps and I can feel the contours of my esophagus and stomach, scorched, as the wine flows through. I lay the clothes from the bag out on the table—the underpants, trousers, socks, the knitted sweater.

I ask Gogo for his pocketknife. He watches me, smiling and drinking, as I cut the old man's clothes. The first few years after we'd moved to Sofia, we had no money for gas to go back to our little town and visit Grandma regularly. We went to see her only twice a year. The second time was in the summer. We found her on the kitchen floor so stiff, Father had to cut her out of her dress and then out of her undergarments with my kindergarten Yakky the Duck scissors. That smell, that sight, stays with you, no phenomenal memory required.

"Help me carry him to the altar," I say.

"To the what?" But Gogo helps me. "I never carried a lighter man," he says once we lay the old man on the clean cloak. "And have you seen paler skin?"

"I wonder what he has," I say. I shake the bread towel from all the crumbs and start to wipe the old man's chest.

"My money is on cancer," Gogo says. He picks up some church cloths from the altar—or rather, something that looks like a long, broad scarf—and he, too, starts to clean the man. The old man moans. I hope he's thankful for our help.

"Why are you laughing?" Gogo says.

I shrug. "I'm not."

"The hell you're not."

I point at the old man's crotch.

"It's a good-sized dick," Gogo says. "Nothing funny about it." He looks at me. "Like you can do better."

The old man's arms are nothing but skin on bone, and I hold them while Gogo struggles to put on the clean shirt. I'm afraid that if I stretched the arms farther back, they'd snap right out of the sockets. "Jesus Christ," Gogo says. His face is all sweaty and red and he wipes it with the shirt. "I can't even get one hand through the sleeve hole."

After the shirt, we manage to put on the tight white drawers, like pants Napoleon's soldiers would have worn. Then woolen pants, then the sweater. I drink more wine.

"I feel great," I say. I step back to have a good look at the man, all nicely dressed, all clean, serene on the altar. I'm proud. I'm happy with myself. "God, am I hungry."

I drink a little more for courage and zigzag to the altar. "Grandpa," I say. "You feel better now? Cleaner?" I hold my face a fist away from his. Gogo leans in.

"I don't think Gramps is breathing," he says. He pinches the old man's nose and holds it pinched.

"How do you know?"

"I'm pinching his nose."

"Don't pinch his nose."

He lets go and we stand very still, waiting. "That doesn't seem to help," he says.

•

The draft is stronger where we sit, down on the floor, leaning against the iconostasis.

"I feel like shit," I say.

Gogo breaks off a piece of bread and lays it in my hands. We eat, we drink.

"Do you feel better now?"

Of course I don't. My throat hurts. My gums feel swollen. The golden candelabra is poking me in the ribs like a spear, but I can't take it out; it's stuck in my shirt and I give up pulling.

I ask Gogo if he thinks we killed the man.

"I'm pretty sure we did," he says. He says if he was lying in his own filth, all skin and bone, he'd pray for death. "Maybe he prayed for us to appear and set him free. You ever thought of that?"

I try to hold the altar, the dead old man, in sight, but both the altar and the man keep swirling in an ugly, quiet dance. The wine keeps rhythm, sloshing in the demijohn.

"If you had to guess," I say, "what did he do for a living? You think he loved his kids? You think he lived an all right life?"

"You think I care?" Gogo says. "You think it matters? Look

at him, *kopche*, the man is dead." He bumps his head against the wooden wall. "This is too much for me. My hands are literally covered in shit: Smell them," he says, and shoves his hands in my face.

"When did I say they weren't?" I push him off.

"Christ, Rado," he goes, "what's the point? The moment I bring home my sweet, sexy TV, Brother will pawn it off again. I'd rather be broke and sleep on the floor." And Gogo chucks away the cup, cross, tray he's tucked in his jacket. One by one they hit something in the gloom, bounce back and roll with a metallic bark.

"I would totally ditch Brother here," Gogo says. "I'd bring him here and leave him behind." He says some other things, but I don't listen.

"You know, Gogo," I say, "this is so silly. Hear me out. The other day we were at this retiree club, my father and I . . . hey, wake up, listen . . . I'm writing this formula on the black board, *r equals p over one plus epsilon times cosine theta*—you know, *the orbit of every planet is an ellipse with the sun at a focus?* So I'm writing it all down just the way I've memorized it, just the way I'd seen it written in that old textbook Father gave me a long time back. I'm proving a point. Some old woman had randomly flashed the page before my eyes twenty minutes earlier and I'm proving my gift now. 'What does the epsilon stand for?' the woman asks me when I'm finished. No one's ever asked me that. 'Come on,' she says, 'if you are really amazing, you ought to know.' Well, fuck it. See, that explanation was on the next page of the book and that page was missing, torn. Turns out the woman was a physics teacher. She goes, 'And what about that Newton's third law you talked about? Do you understand,' she says, 'what that law is really telling us about the world?'"

"Why are you telling me all this?" Gogo says. He tries to stand up but falls right back down, flat on his ass.

"Wait, listen. My father comes to me after we're done. 'Well,' he goes, maybe it's a good thing.' Meaning maybe, after all, we don't need to add new books to our gig. Meaning maybe my memory isn't really good enough for new books. Meaning maybe there was a reason I didn't make the cut to that school. He didn't know the page was missing. So all he says is, 'Well, maybe it's a good thing.'"

"Well," Gogo says, "maybe it *is* a good thing, *kopche*." He lifts the demijohn up and shakes it empty. Three liters of holy wine, gone.

"What did you say?" I go, and he goes, grunting, "See? Case in point."

But I don't see. I don't see anything at all.

"The thing is, *kopche*," Gogo says, "you've memorized some ancient books—history, geography, whatever. You keep an article that says you're great, but aside from this, what have you done? Sure, you've killed an old man in a church, but I mean, what have you really done?"

"How about your aunt? Does your aunt count?"

"The *Amusing* Rado, is that the name you're going for now?"

None of this is funny to me. I say, "Wait a minute, *kopche*. Are you telling me you have some doubts that I am the smartest kid that ever lived?" I get up, stumble, fall down again. I really want to shake my finger in his face, but I don't know if his face is where my finger is shaking. "The last word of the Bible is *Amen*," I say. "The first is *In*. The eye of the ostrich is bigger than its brain. In England, all swans belong to the queen. Winston Churchill was born in a ladies' room during a dance. Stalin never had a mother. He was born by his aunt. Hitler was born with a full set of teeth, including four fillings and a crown."

"Oh, yeah," Gogo says, "the yellow press is a well of knowledge."

"A yellow well," I say, and listen to the wind howling, and to the chanting crowd. Then something, like a cricket, starts chirping in my pocket. It's that rich boy's pager we won at cards. *Come home*, dechko, the page reads. *Mama fried meatballs.*

"Mama fried meatballs," I say, and chuck the pager to the gloom. I repeat this over and over again, until the meaning rots away from the words. *"Kopche,"* I say, "watch my chips. I gotta take a piss, all right?"

I get up somehow. With a swift pull I untuck my shirt and the candelabra rattles at my feet. I try to kick, but miss. I try to open the gates, but can't. There seems to be only one way for me now—up. I can't piss in the church. I'm not like that. So I start climbing this staircase, these wooden steps, and I look for pots of pelargonium. But the neighbors must be keeping all pots under lock and key now. So up I climb, up until there is nothing left to climb, until wind slices my face. I'm where the bells are hanged.

It's snowing big, white chunks. Below me are the willows and the people—one million at my feet, two million, eight million. My Bulgarians.

It would be nice, I think, if someone tolled the bells. A metamorphic gesture. No, *metaphoric* is what I mean. But I just watch the snow fall, and the people still jumping like crickets in my pocket and at my feet.

Jump, my poor sick bastards—or brothers, rather. Mama has fried meatballs for all of us. Jump at my command. At the rise of my hand. Prove that you want change. That you're not Red.

"Gogo," I yell, "are you still doubting? Come see what I can do."

I climb upon the ledge, unzip my pants. My belt hits the rail like a copper tongue.

I'm sorry, my dear Bulgarians. There, you got my apologies beforehand. But I have you all memorized now. Each and every one of you. And so, watch out, my people. This boy has stones in his kidneys.

THE NIGHT HORIZON

1.

She fit like a stone in her father's cupped palm when he first held her. Yellow palm, stained from stringing leaves of tobacco, and she bloody, blind and quiet. She did not scream when her father took her. She did not breathe. A bloody stone was all she was back then. So her father shook her and smacked her face, and then she screamed, and then she breathed.

He raised her up to the ceiling as if God had poor eyesight and wouldn't see her down where she lay. He called her name, Kemal, which was his name, really, the name of his father, and then repeated it, like a proud song, to make sure that up in the Jannah the angel had heard right and had written her name correctly in the big book.

"You cannot give your daughter a man's name," the *hodja* told him.

"It's too late now," her father answered. "It has been written."

2.

Kemal's father made bagpipes up in the Rhodope Mountains. *Kaba gaydi*, they were called—enormous in the arms of the piper, with a low song, monotonous, mournful. He had built himself a workshop in the yard and kept Kemal's cradle there in the workshop, while he drilled chanters and reeds, while he

perforated goat skins and turned them into *meh*s for his bagpipes.

"Let her breathe in the sawdust," he'd tell her mother. "Let it
flow with her blood and let her heart pump it."

When Kemal was still very young, her father sat her down
on a three-legged chair in the corner and placed in her hands a
chisel. He showed her how to carve small half circles on the sides
of a chanter and then he told her to make her own patterns.
"Make them pretty," he told her, and so, day after day, while he
hunched over his lathe, Kemal carved tiny half-moons and dots
like distant stars on a wooden sky. Sometimes she pricked her
fingers, sometimes she cut them. But she never cried. She only set
the tools on the ground and walked to her father and held her
finger up to his lips, the dust red and sticky, so he could suck away
the dirty blood, so he could spit the pain out on the floor. Then
he made her stomp on it, like a snake's head under her heel.

When Kemal grew up a little, her father taught her how to
choose wood for the chanters. He'd take her out of the village,
up the narrow road to the tobacco fields and farther up along
the meadows, scouting for dogwood. If they came to the right
tree, her father would dig his teeth into a branch and taste it and
Kemal, too, would taste it. The more bitter the taste, her father
told her, the tougher the wood. The tougher the wood, the softer
it sang. Only very hard wood could make music. Then he axed
down the tree and pruned its branches, which Kemal roped up
and carried home in an armful. They left the stems to dry in the
workshop, because, to make music, Kemal learned, the wood
had to be dry.

Once, in the winter, they stacked an armful of frozen
branches away in the corner and left them there for a few days, in
the warm hut. Then one morning Kemal saw that the branches
had blossomed: thick white flowers that smelled of dog feces.
"This is an omen," her father told her, and she helped him set
the stack on fire.

3.

Kemal's father kept her head cleanly shaven, though Kemal did not like that. She did not like herself in the mirror. She liked her mother's hair, the thick black tresses that fell like ropes from under the head scarf. But she was not allowed to touch those tresses nor was she allowed to braid them.

"Enough with this nonsense," her father had said once while under the awning Kemal had combed her mother's hair as her mother spun yarn for booties. "The bagpipes are waiting."

The village children made fun of Kemal because her head was shiny like a lizard's, because she smelled like a goat, and because her father was crazy. He must be, they told her, or why else would he give his daughter a boy's name? And if Kemal was really a girl, how come she didn't wear a *shamiya*? Didn't she know that Allah hated women without head scarves? That He sent a plague of hungry maggots to hatch in their brains and eat their innards?

"Nonsense," her father said when Kemal asked him. "You are a bagpipe maker. To make bagpipes, you need a man's name." Then he took her to the mosque and when the *hodja* refused to let her in—when he cried, "You're making Allah angry!"—her father laughed loudly and pushed her inward regardless. Kemal prayed with him, and later, in his workshop, her father taught her verses from the Qu'ran that she recited while she worked on the bagpipes, so the work would flow lighter, so their music would pour out sweeter.

Kemal was six when her father made her her own bagpipe— small enough so she could put her arm around it, so she could squeeze it with her elbow. For months that's all he taught her: how to keep a steady tone; no melody, just air gushing out in an even stream. At first Kemal could not do it. In bed, she held her pillow like a *meh* and squeezed it, not too harshly and not too lightly, until one day her father lay his dusty palm on her shaved head.

"That's it," he told her. One day, he said, she could forget her own name, even, but she'd never forget how to squeeze the bag-pipe. Then he covered the windows with old newspapers, picked up a *kaba gayda* himself and filled it up with air. "Don't think," he said, "just follow."

The shriek exploded—the songs too large for the small hut, the songs longing for sky and meadow. They thrashed, wrecked, shattered and then curled up in the corner, curs who'd recognized their master.

"You are," her father told her, "a conqueror of songs now."

And so they played together, days on end, long hours; they danced in circles around the lathe, with shadows of words on their faces, Kemal's chest ablaze, her fingers enflamed like the roots of sick teeth. And they emerged of the hut reborn, to air fresh and sunsets so sharp, Kemal had to seek refuge in her father's arms or else go blind completely.

But he gave her no refuge. "Hugs are for girls," he'd tell her.

4.

When Kemal was ten, her mother went away to the city. Before she left, she stopped by Kemal's room and made her put aside the bagpipe. "I'm not feeling well," her mother said, and rested a hand on her belly. "Give me a kiss so I'll feel better." Her face was yellow, and when Kemal kissed her, her sweat tasted of dog-wood blossoms. "Do you feel better now?" Kemal asked her. "I feel better," said her mother.

For a whole week after that Kemal's father stayed locked in his workshop. But the lathe didn't turn, and the hammer lay quiet. He wouldn't let Kemal in, no matter how much she begged. She boiled milk and hominy for dinner and every night she left a wooden bowl at the threshold. The hominy always turned chunky—her mother had never really taught her how to cook it properly—but still, in the mornings, she found the bowl empty, washed it and filled it up with breakfast. She fed the chickens, and though a couple died of something, she did well for the most part. She hoed the garden. She watched bats draw nets in the blue night and listened to the *hodja* from the minaret call everyone to prayer. She missed the sawdust and the cold of the chisels. And there was no one to talk to. So sometimes, when the silence got too thick, Kemal walked above the village, above the gorge and the river, and played her bagpipe. Her songs flowed screeching and smashed against the hilltops and bounced back muffled, as if there was another piper blowing in answer, as if it were her father playing back from the hilltops.

On the second week Kemal's father stepped out of the hut another man. He held her up and she tried to tear off his beard, to see if his real face was not hidden beneath it. He took her to the mosque to pray for her mother, but Kemal prayed for other things: she prayed back home he wouldn't lock the workshop; she prayed he'd shave off his beard.

5.

On the first school day Kemal rose up before the cocks crowed. When she stepped out of the house, her father splashed water at her feet, for good luck. He said he wished her mother could see her. Kemal wore a white shirt and black trousers, but her shoes were her cousin's. "Drag your feet a little," her father told her, so she wouldn't walk out of the shoes. In the school yard she was given a paper flag, white-green-red, and lined up with the other children. She chewed on the flag handle, which was like a stick for cotton candy, and so one of the teachers scorned her. *Divak*, the teacher called her, thinking Kemal was a boy, a savage. Kemal was this close to tears. But she remembered what her father said to people. "My daughter," he told them, "does not know tears.

Even when she was born, she didn't cry." So while the teacher wasn't looking, Kemal bit off a chunk of the flag stick, chewed it and swallowed. The splinter was salty from all the hands that had touched it, but by the time they led her inside the classroom she had eaten half of the stick. By the time it was her turn to recite the poem, she was already chewing on the flag. All kids recited the same poem. A teacher had come to Kemal's house a month before this to make sure she had a copy. A classic by Ivan Vazov. *Аз съм българче*, the poem went. I am a little Bulgarian. I live in a free land. I cherish all things Bulgarian. I am the son of a heroic tribe. When Kemal said *heroic tribe* she coughed out a piece of the flag. Her spit had washed the dye away and the piece lay wet on the floor like a cat tongue. All the children started laughing. The teacher sent Kemal home for her father.

"That poem you learned," her father said on the way back from the headmaster's office, "you must forget it. You're not Bulgarian, no matter what people tell you. You were born a Turk and you will stand a Turk before the Almighty when He calls you. '*Kemal*,' the Almighty will tell you, '*recite me a poem.*' What will you tell Him then, Kemal, lest he throw you down in Jahannam to eat thorns from the thorn tree?"

"What poem, Almighty?" Kemal answered, frightened to look up at her father. "I remember no poems."

6.

Kemal's mother, too, came home not her mother.

When Kemal was still very little, her father had asked her to take an old shirt of his and stuff it with hay to make a scarecrow for the garden. And now, when she watched her mother stooped at the threshold, weightless, her hand on her belly, her skin the color of spoiled tobacco, cheekbones like sharp stones and face like a wolf's under the head scarf, Kemal thought of that scarecrow, of how the scarecrow had needed more hay for the stuffing.

From then on, Kemal rarely saw her mother. Her mother ate no breakfast and had no dinners and Kemal was not allowed to talk to her or hold her hand, even. Her mother's room stayed locked at all times.

When Kemal blew up her pipe, hoping they could play together, her father brushed her away and demanded silence. But there was no silence. Doors opening, closing, water running in the bathroom. And in her room Kemal's mother weeping softly, and her father trying to soothe her, his voice calming to her, but to Kemal dreadful. Why wouldn't he talk to Kemal this way? Why was he allowed to hold her mother's hand, while Kemal herself wasn't? And even when her mother didn't weep, her father's voice kept Kemal awake.

At night she held her bagpipe, face buried in the *meh* like in a bosom, and sucked the blow stick, and breathed that goat smell, and prayed Allah to make things quiet.

Once, while her mother was taking a shower, Kemal snuck in her room and rummaged through a drawer of packaged syringes. The whole room smelled like camphor, like piss and shit, and the floor was covered with large sheets on plastic to preserve the rugs from staining. In the corner she found a box of nylon pouches, took one and tried to blow it up, to get it to make music.

The door opened and her mother walked in wearing a bathrobe. Her head was bald, not smoothly shaven like Kemal's, but in patches. Under the robe Kemal could see that her mother held a pouch like the one she was holding.

"Where did your hair go?" Kemal asked her.

"It's not that bad, really," her mother told her.

They watched each other, silent, water dripping from under the robe and the drops drumming on the sheets on plastic.

7.

It was tobacco harvest, so out the window Kemal watched the road, dark now before sunrise, busy with carts and people. She could hear women singing, and their children fussing on their backs, sleepy in rucksacks. Oil lamps shone and torches burned, and as the carts rattled and as the people climbed the mountain they looked like a snake just hacked to pieces, one piece thrashing and chasing the other, no pieces connecting.

But she would not pick tobacco.

Her father had once more taken up making his bagpipes. "We need the money," Kemal had heard him say to her mother. "If you need something," he'd told her, "just blow in this chanter." So in the workshop Kemal helped him fulfill an order: thirty bagpipes for three schools in the region. They worked in the mornings, yet their work did not flow well. Every so often her father stopped and scolded Kemal to be quiet. "Is that," he'd say, "a chanter blowing?" At lunchtime he went to take care of her mother, while Kemal kept on working. Goatskins lay in piles around her and waited to be turned to *meh*s. Old, dry wood sat in the corners, plum, dogwood, and in boxes, for decoration, black buffalo horns, shiny in the noon sun. She felt good in the workshop. She even ate there, goat cheese and white bread, and drank well water from a sweaty jar, while sawdust spiraled and stuck to the jar walls.

"There is one thing," her father said once, "I've heard from the old masters. One hundred bagpipes, if played together over a sick man, chase death away."

One hundred bagpipes, Kemal wanted to tell him, was a lot of bagpipes. How would they find skins, all at once, for a hundred bagpipes?

That night, in the yard, Kemal helped him dig up a cooking pot from under the pear tree, a pot stuffed with rolled bills. With the money, they'd buy more skins. The same week her father canceled the three school orders. But in his telegrams to the headmasters he did not speak of the advances he'd been given, nor of the raw skins he'd already purchased with Party funding.

8.

It was a week after the canceled orders that a militia sergeant stopped by the workshop. They sat him down under the trellised vine, and Kemal's father sent her to draw a pail of well water. She poured a jar for the sergeant and one for her father, and watched her father lift his jar with trembling hands, and the sergeant drink in bird sips.

"Good water, this," the sergeant told her. "I was thirsty."

She kept her eyes on the gun in his holster and said nothing. Her father cleared his throat and asked her for more water.

"There have been Party orders," the sergeant started, "straight from the Politburo. Unfortunate business, but no way around it. I've been walking from door to door all morning, informing people. Now, if you ask me, it's ugly business, but no one asks me. It's Party orders, straight from the Politburo." And he told them: All Turks, Pomaks and other Muslims would be given new, Bulgarian names. If you lived in Bulgaria, he said, then you had to have a Bulgarian name. If you didn't like it, no one stopped you from leaving for Turkey. "Be at the square tomorrow. The buses will take you to town for your new passports."

"*Nachalstvo*, my wife is sick in bed and can't ride buses."

"Nobody asks me," the sergeant said, stood up and saluted.

9.

It rained while they waited for the bus to get them. There was no awning on the square and they did not own umbrellas, so Kemal's father had brought goatskins. He held one with his hand shaking over her mother, but still the rain pounded. Kemal knew all eyes would be on them—look how pale Zeynep is, people would say of her mother, how the sickness has eaten her innards, how Allah has cursed her—so she hid far away under her goatskin, also watching. No wind blew, and still her mother clutched the edges of her head scarf tight in one hand. With the other she held her dress, the nylon pouch underneath it, Kemal imagined. She looked like a spotted goat, poor, sick Zeynep, steaming in the cold, her dress dry in spots and wet in others.

When the bus arrived her father lowered the goatskin and all the rain the skin had collected splashed over her mother. There was laughter, so in the bus Kemal sat back, away from her parents. Everything smelled of wet head scarves, of wet mustaches, and the windows misted with people's breathing. With her sleeve Kemal wiped a tiny pupil and watched the slopes run muddy rivers, until again the window misted. A few times the bus stopped to pick up more people, a few times for her mother to retch in the bushes. Kemal hid under the stinking goatskin and listened.

"Last night I had a dream," a man was saying. "I'm in line waiting for something. My mouth is cracked from thirst and my stomach is churning. The line is long I tell you, not a line but a rope of people. And all I can hear is crying to make your hair stand like budding tobacco. Only it's not crying but a million stomachs churning, hungry from waiting. At last it's my turn at the front, and there before me stands my grandfather—a giant, I tell you, with his mustaches waxed and shiny like oiled hoofs, twirled on the sides the size of ram horns. Behind Grandpa, wide as the world, shine the gates of heaven. I can see in his hand a tray of figs, so ripe their honey flows out of them in rivers, and in his other hand a tray of thorns, the bitter hell fruit. 'What's your name, boy?' Grandpa asks me, and from his voice I go slack in the knees, and from the ripe figs my stomach churns harder. I tell him what my name is. 'It's Mehmed,' I tell him, 'so give me a fig, Grandpa. Let me pass through the good doors.' 'Mehmed, eh?' the giant says. Right then his mustaches unwind, I tell you, and turn to hands, my mother's hands, and hold a thorn ball to my dry lips. "That's a thorn ball, Grandpa," I cry, and the giant starts laughing.

"Well, change its name, then, traitor. Call it a fig and feast on it in the Jahannam."

At this, the women in the bus commenced weeping. But the men, who this rambling had amused more than frightened, clapped their hands in roaring laughter. "Don't listen to this drunkard," an old grandfather told Kemal. He must have seen her shiver under the goatskin. Her lips were chapped with thirst and her stomach was churning. Then the old man twisted his mustache, leaned in and asked her, "What's your name, boy?" and around her the men once more burst laughing.

10.

In the militia department the line went up for three stories. Kemal was forced to wait beside her mother. It was dim in the hallway and Kemal could see no colors, no sharp edges, and so her mother seemed almost peaceful for the first time in a whole year. She wanted to hold her hand then, and tell her not to grip the scarf so hard, not to mind a head without hair. Instead, she held a notebook someone gave her, and in the notebook, pages and pages of first names. Proper. Bulgarian. *Aleksandra, Anelia, Anna, Borislava, Boryana, Vanya, Vesselina, Vyara.*

It was three hours before she stood at the front of the line.

"Whatever happens in there," her father said, "you must forget it." Then Kemal stepped in a room, with a desk, with a man behind it writing names in a book, with a dead ficus in the corner, with a portrait of Todor Zhivkov askew on the wall, with a floor muddy from the boots of other people.

"What name did you choose?" the man asked her, licked his fingers and turned a page, not looking. She told him she already had a name. That no one could force her. No Party, no militia.

"There are four hundred people waiting behind you," the man said, finally looking.

So she said, "Vyara," and the man wrote that in the big book.

On the drive home, she kept repeating that new name, watching her face in the window—and beyond the window, the mountain, her head too in a head scarf, her face veiled in cloth of rain fog. It wasn't a bad name, the new one, she thought, and kept repeating it. Then she remembered how her father had pulled the goatskin, and how the water had soaked her mother. She started laughing. And laughing she walked to their seat and sat between them.

She had expected to see her father outraged, angry. Instead, quiet, he stared out the window. A different man already, Kemal thought, and put one hand on his knee, and one on her mother's. "Nice to meet you," she told them. "Who are you now?"

11.

It wasn't only the living.

They were making bagpipes when a neighbor told them.

"Shame on you, Rouffat, for spreading cheap lies," Kemal's father said, but all the same, still holding an awl, he ran out the village. Kemal ran in his footsteps.

Every stone on every grave had been plastered over. They had chiseled new names on some stones and left others empty. Kemal's grandfather had been given a new name. Her grandmother had been left nameless. Her father kneeled beside another, smaller headstone and ran his fingers across the fresh plaster. More and more people gathered, and up the row Kemal saw a man with a mattock beat the stone of his father. The man broke the stone to pieces and started digging.

Her father stabbed the stone before him with the chisel until the plaster crumbled. And once he licked his fingers and polished each letter, it was Kemal's old name she saw in the tombstone. Her father polished the years. But this grave was not her grave, and she figured the boy who lay in it had never lived to be half her age, even.

Up the row the man with the mattock, now shirtless, his hands sticky with mud to the elbows, pulled out bones from the ground and lay them one by one in the shirt beside him.

12.

They worked on the bagpipes. Day and night without rest. When Kemal's fingers bled, her father no longer kissed them. "My fingers, too, are bleeding," he'd tell her. He started drinking, despite the Qu'ran and his own judgment. Sometimes, tired, Kemal pierced a hole too broad in the chanter, butchered a reed, snapped a mouthpiece.

"It's that new name they gave you that makes you clumsy," her father would say, flaming. "To make bagpipes you need a man's name." At first it was a quick blow behind the neck he dealt her, but soon his hand loosened further. No day rolled by without a beating.

The money they'd dug up was not enough for a hundred skins, so one night her father took her up to the goat pens to steal kid goats.

There was no moon when they walked out of the village. Hot wind blew in their faces, a gust from the White Sea, and Kemal's lips cracked the more she licked them. So she kept licking, the salt and seaweed, so clean after the stench of her mother. They climbed a hill and crossed a meadow. The wind turned musky. In the distance they could see a scatter of sparks from a fire, tall and bursting with pinewood. Around that fire, Kemal knew, the shepherds lay too drunk to notice them coming. The dogs started, but when the wind threw the familiar smells at their muzzles, the dogs fell once again silent. This was the pen Kemal's father came to when he bought *meh* skins. These were the dogs Kemal played with, the dogs she rode like mules, the dogs that had once licked her body clean when, as a baby, her father had bathed her in a trough of goat milk by this same fire.

At the pen hedge Kemal clamped the knife in her teeth, and hoisted herself over. She stood silent amidst the herd, sleeping goats dreamily munching, flickering ears. She could see the fire over the hedge and hear the shepherds snoring, the dogs whimpering, lazy, the wind gusting muffled between the twined hedgerows. In the dark her father was looking for kid goats. Only kid goats could turn *meh*s for a bagpipe. An older goat, ready for mating, reeked so bad, not even rose oil could cure it.

Kemal waded through the darkness on all fours, still biting the knife, her spit drooling. She came to a kid goat and like her father had taught her, rolled it flat on its back, sat on its hind legs, clenched the front in her fist. The goat did not scream even when she cut a hole in its belly. She breathed the stench in. The goat flapped its ears. Kemal buried her hand deep inside it and the wet heat stunned her fingers the way snail horns are stunned when you touch them. She felt her way around the stomach, a *meh* bloated with half-grazed grass instead of air. Then she caught the goat's heart, midway in its beating. The goat kicked lightly, its neck stretching when she clamped its muzzle.

In the dark, she could hear her father dragging his belly across the short grass, stopping goat hearts. His nose whistling, stuffed from hay and flower, his breaths deep and even, regular knocking. She could not see him nor did she need to. She could not imagine that this same hand could hit her. In the dark, he was the way Kemal would always remember.

From that night on, she began to sleep in the workshop on the piles of stolen goatskins and in her dreams she saw hubs, reeds, chanters, *meh*s, like hearts beating in her clenched fists. And in her dream, it was her mother's heart she was clenching, and so she clenched tighter.

13.

They were up to seventy bagpipes when the militia car came back to the workshop. Three men and the sergeant Kemal had treated with well water. "Now listen up, comrade," the sergeant told her father. "The shepherds called from the goat pens to say some goats were stolen. So we followed the wool thread, if you permit the expression, and guess where that thread led us? Show us, kindly, the receipts for these skins you've purchased."

"I've lost them," Kemal's father answered.

"And your passport?"

"I might have burned it."

"*Losho, drugaryu,*" the sergeant told him. "That's too bad, comrade." He walked between the boxes and kicked them over gently, and Kemal watched the reeds and chanters spill out on the wood floor. He leaned down a little to face her better, then licked his thumb and wiped the dried blood from her split lip. "Why is your lip split?" he asked her, then took her hands and examined her fingers. "And why are your fingers bleeding? Is Father trying to make a quick buck?" The sergeant kept pacing and counting the bagpipes. Then he suggested Father come back to the station to have some coffee—some Turkish delight, even—and talk things over. He handed a pair of handcuffs to Kemal's father and asked, kindly, for him to snap them on his own wrists.

14.

From then on, it was Kemal who took care of her mother. When the dark fell, she jumped over the fence to their neighbors and squeezed what little milk they'd left in their goats—half a jar, a whole jar sometimes. She felt no remorse for stealing. No neighbor had come to ask how Kemal managed, now that her father was taken. How her mother was feeling. So she cooked lumpy hominy or *popara*, and though her mother refused to eat, Kemal forced her—twenty spoonfuls at dinner and ten at lunchtime.

They kept waiting for the militia car to bring back Kemal's father.

"Is that," her mother often said, "an engine I hear?"

In the shower, Kemal brought the three-legged chair for her mother to sit on. She could not stand to see her mother naked— how thin her arms were, her legs, how swollen her kneecaps, how her bald skull glistened, and the hole in her belly where the pouch connected.

"It's not that bad, really," her mother told her. "I'm doing . much better."

Kemal could no longer stand to see her own skull in the mirror. So she let her hair grow longer—thick and prickly at first, like pig bristle, then much softer. She did not like the way her hair tickled her neck, cheeks, eyelids, but she liked to run her fingers through the locks and twirl them. Her mother had given her an old comb, and for an hour each morning Kemal combed at the threshold.

"Let me touch your hair," her mother asked sometimes, but never dared raise her hand to touch it. She'd only smooth a crease on the blanket. "Beautiful hair, Kemal. Down to my waist. Do you remember?"

Sometimes Kemal took her bagpipe above the village to play with the echo. Once, she saw cars on the road below her, bumper to bumper, with mattresses, chairs, wooden cribs roped to their tops—blue, green, yellow, red cars, blood flowing away from the mountain. She'd heard men talking of fleeing to Turkey, so she tried to imagine herself in a red car, and the car speeding, and only the road before them, clean, smooth, endless. Her father was driving, her mother beside him, and in the back Kemal played the one song she loved most.

Down the slope she watched people from the upper hamlets haul their households on their backs like camels. Men and women and children loaded. She watched a woman trip and all the things tied to her back snap loose and roll down the slope with her body. Pans and pots and spoons and ladles and metal plates jumping wildly and catching the sun like gold coins. So Kemal struck her song with the bagpipe: *A little pebble rolled down the mountain, gathered its brothers. Down in the valley Stoyan was herding a hundred white sheep. "Don't roll, little pebble," Stoyan begged it. "Don't gather your brothers. I'll give you my two sons, little pebble, just spare my white sheep."*

15.

One night Kemal's mother called her over. "Listen, Kemal, I'll be facing the Merciful soon, so do me a favor. Bring me a bagpipe. I want to blow into it." When Kemal brought her own bagpipe, her mother cradled the bag in her arms like a baby and touched her lips to the blow pipe. A frail breath escaped her and the bag expanded, just slightly. "Have I told you, Kemal, how I met your father? I was a young girl then, sixteen, but my father had already promised me in marriage. I was to marry a neighbor, twice my age, but a rich man—he owned five fields and had traveled to Mecca. Well, one summer evening I go to the fountains—there were fountains, Kemal, outside my village where the water was softer—and I begin to fill the coppers. I hear footsteps behind me, and when I turn around I see your father. His shirt unbuttoned, his hair disheveled and his face sweaty and covered with sawdust. In his arms—two bagpipes. 'I'm a bagpipe maker,' he says. 'Blow up one bagpipe and I'll blow up the other. I want to hear,' he says, 'how they sound together.' So I blow up one bagpipe and he blows up the other. In two breaths—that's how quickly he did it. 'Have you seen,' he says, 'a man blow up a bagpipe faster?' 'My husband,' I tell him, 'needs only a single breath to do it.' 'I'll be your husband,' he says, and sets the bagpipes to screaming. He holds one under each arm, squeezes and dances. And I can't stop laughing. But I did stop when I saw, running toward us, my brothers, back from the tobacco. They'd seen your father courting me, and they didn't need to see more. They gave him a good thrashing. Split the bagpipes, tore his girdle belt. That night, a pebble knocks on our window pane. 'I'm stealing you,' your father says when I meet him under the shed, 'and tomorrow we're getting married.' Zeynep, Zeynep, I told myself, you're a promised bride and your father will kill you. But if you live, your life will be a song with this man, a merry man, a bagpipe maker."

Then in one swing her mother threw the bag down on the floor. "Take me to his workshop, Kemal," she said. "In fifteen years he never let me set my foot there."

And Kemal took her.

"So many skins," her mother said, "so many chanters. One hundred bagpipes, your father told me before they took him." Then she looked at Kemal and her eyes misted just enough. "Do you think that maybe—"

In the morning, Kemal moved her mother's bed to the workshop. And she started making bagpipes. But she butchered the wood parts, ripped holes too large in the goat skins. None of the bags she'd crafted could make music. What they made was screeching, hoarse and ugly.

16.

Days on end Kemal worked, and because the silence scared them, they left the old radio playing. They listened to the news from foreign places, to a voice reading the Danube levels. *Povishenie edinatsa,* the voice read in Russian. *Onze centimeters,* in French. Kemal had never seen the Danube, never would see it, but she wondered how big of a river it was and what it meant for its waters to be up by eleven. Was this a good thing or a bad thing? To whom did it matter?

At night, they listened to a program called *Night Horizon.* People could phone that program and talk on air about the things that hurt them. One engineer from Plovdiv called every night to say he could not sleep. "Dear Party," he always began his confessions, "I haven't slept in fifteen years." He kept a close count—"and three months, and four months, and ten days, nine hours, twenty-one, no, twenty-two minutes." An old man from Pleven recited children's poetry to his daughter. After each poem he begged her to phone him in the morning. His daughter never phoned him in the morning and so he kept reciting. But there was a woman from Vidin who Kemal and her mother liked to listen to above all. That woman read letters she'd written to herself, mostly, but sometimes also to other people. *I am outraged, comrades,* the woman read from one letter, *because there were green peppers on sale at the farmer's market today and no one told me. All my neighbors bought green peppers. Stuffed jars for the winter. I can still smell the peppers roasting and no one told me.*

Kemal's mother laughed at that one. "Peppers in November," she said, and asked Kemal to throw more wood in the fire, to keep it burning a little longer. By the stove, Kemal kept waiting for the woman to mention the Danube. Could the woman see it outside her window, Kemal wondered, the way they could see the peaks of Rhodopa? And what did Kemal's father see out his window? She hoped he had one. She hoped they let him listen to the *Night Horizon.*

"I want to call that program," Kemal said, "and play Father my bagpipes. I want him to tell me how to make them better. I need a man's name, Mother, don't I, to make bagpipes?"

"My dear Kemal," said her mother, "I had forgotten how pretty your voice was."

17.

So, like the pepper woman, Kemal began to write letters. She wrote in copying pencil and taped up notes all over the village, mostly outside the village hall, where people could see them. *"Dear Party, a Turk cannot become Bulgarian. Give us back our old names so we can eat figs and go to the Jannah."*

But nothing happened. So one day she wrote a new note and nailed it to the well bucket, down on the square of a Christian village. *Dear Party, a large amount of poison has been dumped into the well. Do NOT drink water and give us back our old names.*

In daylight, from up the road she watched a crowd surround the well. A man splashed two buckets on the pavement and all stood over the puddle as if over a deep hole. A woman began wailing. At last two militia Ladas arrived from the city, blue jars spinning. Kemal did not know if these were the people who'd taken her father—she could not tell one from the other—but she watched them scratch their heads under the blue caps and stare into the puddle like they could see the poison.

To see them so puzzled and stupid gave her a sense of lightness. She would write more notes like this one.

18.

A few drops of blood rolled down her mother's shoulder and Kemal licked them. She watched more drops gather and wondered if her blood knew yet, if it had sensed death had come. She had moved the body back to the old room, but had nicked a spot when cutting the dress to remove it. She filled up a wooden pail with water and gathered clean gauzes from a box in the corner, and washed her mother's arms, chest, legs. After she'd washed her, she dressed her in her other good dress. She rolled her to her father's side of the bed and spread newspapers over where she'd just lain, to soak up the water. She brought her bagpipe but didn't play it. Instead she lay on the newspapers, held the bag and thought of how her mother's breath had filled it slightly. She spread out her fingers and watched them. The more she watched them, the more they looked like another girl's. They felt borrowed, cold, swollen, and they crafted lousy bagpipes. She spoke her old name—Kemal—and the more she repeated it, the more it flowed in itself, the deeper it bit its own tail. She repeated her new name, Vyara, and kept repeating—the old name, the new name, until one devoured the other. Until both felt foreign.

Her body was not her body. Her name was not hers.

19.

Next morning, she wrapped her mother in white sheets. She dragged the bundle out in the yard and onto the two-wheeled carriage they used to haul raw skins from the pens. There were still skins in the carriage, so she spread those for a cushion. She fixed a shovel beside the body and pulled on the carriage. It wasn't heavy.

She could see shapes behind curtains, ghosts without names and honor. By the time she reached the graveyard, the sun was as high as it would be. By the time she dug the hole up, the sun was setting. She lined the bottom with goatskins so her mother wouldn't be too cold. She stained the sheets when she rolled her over; her hands had blistered from digging.

It was in that boy's grave that Kemal lay her. But she would not let the boy rest beside her. So later, after she'd piled back the earth in a black heap, Kemal chucked his bones at the sun to feed its burning a little longer.

20.

That night, Kemal sheared her hair with the kitchen knife. Then, in the workshop, she gathered up all bagpipes—eighty-seven, she counted—and began to inflate them. One after the other the bagpipes let out their pointless screeching. Then, one after the other, Kemal set the woodpiles, boxes, skins, on fire. Out in the yard, she held her own bagpipe and squeezed her elbow, and let the pipe draw flat lines of sound, terrible, stabbing. She watched the flames fatten, and sparks exploding, the hut collapsing and hissing pipes and chanters shooting up in ashen showers.

All over the village dogs were barking. Once more Kemal could see shadows from dim-lit windows, and once more no one stepped out, not even to curse at her for all the clamor.

She stuffed her sweater with gauze and old newspapers, then crawled out of the village toward the cooperative haylofts. The guards were already drunk in their barrack, and even when Kemal nailed her new note on their door, they did not wake up.

Dear Party, give back my parents.

Two tractors stood in the dark, and Kemal remembered what her father had once told her: a day would come when from the east a white ram would rush, sprinting, and from the west a black ram. Both enormous, with horns like nesting snakes, like serpents of bone scattering lightning and fire. The earth would tremble with their hoofs and young and old would gather to see them. Some would hop on the white ram and up it would take them, up to the Jannah, so they could glide with the eagles. But others, vile and wretched, would crawl onto the black ram. Down the black ram would drag them, down to the low earth, to creep with the maggots.

Kemal crouched by the black ram and pressed her face against its bumper. She stuffed its mouth with gauze and paper. Lit a match, let the flame loom from under her fingers. Hid far away by the hayloft and waited for something to happen. For some time nothing happened.

Then, in pyre and lightning, the horns uncoiled and heavy hoofs made the earth tremble. She saw the black ram collide with the white ram and the guards stumble drunk and dreamy out of their barrack. Which ram would take them, she wondered, and which would take her?

DEVSHIRMEH

I.

It's Friday afternoon and John Martin is driving me to my wife's. We're picking up my daughter for the weekend and I don't want us to be late again. I'm tired of my wife rolling her eyes, arms crossed over that heavenly chest, and tapping her foot in some maddening rhythm only she can hear. I'm tired of making her new husband look good in comparison.

I crane my neck to see how fast we're going and tell John Martin to step on the gas.

"You want speed?" John Martin says, "Get your own damn car," and cranks the heat higher. It's a hundred and five outside, and John's truck, the same one he bought after he came back from Vietnam, has trouble staying cool. Sometimes, when he drives me to Wal-Mart, he pulls over to the shoulder, pops the hood up and like shipwreck survivors on a raft with a flat sail we wait for wind to cool down the engine. But there is no time for wind now.

"How does this help, exactly?" I say, and hold my hand against the stream of hot air.

"It's specific science," John Martin says. "You won't understand it." His eyebrow twitches on an otherwise calm face, and I take this as my cue to keep pushing. "Some shortcut this is, John."

Out the rolled down window I can see a thin strip of scorched Texas earth and yellow grass. The rest is sky, so large and dull I get angry just watching it. I look at my wrist, an old habit from the days when I still owned a watch, then I look at John Martin's wrist. That's where my watch is now: an original Seiko I bought, once upon a time as a student of English philology in Sofia, from an Algerian fellow for a demijohn of Father's *rakia* and a pallet of Mother's canned tomatoes. I sold the watch to John Martin and with the money took Elli to Six Flags; a great experience, if it hadn't been for all the hitchhiking. When we returned to the house, John Martin had thrown my bed out in the front yard and piled all my clothes on top. He'd left a spiteful note on the pile, in case the message wasn't clear enough. *Pay rent, Commie.* So I sent Elli in to melt his heart with some sweet talk about how much all that bonding time in line for the Judge Roy Scream ride at the Goodtimes Square had meant to her. Later she told me John Martin wept while she talked, that's how touched he was.

Now I tilt my head to see the time better. As expected, we are already ten minutes late.

"God damn it, John. This car is absolute rubbish."

Like that, John Martin slams on the brakes. We slide along the gravel, and when we finally come to a halt, the dust we've roused catches up in a thick cloud. I try to roll up my window, but that's no good. I'm dust-slapped already, I can feel it on my face and hair and on my shirt.

"You little Communist shit," John Martin says. He stares me down and I can't get my eyes off his epileptic eyebrow. I try hard not to laugh. "This here truck is an American truck," he says, in case I ever doubted it. The statement alone is meant to refute the shittiness of the vehicle and put a full stop to any further discussions. "Like you ever drove something as fine in Russia."

"I drove a tank, John," I say. "And you know I'm not Russian."

"You're all alike to me."

"Cool it, John," I say. "God is watching." I nod at the cross that dangles from the rearview mirror—a tiny wooden crucifix on a black string John Martin received as a gift from the fifty-year-old Mexican widow he's in love with at his church.

He grabs the cross and kisses it. "Shame on you," he says, and I apologize right away. I tell him I didn't mean anything, really, that I was just yapping, nervous because of my daughter. Because we're late. His truck is fine, a fine American truck. "Here," I say, "Peace," and hand him a beer from the cooler at my feet. Miller High Life. America's finest. The Champagne of Beers. He rolls the can against his neck, cheeks, forehead, and sweat runs in dirty creeks. We both slurp hoglike and wait for the car to cool. I watch a flock of Texas crows land far in the field and I can see their heads twisting to peck dead earth.

"You should call her tonight," I say, meaning Anna Maria, the widow from church. "You should take her on a date. Taco Bueno? Taco Bell, even."

"I don't know," John Martin says, and takes a big gulp from the beer. He watches the heat gauge still in the red. "It might be too early for that."

"It's never too early for Taco Bell."

He crushes his can and throws it back in the cooler. "You don't know shit," he says. He raps his fingers on the steering wheel. "Last time I checked," he says, "another dude was boning your wife."

"Great talk, John," I say. I say, "God is watching. Besides," I say, "I'm working the situation. It's all a temporary matter. I'm getting her back, one step at a time, even as we speak."

"One step?" He shakes his head. "Look at yourself. At least shave that stupid mug of yours. Wear a shirt that's not brown with dust. You don't get women back like this, man. Especially one married to a doctor."

"Why bring up his occupation?" I say. And I tell him, less time spent listening to Delilah on the radio might do him good. He starts the truck and we're back in motion. Across the field the crows, too, rise up and head in the opposite direction, flapping chaotically. "I swear, man," John goes, "I feel sorry for you. That's the only reason I put up with your shit."

"You know it," I say. "And it's God that puts this pity in your heart, don't forget. Love thy neighbor. Love, love." John Martin first started going to church in hopes of finding a wife. That's a fact, he told me so. To look good, an eligible bachelor, he assumed the role of a pious Bible abider. Soon he grew into that role and finally convinced even himself. John Martin is not a religious man, he's not a believer. But he doesn't know it yet and that's exactly what I'm banking on.

We pull outside my wife's house half an hour late. I step out and the heat feels cool after the sauna of the truck.

"Five minutes," John Martin says. I take a swig from the canteen in my back pocket and he shakes his head again disapprovingly. At the door I smooth my hair over, brush my face with a sweaty palm. I pop a mint in my mouth and check my breath.

No one answers the bell for five minutes. When I look back, John Martin is drinking beer against the truck, its hood open. He taps my watch. I ring the bell again and finally there is a voice on the other side. "Buddy, buddy," I hear, a thick, ugly, stupid Bulgarian accent. "Sit. Good boy." One lock turns, then another, then a chain falls.

My wife's new husband emerges before me, absurdly obese in the door frame. He's wearing flip-flops, American ones, a single string between his wet, puffy toes, long shorts that drip water on the parquet, and a cell phone clipped to his waistband. He has no shirt on, and his chest hair, and the hair on his legs, is smoothly glued to his body, layer upon dripping layer. By his side is an equally obese, equally wet dog whose breed I can never remember.

"Buddy!" he yells at me in English. "What's going on! You're late. We've been waiting."

"Traffic," I say.

"Oh, no, buddy. English. We speak English here."

"Traffic," I repeat. "That's an international word."

He swats a mosquito on his shoulder with a thick slap of his meaty palm. Droplets splash my face. "Well, get in," he says. "Hurry, hurry."

I bet he's eager to get back to the pool before my wife has seen him inside, all wet and with that dog. I know she'd be furious if I ever did such a thing. So I stand where I am and tell him all is well, that I'm only here to pick up Elli, that I don't want to impose. I keep peeking behind him, hard as that is, waiting for my wife to show, waiting for the parquet to get well soaked and start peeling up. I even reach for the dog and my heart melts with joy when the dog growls and shakes its shaggy coat, sending water all over the shoe rack.

At last my wife appears from behind Buddy, in a two-piece red swimsuit, her bronze skin oiled up and gleaming. She's trying to dry her hair with a towel, but it's not her hair I'm looking at. Somehow she manages to squeeze herself between Buddy and the door frame and attempts to put an arm around his waist—an impossible gesture, really. "We've been waiting," she says, also in English.

I don't know what to say.

"Buddy, hey, buddy," Buddy says. "Up here," he says and snaps his fingers. "Yeah? You like those? Ten grand each. We got them done in Dallas. Best investment I ever made, if you know what I mean."

I want to ask him why, but they're already walking through the house. I wave at John Martin.

"Five minutes!" John yells, licks his finger and touches his sweaty shoulder with a gesture that's meant to convey eroticism, among other things. As I start through the living room my wife orders me to take my shoes off and keep the floor clean. Shoes in hand, I follow them to the pool.

Their yard is full of people—all in swimsuits, all holding broad, stemmed glasses, margaritas, martinis. There are people in lounge chairs, on towels spread in the grass, on the concrete by the pool. A large grill on one side sizzles with burgers and steaks. Everyone turns to me, and all conversation seems to hang in the heat, but only for a moment.

My wife brings me a Dr Pepper. "Have a Dr Pepper," she says. I'd rather not, but I take it. "What's the occasion?" I say. She sticks out her chest, in case I didn't get it. I get it all right, but I refuse to stare. Instead, I search for Elli, who's nowhere to be found, not even in the pool with all the other splishy-splashy children. I ask where she's gone.

"It was Buddy's idea," my wife says. Maybe she doesn't say it exactly like this, maybe she calls him Todor or whatever his real name is, but it sounds like Buddy to me.

"You shouldn't have," I tell her. "They were great to begin with."

"What? No," she says, "no, these were my idea, a self-esteem issue. I mean the scuba set. Buddy thought of that." And then I see it—through the crystal-clear water, at the bottom of the deep end of the pool—my daughter with a tiny oxygen tank on her back.

"It's all safe," my wife says. "We hired a diving instructor. You see him down there? All Buddy's idea," and laughs as if she's cracked a great joke. So much for working the situation. I have no desire to talk to her now; all the little lies I planned on telling her—that I was declared employee of the month yet again, that I found a great little place I'm thinking of moving to—will now remain unspoken. All I want now is to pick up Elli and get the hell out.

"Tell her I'm here," I say, and my wife lets me know there is another twenty minutes on the diving lesson. "Have a seat," she says, "have another Dr."

"John Martin," I say, but as before, she's already drifting away. I find a chair with a broken leg far from the pool and pour some vodka into the soda can. Then I watch Buddy, flipping steaks with one hand and with the other holding the cell phone to his mouth like a walkie-talkie. He drops a chunk of ham-

burger meat to the dog and the dog pushes the chunk with its
muzzle, licks it and refuses to eat. I could go for a burger right
about now. Most likely John Martin, too, could go for a burger,
out in the truck. I drink more and wait for the lesson to be over,
for my daughter to reemerge from the deep. She does that at last.
My wife helps her out of the pool and the instructor removes the
oxygen tank from her back. I would never make my daughter
carry anything of such weight. Then my wife tells Elli something
and Elli looks about and sees me in the corner. She runs to me
and, one hundred words a minute, asks if I saw her scuba diving,
with a tank and all, down there in the pool, breathing under-
water like a mermaid, like a real mermaid, in the pool.

"Elli, Elli, Elli," I say. "Slow down, baby," I say. "*Na bulgar-
ski, taté*. Tell me all this, but in Bulgarian."

I keep drinking while Elli is changing up in her room, while
my wife is packing her a bag for the weekend, because it is just
so hard to have the bag packed already. I watch the diving instructor teach a freckled woman how to suck air through a snor-
kel. Then I watch Buddy by the grill in his flip-flops, dry now, with
his fur all bristly, forking meats, taking their temperature with a
stick, talking to the dog in his stupid accented English. I feel so
utterly out of place here, so stranded I can't even hate him right.
I can't even envy him properly for all the things he has that I
don't. This is not the way I imagined it. This life. Sometimes, at
night, long after John Martin has gone to bed, I sit on his back
porch and I drink his beers and chuck empty cans at the dark
and I wonder—this everything. Is it worth staying?

Then Elli emerges, with a bag in her hand.

"I'm ready," she says. Buddy comes for a good-bye and she
gives him a kiss on the lips. He asks me if I want some steak and
I tell him I'd already had plenty of steaks today—for breakfast,
for lunch, for an afternoon snack—all steaks, rare, medium, well
done. Elli pets the dog and it licks her fingers while my wife
whispers something in her ear, all the while watching me with a

serious face. "Michael," she tells me, though she knows this is not how my name should sound. "Take good care of her." As if such instructions are ever needed.

By the time we walk out, the sun is slipping behind the scorched earthline. John Martin pushes himself off the truck with a dusty boot and shuts the hood closed. I tell Elli to get in, because she'll be riding between us, and as I climb in I see that John hasn't touched any more beers from the cooler, that they are all floating like dead fish in what was once ice.

"Jesus Christ, John," I say. "I'm really sorry for the wait."

"It's okay, man," he says and closes his· door gently. "Hi, beautiful," he tells Elli. He tousles her wet hair. "Hi, Princess."

II.

We came to the U.S. seven years ago. Maya, the baby and I—despite the slim chances—proud winners of green cards. I submitted our lottery applications on the day Elli was born. Ten months later, we passed the interview at the embassy, and two weeks after Elli turned one we flew to New York City. There was very little fear when we left Sofia. We figured if we had to be poor—and we were, very, both of us English teachers at neighborhood schools—we might as well be poor in America. We left in hopes of a better life, I suppose—not for us, but for the baby. And I suppose a better life is what we got. Certainly not me, but the baby. Perhaps. And, as much as I hate to admit it, Maya as well.

Maya's first cousin had already lived in New York for fifteen years and he let us stay at his place—a one bedroom in Bronx—until we rented our own one bedroom above his one bedroom.

The cousin helped me get a job as a cashier at a Russian convenience store during the days and another at night, as a 7-Eleven clerk, three times a week. I worked like this for four months until, one morning, I came home after a long shift with a high fever and abdominal pain so sharp, I cried louder than the baby. Five hours later I lay in a hospital room without an appendix. The operation cost us twenty-five thousand, out of which we could pay zero. We decided to save up for a few months, buy tickets to Bulgaria and vamoose. But while Maya had been waiting in the hospital, she had, entirely by accident, as these things are prone to happen, overheard a Bulgarian name mispronounced over the intercom. She'd seen a doctor rush down the hallway and chased him to the elevator. She'd read his tag. And lo and behold . . . Buddy Milanov, M.D.

For months I thought of Buddy as my Christ, my God-sent Savior: he called insurance companies for us, filed claims on our behalf and finally, because we were so officially poor, managed to get ninety percent of our hospital fees remitted. We made him Elli's godfather. We invited him for *musaka* on the weekends. We even hiked up our skirts so he could bend us properly over the kitchen counter. With the baby in the room.

After I walked in on them, Maya moved on the offensive. She blamed me for this, and that, and for other things. A week of fighting later, she had already taken Elli to Buddy's apartment— overlooking the river, with plenty of rooms and a granite counter in the kitchen.

I decided to kill Buddy. I quit my night job so I could wait for him outside the hospital with a knife in my pocket. I waited for a week, watching him call cab after cab, until it became clear I'm not, alas, a real man from the Balkans. So like a slug I began to befriend him again. Buddy, my friend, what's going on, pal? Let bygones be bygones. I knew that if I could talk to Maya, reason with her over time, she would undoubtedly come home with me.

Five years went by. Last March my wife informed me that Buddy had found a job in some clinic in Texas and that they were all moving. They would graciously pay for my plane tickets, twice a year, so I could come down and visit Elli at dates of my convenience.

I decided it was time to kill Buddy again. I sharpened the knife, polished its thick, wooden handle. Then I poured myself some vodka and made a tomato salad with too much vinegar and a lot of onions and ate the salad and drank the vodka, and sharpened the knife. I stared at my Seiko until the phone rang, eight in the evening.

"*Taté*," Elli said on the other side, "we just rode an airplane." And after, when I hung up, I could not breathe, could not move, knowing she was there and I here. I could not imagine where she was. I could not see the things she saw, did not understand what she meant by a huge sky and no tall trees. After I finished the bottle I called my mother back home, in Bulgaria.

She did not recognize my voice right away.

"Mother," I said, "I'm moving to Texas."

"Good for you," she said. "Are you thinking . . ." she said, "are you considering . . ."

I told her I was not. I had no money, no time for trips to Bulgaria.

"Of course," she said. "Money and time. I know how it is."

III.

We're kicking the ball in John Martin's backyard, catching the last sun of the day, while he sways in his rocker—one hand holding a beer, the other one swatting mosquitoes. The rocker creaks and every now and then there is the sound of crushed metal, of his boots knocking on the planks, as he reaches over for a new can from the cooler.

We play a quick game, which I win, ten goals to seven. Then, when it's too dark for playing, I teach her how to dive for penalties, how to kick her own heel and roll to the ground with an agonizing yell.

"Always seek contact," I say, "but if there is none, kick yourself to the ground. Make this a rule: you must dive for a penalty at least once every game."

She listens and, like a great sport, runs, kicks her heel and rolls in the grass.

"It hurts," she says and rubs her knee.

"What can you do?" I tell her. "Life."

Then John Martin brings his beer down to the pitch. "I can't understand your Bulgarian gibberish," he says, "but goddamn it, Princess, is he teaching you to cheat?"

"No, John," I say. "I'm teaching her to play the game."

"Some game this is," he says, and pokes the ball with the tip of his cowboy boot. "Come on, Princess, let's play a real sport."

"John Martin," I say, "American football is not for girls."

"My daughter loved it," he says. "I threw the ball with my daughter every day, in this very yard, for nine years and she loved every minute of it. Come on, Princess. I'll teach you to throw."

He wobbles back to the house and reemerges a few minutes later with a half-deflated eggball in hand. I step to the side and open a beer while he positions Elli at the right spot, while he throws the ball so far away from her it's embarrassing to watch.

"Just warming up the old joints," he says, and sways his arms madly about, forgetting he's holding a can. Beer splashes all over him. "Come on, Princess, throw it back," he yelps, dripping, clapping his hands, stomping his boots. Elli giggles and looks at me for the green light.

I tap my nose with a finger a few times. "At his mug," I clarify in Bulgarian.

"Quiet, Commie!" John Martin yells. "We're playing ball now. Come on, Princess. Throw."

With a light grip, just the way I've taught her, Elli raises the ball to her ear, shoulders parallel to John's body, left foot forward. Then she extends her arm back gracefully, and with a swift half circle, rotating her shoulder for maximum velocity, chucks the ball straight into his face.

The ball knocks him flat on his ass.

"Jesus Christ," he says. He sits panting and wipes his bloodied nose. He starts laughing. "Jesus Christ, that was a cannon. I did not see that coming."

Elli runs to the house for napkins and I help John up and pass him my beer.

"I told you American football was not for girls," I say, and he shakes his head.

"She's good," he says. "Jesus Christ." Then he figures Elli was not the girl I meant.

•

After three boxes of macaroni and cheese for dinner, John Martin unfolds the flat earth of his Risk game and we battle each other for all the continents of the world. As always John Martin conquers Asia. He clusters the majority of his troops in Siam, now officially amended to Vietnam with a pen. Elli holds the Americas and I'm spreading the Great Bulgarian Empire.

"Watch out, John Martin," I tell him. "The Great Bulgarian Empire is spreading."

"Bring it on, Commie," he says. He arranges some of his manned cannons in a row, like that would help him. I pet the musket of one of my soldiers. "Avtomat Kalashnikov," I say, "Bulgarian-made."

He pushes forward a soldier of his own. "Napalm, mother fucker. American as apple pie." Then he looks at Elli and his big, square face is flaming red from swearing.

We have never finished a game. After an hour John Martin is too drunk to keep rolling the dice. He retires to his recliner and watches us for a while, every now and then, yelling, "Kick his Communist ass," or "Atta girl." Sometimes he takes the phone and cradles it in his lap. Sometimes he fondles it until he falls asleep.

"He wants to call his daughter, doesn't he?" Elli asks, and

sometimes I suppose that's exactly what he wants to do. Either his daughter or Anna Maria, the Mexican widow. With John Martin there is no telling. We lay the board and all the tiny soldiers back in their box. Elli pulls the stinky boots off John Martin's feet, and while I take them out to the porch she throws a blanket over him. Then she takes a shower and brushes her teeth.

In my room we read Bulgarian books, mostly fairy tales of *samodivi* in beautiful garments, of men with scales and dragon wings, of *vampiri, karakonjuli, talasumi*. But we've read those books so many times, there is no surprise in the stories, no heart left.

So sometimes Elli asks me to tell her a story. And I tell her. I make things up about the old khans, about the glorious battles. I teach her history as I remember it from school. Important dates, memorable moments: how they made the Cyrillic alphabet, how we defeated the knights and kept their emperor imprisoned in our castle until finally we decided to push him off the tower to die a deserved death.

"Have you seen this tower, *taté?*" she asks me, and I tell her, of course I have. All Bulgarians have, it's there, part of the castle.

"When can I see it?"

And I don't know what to tell her, because the way my wife is raising her, the way Buddy dictates things, I can never see them actually going back to Bulgaria, even as tourists. For Christ's sake, they won't let her speak her own language out of fear it'll ruin her English. In their eyes, my daughter is capable of speaking a single language only.

Tonight Elli asks me for another tale. I change into my sleeping T-shirt and jump in bed, but she remembers something and takes a cell phone from her jeans on the chair. She hammers a quick text message, and twenty seconds later comes the reply. *Sweet dreams, angel. XOXO.*

"What the hell is XO?" I say. "What the hell is this phone for?"

"To keep contact," she says and slips the phone back in her jeans. "Hugs and kisses."

"Remember," I tell her as she gets back to bed. "Even if there is no contact . . ."

"Kick your heel, and fall for penalty. I remember."

"Atta girl," I say and we laugh. "What story do you want to hear?"

"Any story. Something nice. About our family. Back home."

Back home. I kiss her on the forehead. "Okay," I say. I take a deep breath while she lies on my chest and prepares to listen. "And so this story, this story, too, begins with blood," I say. "And with blood it ends. Blood binds those in it and blood divides them. Many have told it before and many have sung about it, but I didn't learn it from them. I was born and I knew it. It was in the earth and in the water, in the air and in the milk of my mother. But it was not in your mother's milk and not in your air, so you must listen now as I tell you."

I can feel her breath, tiny and warm against my neck. I rest a hand on her hair.

"See now," I say, "how black smoke plasters the sky of Klisura. Feel the fires that burn the flimsy houses. Hear the children screaming and their mothers weeping. Ali Ibrahim is converting slaves to the true faith. 'Who else will refuse to put a fez on his head?' Ali says, and his deep voice cuts through the air like a damascene sword. He sits on his black stallion not far away from a chopping log, in a yard filled with soldiers and poor peasants. Dark blood has soaked into the log, and only five more heads must be cut for the blood to finally reach the feet of Ali Ibrahim's horse.

"'Whose head will roll next?' Ali asks. Weeping rises above the crowd. A young girl steps forward. She moves slowly; she swims above the ground. Her hair is long, so long that it trails in the dirt behind her and winds out of the yard like a river. Snowdrops wreath her head, and a white gown envelops her in a ghostly cocoon. Her blue eyes cut through the darkness around Ali and search for his face.

"He watches as she comes near.

" 'Why, my poor brother,' the girl asks him, 'have you forgotten your own? It is your blood you shed as you slay them, my brother. It is your blood you spill.'

"Ali takes out his yataghan and jumps off the horse to cut the girl. The frightened eyes of the villagers—Christians he has sworn before the sultan to convert to Islam—follow him as he swings the sword through the air, desperately trying to butcher this apparition. But, as usual, the girl is gone. She has sunk back in his mind, only to return again on some other occasion and in some other form."

I stop for a moment to catch my breath.

"*Taté?*" Elli says. "How is this story about our family?"

"Wait," I say. "Just listen. And try to fall asleep. It's getting late. So this story," I say, "does not begin with Ali Ibrahim, really, although it ends with him. It begins eighteen years earlier with the birth of my great-grandmother—the prettiest woman who ever lived.

"It is well known, even before her birth, that my great-grandmother would be the most beautiful woman in the world. So on the day she draws her first breath, men from all over come to pay her tribute. The line in front of the house is so long that it takes the last man twelve years before he finally falls at her feet and presents his gifts of honor.

"Because of my great-grandmother's supreme beauty, the laws of cause and effect in the village break down for a while. An event is no longer followed by its usual consequence but instead leads to something completely unexpected. This is first noticed when a few of the men waiting to see the newborn get so anxious that they start throwing stones at the house. Contrary to all expectations, the windows do not shatter, but the leaves on the nearby trees momentarily turn red and begin falling as if autumn

has come months before its time. Five houses down, a girl desperately falls in love with her uncle because two kids try to
drown a bag of black kittens in the river, and an old woman is
run over by a bull because on the other end of the village a
housewife forgets to put potatoes in the stew.

"Word that the child destined to be the most beautiful woman
has been born spreads quickly. It travels from the steep banks of
the Danube through the snowcapped peaks of the Balkan range
to the vast rose valleys of Kazanlak and the strait of the Bospo-
rus until it finally reaches the ears of the great sultan in Istanbul.
His Greatness immediately loses sleep over the beauty of my
great-grandmother simply by listening to others talk about her.
For days, a wretched shadow, he sits under the fig trees longing
for her, and nothing seems to bring him pleasure anymore. The
songs of the most exotic canaries of Singapore are but dreadful
noise to his ears. The caresses of the prettiest of his wives chill
him to his bones and make him want to weep in solitude. Eating
is his only way out of the misery. With every sunrise the sultan
devours a dozen dishes of baklava, each one more soaked in
honey than the one before. With every noon he feasts on three
roasted lambs garnished with trout liver and woodpecker hearts,
and when the sun sets behind the palace he seeks comfort in the
meat of twenty ducks and two baby calves. All this food makes
him so obese, so absolutely humongous, that nothing within a
hundred steps can escape his shadow."

"He's a fat bastard," Elli says, and giggles. "Like in the
movie."

"Exactly," I say. "*Fat bastard* describes him spot on. For eighteen long years this fat bastard of a sultan prays to Allah to give
him good health so he can live long enough to hold the most
beautiful of all women in his arms. On one misty spring morning after almost two decades of suffering, the sultan disbands
his harem and sends his servants to call for the great vizier.

"'It is obvious that I have lost my mind over this woman,' the sultan tells him. 'I have waited long enough for her to grow up, and now I should finally hold her in my arms. Tell the best silk weaver to make the finest black *feredje*. Then send our most merciless janissary along with one hundred soldiers to take her from her house. Tell them to veil her with the *feredje* and never to look at her face, because whoever lays eyes upon my bird I will punish with blindness.'

"The vizier signs a *firman* and puts the sultan's red seal on it, then gives it to the best rider with the swiftest Arabian steed and tells him: 'Run all day and all night until you reach the village of Klisura, where Ali Ibrahim is converting slaves by the sword to our true faith. Find him and give him this *firman*. Tell him to obey every word in it lest he lose his head. Be back in one moon and the sultan will give you your weight in gold. Come a day later and your head will roll in the dirt.'

"The rider finds Ali Ibrahim waving his yataghan through the air near the chopping log in the yard filled with peasants and soldiers. He gives Ali the *firman* and waits for him to read it.

" 'Never have I been more humiliated,' Ali Ibrahim says, and throws the letter at the feet of the notice bringer. 'I should at least take the pleasure of killing you for bringing me such news. Go back to His Greatness and tell him that Ali Ibrahim will bring him the most beautiful of all women. But along with her, you tell him, Ali Ibrahim will turn her whole village to the true faith; for Ali has sworn to reveal the face of Allah to the slaves, not to chase harlots for the sultan.'

"After these words he jumps back on his black stallion and casts a last glance at the yard washed in red and the crowd of trembling faces. He orders half of his men to carry on with the conversion, while the remaining hundred soldiers he leads out of the valley, heading for the village of my great-grandmother, the most beautiful woman in the world."

Elli's breathing has become soft and even, but she isn't sleeping yet. She's just dozing off and coming to again. I lie quiet for some time until suddenly she perks up, surprised at herself for dozing. "Ali Ibrahim," she chatters. "Who is he, *taté*? Who is Ali Ibrahim?"

I pet her cheek and hair and tell her to lie down and close her eyes.

"Ali Ibrahim is a janissary," I say. "It is Bulgarian blood that runs in his veins. According to the orders of the sultan, every five years the slaves have to pay their blood tribute—the *devshirmeh*. No one can escape the recruitment; the most capable boys are taken away to become part of the imperial army, and those parents who try to hide their sons are punished with death.

"Ali was parted from his mother when he was twelve, when he still had his Bulgarian name and still believed in the power of the Holy Cross. At dawn one morning, the recruiting soldiers came like crows of darkness, and by the time the sun died behind the Balkan Mountains they had selected forty of the healthiest and strongest boys in the village to take away. Ali Ibrahim was not among them. But it was his mother who chased the soldiers and fell at their feet and begged them to take him. She was a widow and meant well for her boy: as a peasant, she knew, he had no future, he was destined to die a slave. But as a soldier, as a janissary, the whole world could be his. 'Take him, Aga,' she cried, and pushed the boy forward, and the boy did not know why his mother did this, could not understand.

"For weeks, then, the convoy of boys, guarded by fifty soldiers, walked the path to Istanbul—south through the Rhodope Mountains and east through Edirne, then farther east. In Istanbul the boys were bathed, their hair was shorn and torched. The names of their fathers were erased and they were given good Muslim names. No past lay behind them: they were faceless in the hands of the sultan. Humble servants in the name of the true God.

"Ali Ibrahim was sent to a small village in Anatolia where he served in the house of a linen merchant. An old man, who'd once fought the Siamese to the east. There Ali Ibrahim was taught the foreign tongue and the new faith. There he was taught to hate all he once loved.

"Ali Ibrahim's mind is haunted, Elli. The invisible pull of his wicked heart is so strong that none of those he has slain has ever managed to escape it. Fettered to his body, the dead follow wherever he goes. A never-ending chain of wretched souls trails behind him, and no one else can hear their cries. Behind his back, his soldiers call him 'Deli Ali,' which in Turkish means Crazy Ali, but no one dares say that up front, for they also know him to be Merciless Ali, who never hesitates to take a head. Some say that during a conversion in his native village, among the nonbelievers who refused to recognize the greatness of Allah, Ali killed his own sister and his own mother."

Then I'm quiet for a long time. Elli is asleep on my chest and I have to get up, to turn the light off. But I don't want to get up. I lie and I think of my own mother, of how I haven't seen her in seven years; of my sister, who had a baby last spring. I listen to Elli's even breathing and wish for things that can't be.

IV.

Next morning I ask John Martin if he'd let us borrow his truck to go to the zoo.

"Over my cold, stiff body," he says, rocking in the recliner, and behind him Elli mouths off his words exactly as he says them.

"But I'll take you fishing," he says, "if you pay for gas."

I look at Elli and she shrugs a *Why not?* So I tell John to put it on my tab and hurry off to get us ready before he's had the time for some clever reply. Half an hour later we're loading his boat behind the truck. Another half hour after that, I'm dipping my toes in the lake.

"Get your toes out," John Martin scolds me, "you're slowing us down."

In the back of the boat he holds the handle-looking thing on the motor and steers us forward. I know nothing of fishing or boats. What I do know is that this boat looks about as sturdy as the ones the Russians must have used when crossing the Danube to attack the Turks in 1878. But this boat is John's jewel, dearer to him than his truck, even. He has named it *Sarah*, and that there says it all.

My own daughter sits at the nose, or the stern, or however you call it, and points at distant spots across the lake where she thinks fish will be hiding. But John Martin never listens. He always takes us to the same place on the far end of the horseshoe, by an abandoned, half-collapsed wooden dock where the water, only three feet shallow, is filthy with osier, lilies and grass, where there is a permanent fog of mosquitoes and large, black turtles snap on the oars, where dipping your toes is completely out of the question.

"Jesus Christ, John," I tell him when I realize that's where we're heading again. I smear mosquito repellent on Elli's neck, legs, arms. "Take us someplace else, will you? There, by that concrete tower, or by that island. Anywhere else but the dock."

"The dock," John Martin says, and once more Elli mouths off his words as he speaks them, "is where the fish are situated. The dock is where I've been going for fifteen years and where I'll be going for another fifteen if the good Lord wills it. That's where Sarah took that ten-pounder, and if it was good enough for Sarah, by golly . . ."

But I'm not listening anymore. The sun is climbing steadily toward mid-sky, and there is no shade for us to hide in, no good trees along the banks. Here and there across the lake I can see other boats, all larger than ours, with faster motors. I can see expensive rods bending, and waves splashing, and men pulling out fish as large as calves, or at least baby lambs.

The first few times I took Elli to fish with John Martin—the first few times when we gutted the bass and cleaned them, when Elli peed behind a bush, once upon a time—those first few times were fun and I enjoyed them. I could lie in the boat and look at my daughter and feel empty inside, free of regret, of envy. It didn't matter that I saw her only on the weekends. It didn't matter that my wife lived with another man now, and even that man himself didn't matter. So what if I didn't own a car? So what if I lived at John Martin's, drank his beer and ate his macaroni? At least I had Elli.

But now our weekends have become repetitions of those first weekends of fun. Only, we've murdered the fun. Sure, Elli seems to enjoy them, but I no longer lie in the boat free of hatred. Oh, how I hate now. Nothing seems enough.

"Don't you just hate them, John Martin?" I ask him. "Don't you just envy the shit out of these people in their fancy boats?"

"No, sir, I sure don't," he tells me, and keeps steering.

"Well, I hate them," I say. "I feel this thing called *yad* when I watch them. So much *yad*, my chest gets constricted. Elli?" I say and gently nudge her on the back with my toe. "Do you feel *yad* when you watch them?"

"Not really," she says.

"You should, honey. You ought to. *Yad*, John Martin," I explain, "is what lines the insides of every Bulgarian soul. It's *yad* that propels us, like a motor, onward. *Yad* is like envy, but it's not simply that. It's like spite, rage, anger, but more elegant, more complicated. It's like pity for someone, regret for something you did or did not do, for a chance you missed, for an opportunity you squandered. All those feelings in one beautiful word. *Yad*. Can you say it?"

But he doesn't say it. "Let me give you," he says instead, "one word of my own. Elli, Princess, cover your ears."

Then Elli turns around and looks at him. "Bullshit," she says. "Is that the word, John Martin?"

•

We take six bass. Or rather, Elli catches two and the rest are John Martin's. I drink my Champagne of Beers at the back, while John teaches my daughter flippin' and pitchin' and other neat angler tricks. It's a bit creepy how he pets her head, how he calls her "Princess" over and over, but the lesson is worth it and I decide not to intervene.

Finally, Elli says she can't hold it much longer. And would I please quit asking her to go over the side: girls don't go over sides like that. John Martin orders me to retrieve the cinder block we use for an anchor and I pull on the rope, but the anchor is stuck in the mud below us. With a sigh John takes the rope and pulls, as if he can do better, and his face turns tomato. "God damn it," he says.

"That's right," I say. "Every time."

We pull on the rope for a while, left, right, in circles. Elli has clenched her legs crossed and, eyes shut, she's biting her lip. John Martin curses and I curse a little as expected.

"Come on, now," he says, and twines the rope around his hand. "Come on."

We pull for fifteen minutes, give or take.

"I can't hold it much longer!" Elli cries. So John Martin jumps out on one side of the boat and I jump on the other. The water is up to my chest, waist for him, and it gets up to our chins when we kneel and grope in the warm mud for the anchor. We puff, we work the mud, we kick on the block until it finally loosens. With a yelp John Martin lifts the block up and lays it enormous in the boat, a chunk of lake, and weeds, and slimy brown leaves.

Then, after seven pulls of the cord, the motor is roaring and we fly, four miles an hour, toward the closest bank. Elli hops out of the boat and splashes to seek cover behind some mangy bush.

"Jesus Christ, that was close," John Martin says, and searches the cooler for full cans. He begins to roll one against his cheeks to cool them. I look at his neck.

"John," I say, "there is a leech the size of a five-year-old Gypsy's dick on your neck."

"God damn it, Michael, not again," he says. Then he leans backward and stretches his neck to allow me easier access.

V.

"The news that Crazy Ali is coming to take her away reaches my great-grandmother as she is washing clothes in the river. Panic seizes all other girls, but great-grandmother never loses her calm. She wrings out a shirt and washes another.

" 'I have no time to be frightened,' she tells them. 'Work waits for no one.'

"A bright moon blooms in the sky. Ali Ibrahim and the hundred soldiers stop before the wooden gates. Ali dismounts, takes out his yataghan, and knocks three times with the ivory handle.

" 'I have come for your daughter,' he tells the man who opens the gate. He brings his sword to the man's face, and on the tip of the blade hangs the black imperial *feredje*. 'Go veil her face and bring her here. We have much road ahead and time is short.'

"The man takes the kerchief and walks to the cattle shed where the most beautiful of all women is milking the cows. He hands her the black cloth, which flickers like a wounded pigeon in his trembling hand.

"My great-grandmother narrows her eyes, takes the kerchief, and throws it in the dirt. She then finishes milking a cow and jumps on the only horse in the shed.

" *'Az litse si ne zabulyam,'* she says: 'I shall never veil my face.' She whispers something to the horse and grabs him by the mane.

"People say that right then a great storm rose from the west, and that when my great-grandmother vaulted over the yard walls, over Ali and his soldiers in a cloud of dust with her long hair flowing, her beauty was astounding.

"For a long time Ali stands in disbelief. His face is calm except his right eyebrow, which twitches every now and then. He mounts his horse and puts the yataghan in the sheath.

" 'Bring me the *feredje*,' he says. And when the soldiers bring him the black kerchief from the cattle shed, he commands them, 'Chop all heads if you have to, but when I come back I want to hear a *hodja* chanting in the name of Allah.'

"Then at an even trot he makes after the cloud of dust that my great-grandmother has left behind."

We're on the bed again. It's raining, like never. Even on the way back from the lake, clouds were already lining the sky in thick chunks. We stopped at Dairy Queen and I bought Elli a milk shake. I bought one for John Martin. "You asshole," he said. "You know I can't have milk." But he drank it in gluttonous gulps. We had to stop at gas stations twice before we reached home and once we were in the driveway, John Martin sprinted out to the bathroom with the truck's engine still running. Involuntarily he granted me the honor of parking under the shed. After he was finished, forty minutes later, pale and sweaty, he went out in the rain to make sure I'd turned the headlights off and straightened the tires. Which I had forgotten to do.

Now on the bed Elli throws a final glance at her cell phone. She's already texted her mother and gotten her hugs and kisses.

"Keep talking, *taté*," she says at last. "What happens next? Does Ali Ibrahim catch her?"

•

"For two days my great-grandmother rides without any rest and for two days Ali Ibrahim follows in her steps. Like a hound he goes after her scent, shortening the distance that stands between them. As he gets closer, as the smell of lilies gets stronger, his heart beats faster, his throat gets drier, and his palms sweat more and more on the handle of the yataghan. With every step the air feels thicker. To Ali Ibrahim it seems as if he were making his way through a rushing stream.

"On the third day, my great-grandmother understands that she cannot outrun the janissary, so she decides to defeat him with her beauty. She sits on a rock in the middle of a river, and this is where he finds her, combing her hair with her fingers.

" 'So you are Ali Ibrahim,' she says without looking. 'Crazy Ali—the one who sacrifices his own in the name of a fake god.'

"Ali stands on the bank and his fingers rub the ivory handle of the sword.

" 'Well, Ali,' she says, 'don't stand there like that. Come help me braid my hair.' He takes out the sword and lowers it so when he walks through the slow river, the blade scrapes the stones on the bottom. My great-grandmother is still combing her hair, not yet looking at Ali, whose face is as calm as before, although his right eyebrow has started twitching again. He stops in front of her and takes a tress of black hair in his hand. He is ready to cut it, but just then my great-grandmother looks up and her eyes rest upon his face.

"Ali's hand goes numb and he drops the sword. He takes a step back, stumbles on a stone, and falls on his back in the river. My great-grandmother starts laughing while Ali, lying in the stream, watches her.

" 'You are not the first man who fell before me,' she tells him, 'and you will not be the last. But you are, by far, the most handsome one I've seen.'

"Ali says nothing. He stares at her and licks his lips.

" 'What's the matter with you?' she asks lightly. 'If I didn't know you were Ali Ibrahim, I'd think you were frightened of something.'

"Ali Ibrahim finally manages to rise and get a grip on his yataghan.

" 'Stand up,' he tells her. 'I'm taking you to the sultan.'

"My great-grandmother laughs again and tosses back her hair. She will never let him take her to Istanbul, but she knows it's pointless to show resistance now. She'll obey him until her moment comes.

" 'All right, then,' she says. 'Take me. But I can't appear before His Greatness like this. You must help me braid.'

"When he touches the dark hair, a shiver runs through his body. He starts braiding slowly, with skill never forgotten."

•

"They ride together side by side. Every time the horses step on a broader road, my great-grandmother starts singing. She lets her voice rise high in hopes that it will attract the attention of someone who can help her. For three days they don't meet a soul, and for three days Ali Ibrahim doesn't utter a word.

" 'Is it possible,' my great-grandmother wonders, 'that my beauty has no power upon him?' Every now and then she sprints a few feet forward so her raven braids sway, so Ali could watch her.

"He stays unchanged on the outside. He rides tall on his horse, proud and fierce as always. But on the inside pyres burn him, tempests devastate him and he is weak—just the way a man should feel when he has fallen for the most beautiful woman in the world.

"On the fourth night, they find a glade amid the thick pine woods and stop there to wait for sunrise. Ali gathers dry twigs and builds a fire. The twigs crackle in the darkness and my great-grandmother shivers.

"Ali speaks at last. 'Eat,' he says, and hands her a piece of meat he has roasted on the flames.

" 'I don't eat meat,' my great-grandmother tells him, even though she is starving. 'I eat only white bread and honey. I drink fresh milk.'

"They sit quiet for a long time, the blazing fire like a living wall between them. Ali watches her—lips, nose, eyes. She also watches. His dark gaze fills her with fear and coldness, and with something she has never felt before. And she hates him.

" 'Tell me, Ali,' she says, and holds a tress of her hair, 'why should hands that can touch so gently bring so much death and pain?'

" 'This is God's way,' he tells her. 'Even the whitest shirt has a bit of gray in it. Even the darkest night conceals something shining in its gown.'

"And then, when my great-grandmother is about to speak again, a shadow emerges from the dark. A woman in a black dress wearing a black apron and a black cloth on her hair walks toward them and sits by the fire. Two dark holes gape in her face. She has no lips and no nose. The apparition loosens her hair and combs it with a wooden comb. From underneath the fall of tresses, she seems to look at my great-grandmother and then at Ali.

" 'Sunshine,' she cries out, 'why did you do it?'

"Ali grabs a burning brand from the fire and tosses it at the apparition. The twig blazes through the air, falls in the grass and slowly sinks in darkness. The apparition is gone, and where she was sitting there now blossoms a tiny snowdrop.

" 'They follow wherever I go,' Ali tells my great-grandmother. 'All those I have killed. They are chained to me.'

" 'And the one we saw now? Whose shadow was she?' "

VI.

The rain is no longer so bad, but the wind has kicked up into a storm. I move Elli to the side and tuck her in. She stirs in her sleep but doesn't wake. I kiss her smooth forehead. I listen to the gusts slam sheets of rain against the glass, and to the AC unit oscillating just outside my window. A car whizzes by in the dark and its tires howl as they push water away from the road.

I wouldn't mind if like in some cheap movie with a twist John Martin turns out to be a figment of my imagination. If the truck is all mine and I drive it alone, a maniac talking to himself, up and down the dirt roads of Texas; if somewhere along those roads, from grief and envy, I lose my mind. I wouldn't mind some help from ghosts and shadows is all, I suppose. Like in the fairy tales I read to Elli.

And I wouldn't mind if we were on the road right now, just me and her, in John Martin's truck. Heading to the ocean, or to Mexico, even. We'll make it across the border somehow, down in El Paso. We'll buy tickets to one of those enormous cruise ships and sail across the Atlantic.

When we first moved to the U.S. our idea was to save up some money, buy our own place and later, when we received citizenship, bring our parents over to the better life—Diet Coke and fried okra, and five-minute commercial breaks on TV every ten minutes. They would be retired by then and would quietly take care of Elli when both Maya and I went to work. They would teach her proper Bulgarian, how to read and write. They would keep all the roots from withering. But it was too expensive to even maintain a phone and so we wrote letters. It took the letters two weeks to arrive from Bulgaria, and from the States—if the envelopes were too bulgy, if they looked like there could be dollars stuffed inside—the letters never arrived. So we wrote shorter notes. And those notes thinned in meaning. Yes, a letter from your sister is always something you hold dear, but they told us nothing of substance, these notes, only the big facts that can never paint a living picture. What do I care that the family vacationed on the sea? That the other day, while buying lettuce, my mother met an old friend who said hi? That my niece was born? I'm here now, so far away I can't really know how warm the sea was, whether my mother bought the lettuce at a good price, whether it snowed on the day my niece took her first breath. I don't know who held the umbrella over my sister when she carried the baby to the car. I know it wasn't me, and sometimes that's all I have to know.

This is a natural occurrence, Maya's cousin, the one who lived in the Bronx apartment below us, once said. Do yourself a favor, he said, and kill the things that pull you back. He hadn't heard from his brothers in three years and look at him: he was a perfectly happy human being. Fewer stones to carry, so to speak. Onward and upward. Never look back. Nothing good, he told me, ever came from looking behind you. You either turned to a pillar of salt or lost your beloved into Hades. He, too, was a schoolteacher, the poor guy, and now a fine cabdriver in New York.

I lie in bed and watch the wind whose howls are so strong now they turn to shapes, and I can't hear Elli's breathing over the beating of their wings. Then my thoughts get mixed up a little. I'm on the street in Sofia buying sunflower seeds from an old man with no teeth because I want to feed the pigeons, a thick, black mass on the square around us. But the old man won't give me the seeds I've paid for. No, no, he tells me. You haven't paid. He's holding red balloons now and I snatch a bunch and he yells with a lisp *Ffnimanie! Ffnimanie! Attention!* And then I'm in a parade, with children marching and waving paper flags and a siren, a loud, ugly war siren cuts through the rain, because of Chernobyl, maybe, because they want us off the streets and it's raining.

"*Taté*," I hear and someone's shaking my shoulder. I see Elli, but it's John Martin who has me in his grip.

"Wake up, goddamn it," he says, and Elli repeats it. "Tornado."

VII.

"Sometimes when he was still young, Ali Ibrahim dreamed of his mother. He saw her sitting on a rock in the middle of the river, combing her long black hair. In the dream it is raining.

" 'Come, my sunshine,' she calls to him, 'come help me braid.'

"The river is low and he can walk to the rock in the middle, following a path of white stones. But the rain falls harder. The waters rise, the stream becomes turbulent and the path to his mother is closed for Ali. Soon the flow starts to drag dead bodies, and they all float with their backs facing the dark sky. His mother still sits on the rock and still she combs her hair. It's raining blood now.

" 'Come, my sunshine,' she calls again, 'come help me braid.' But her face is no longer there: the rain has washed it away.

"Every night that he dreamed this vision, Ali remembered less and less of his mother. Until one night there is no one on the rock, only the bodies floating in the stream, bodies whose faces he cannot see."

VIII.

"We're getting the hell out of here," John Martin says. He slices a package of bologna, then a package of bread, and begins to fix sandwiches on the kitchen counter. Elli wraps the sandwiches in the stack of napkins we took from the Dairy Queen and I watch them work as a team for a while. The TV is booming one warning after the other, but I can't get my eyes to focus. They caught me in the thickest of sleep, and now even that lobotomizing siren can't seem to screw my head back in its place.

I finish a can of beer on the table, a few warm sips that now taste almost as bad as a Dr Pepper. "Listen," I tell them. I nod at the TV. "It's just a warning. Relax."

"No way, man," John Martin says, and wipes the knife in his jeans, then folds it. "I ain't relaxing with this siren going. You can stay if you want, but I'm going."

He blows up a Wal-Mart bag to make sure there are no large holes in it and lays the sandwiches inside. He fills up with tap water an empty sweet-tea jug and that, too, goes in a Wal-Mart bag. The prerecorded voice on TV tells us that a warning has been issued for northwestern Buddyville County, for Buddyview County, for Buddysonville . . . and I can't decide whether I should be hopeful or fearful to hear my wife's new house mentioned. Relieved not to hear John's house on the news, or thankful that I've heard it? Because right now, the way things have been going, some total destruction, some utter annihilation, might not be too bad for me.

The tornado, we hear, has touched ground two counties north from us and away from my wife's. We'll drive south, John tells us, five, ten miles, just out of town to a McDonald's. He'll buy us McGriddles, coffee, orange juice for the Princess. We'll sit there and wait this all out in peace and quiet. Then we'll come back here and clean the yard of branches and leaves. But for Christ's sake, let's get going.

We grab Elli's bag, the way my wife packed it, and as for me—I have nothing worth taking that you can put in a bag.

It's beginning to dawn. The sky is strangely green this early in the morning and the wind has stopped almost completely. The air smells bad, like a stinkbug on a raspberry bush, I suppose from the ozone. Far away we can see lighting and feel the roar of thunder, muffled at times and louder at others with the distant wind changing direction. We stand on the front porch while John Martin, the two bags in hand, runs to the truck to get it ready. It's then that Elli's cell phone starts ringing in my pocket.

I've already answered it before she can ask how I have it.

"Elli, honey, are you okay? How's the weather?"

"Turbo sunshine," I say in an authentic Bulgarian peasant

dialect. We run through the yard and John Martin pushes the door open. Elli hops in the middle and I follow.

"Michael," my wife says so loudly even John Martin flinches, "what's going on? Are you down in the shelter?"

"We don't have a shelter," I tell her. "Listen. We're fine. Don't worry about us."

"Get to the shelter," she says, and her voice breaks up with static and an ugly accent. "Michael," she says, and I'm thinking, seven years in the States and already calling her husband by a name that is not his. And then it strikes me: I am not her husband—and this thought seems so new at first it's like someone else's.

"You're breaking up," I say.

"Michael," she says, "is that a truck engine? Are you driving?"

"We have to go down to the shelter. Here's Elli." But before I pass the phone my thumb ends the call.

Elli shouts to her mother, into the dead receiver. "We need to dial again," she says. "I want to talk to Mommy."

I hide the phone in my pocket and tell her there is no reception. I help her buckle up and hug her tightly. "But I'm here. I'm right here, Elli."

"I want to talk to Mommy," she says. Then, like that, she starts crying. All in English, too. "I wanna go to Mommy. Take me to Mommy."

"Hush, hush," I say. I try to kiss her on the forehead, but she pushes me away. So I say, "God damn it, John Martin, drive the fucking truck already," and Elli begins to wail louder. I start with that tale I've been telling her, but she won't listen. Not even when John Martin begs her. On she cries, a siren of our own in the car. It's like this that we drive, the green sky thickening greener above us, a blinding thing. It's raining again.

"Don't look back," I tell John Martin when he steals a peek at his house in the rearview mirror. I am speaking, of course, of pillars of salt.

IX.

"They arrive at the mountain path a day later when the sun is high above the horizon. The trail is narrow, with steep slopes on both sides; if you roll a stone over the edge, it will crumble to sand before it has reached the bottom. One wrong step and both the horse and its rider fall in the abyss. Ali Ibrahim leads. My great-grandmother follows.

"'I'm exhausted,' she says and stops her horse. 'When I appear before the sultan, I must be at my best.'

"Ali dismounts his horse and, while she hides in the shadow of hers, sharpens his yataghan.

"'The sun is too strong,' my great-grandmother says, 'and my skin is too fair. Give me the *feredje* so I can veil my face.' Ali sighs deeply, puts the yataghan back in the sheath and takes the black kerchief out of his saddlebag. He hands the *feredje* to my great-grandmother, but she drops it, and the precious silk kerchief flies off the trail and down the steep slope, the wind tossing it toward the bottom of the abyss. Ali knows he can't bring my great-grandmother to the sultan without the special silk covering her face, so very carefully he descends after the *feredje*.

"Narrow trail, steep slopes. The *feredje* jumps in the air like a bird; Ali stalks it—slowly, measuring his steps, seeking footing in the weeds that grow in between the rocks. Then he trips. He rolls down the slope.

"The moment she sees this, my great-grandmother leaps on her horse and spurs it on. She rides swiftly down the mountains, but the farther she gets, the sharper the pain in her chest becomes. She despises Ali—his face, his eyes, his voice—yet, something pulls her back. It begins to feel like her own blood she's spilled.

"Once on a broader road, she stops the horse.

"'If I see a sign,' she whispers, 'if I see a pink lark, I'll go back and help him.'

"At that moment, a shower of larks pours from the sky. When she turns her horse back and spurs it toward the mountain, its hoofs squash the tiny bodies.

"She finds Ali half buried in stones. His face is bloody; pebbles embedded in his cheeks glisten underneath his skin. His arms are bruised, his knees mangled; his clothes have turned to rags. My great-grandmother kneels and strains to pick him up. She puts his arm around her shoulder and, bent in two under his weight, attempts to walk toward her horse.

"She sinks to the ground. Ali crushes her, his face upon her chest. My great-grandmother rises. She drags him five more feet and once again collapses. The rocks cut through her dress. Her knees, her elbows, palms are bleeding. She stands up again. Her hair, now sticky with Ali's blood and her own, falls loosely over her shoulders.

" *'Ela, konche!'* she calls for the horse. The horse kneels down and she drops Ali on the saddle. The sun pours fire upon the gorge. The Mountain rises in the distance, its peaks still snowy.

" 'I can't go on the road like this,' she says. 'If people see us, they'll kill him.'

"She takes the reins and calls out at the Mountain, *'Oy, Planino*, hide us in your bosom, your precious children.' "

·

"My great-grandmother leads the horse up the Mountain trails. Snowdrops blossom in a line at her feet and she follows.

"Before sunset she reaches a shepherd's hut. There is no one in the meadow, the house is deserted and fifty sheep bleat in a pen. Inside the hut, she finds the fireplace burning. Water is boiling in a copper, and an armful of white towels lie on the solitary bed.

"My great-grandmother lays Ali down. His eyes shiver under closed lids, and every now and then he mumbles words she cannot tell apart. She unbuttons his torn shirt, takes off the shreds of his trousers, his red boots, his blood-soaked belt. The yataghan falls to the floor, and when she touches the ivory handle, cold waves pass through her body: a thousand mournful screams. She flings the sword away. She soaks a towel in the hot water, then washes him. He cries in pain every time she touches his broken limbs and his cries echo in the falling night. Only the sheep bleat from the pen. The Mountain is quiet."

•

"For a month my great-grandmother takes care of Ali. She changes his bandages, tightens the splints, washes out his wounds and smears them with crushed centaury and boiled crowfoots. Once a day she bathes him outside on the meadow. Because the spring she draws water from is far away, she bathes him in sheep milk. She makes cheese and yogurt to feed him, she kindles the fire at night to keep him warm, she sings to him when the silence around them gets heavy. And through this care, despite her hatred, she grows to love him.

"It is always strange when a woman falls in love, and it is stranger still when she is the most beautiful in the world. The laws of cause and effect break down again. Every time my great-grandmother milks a sheep, the grass on the meadow grows taller. Every time she lights the fire, an avalanche of stones rumbles down the distant peaks. Her love for Ali grows stronger with each day, and it is her love that cures him."

•

"Nine months after they lie by the fire, the prettiest woman in the world bears an equally beautiful girl. Ali shepherds the fifty sheep along the lush pastures. He no longer carries his yataghan, which now lies locked in a wooden chest. My great-grandmother takes care of the baby, makes the cheese and yogurt, and it seems like the sun will never set upon their home. But this story starts with blood, and so with blood it must end."

Ꚍ.

John Martin takes us on a shortcut, a thin dirt road south through an endless field. Elli is no longer crying, but she refuses to speak. We drive past someone's ranch, separated with a barbed wire from the rest of the world. There are cows on the other side—big brown cows, and calves with long wet coats—all huddled together next to a large hole in the ground filled with bubbling, green water. As we drive by, they stomp their hoofs, stretch their necks restlessly, and I can see their blue tongues tasting air, as if the ozone were salt for the licking.

Behind us, far in the distance, the rain is thickness and the sky flashes with lightning. But the sky ahead is just as green, just as flashing. We drive for six miles before the truck overheats and John Martin pulls over in the grass.

"Why don't you turn the heat on?" I ask him, and he nods ahead.

"No sense of rushing that way."

I let out a sigh that is perhaps more tortured than it should be. "Why did I listen to you?" I say. I know exactly what will follow, but right now I don't care. "We should've stayed in the house."

John Martin nods. He rubs his chin and bites his lip.

"What a terrible idea this was. Why did I listen to you?"

And then he opens his door. "I've had enough," he says. "Princess," he says, and tips the rim of an invisible hat. He steps out into the rain and gently closes the door. Then he walks away back down the road, blurring almost immediately. I call after him. I honk the horn. "John Martin!" Elli shouts, but he keeps on walking, hands in his pockets, an apparition in the storm.

I let out a curse, step over Elli and get the truck running and turned around. I roll my window down and, once leveled with John, I tell him to knock it off. I do apologize. "Witness the tears of repentance," I say, and wipe the rain on my face with my sleeve. Behind me Elli adds to the pleading until at last John Martin is back in the truck, soaked and dripping.

"What the hell was I thinking?" he says. "It's crazy out there." I know I shouldn't. But still I say, "We should have stayed." And then softly, without animosity, John asks me what in the Lord's holy name is wrong with me. At least, I'd like to think that's how he asks it. And suddenly I feel obligated to answer, not for his sake, but for mine.

"Quite honestly, John," I say, "I really hate it here. I think that's what it boils down to. We should have never come. The States, I mean—not just Texas, not just this road." I pet Elli's shoulder, but she shrugs my hand off. "There are no tornadoes in Bulgaria, and that's a fact." And then I tell them how I cannot look at people who smile, at young, beautiful couples, at fathers with daughters, and old men with their old wives, healthy together, full of some life that I have been robbed of. It's a ridiculous feeling, this *yad*. I know that much. "It's so bad," I say, "that sometimes, when I've had a few, I actually regret losing my appendix. I miss it. I feel incomplete without it."

"You are a sad human being, Michael," John Martin says, and leans forward to kiss the cross.

"Also," I say. "My name is Mihail. Not Michael."

"Listen, Michael," John goes on. "No one made you leave the house this morning. And no one made you leave your country. Those were your choices and you should be man enough to stand behind them. You make a decision, you accept the consequences. You move on. This, Princess," he says, "is life. You don't win by tripping yourself and rolling in the grass. You stay on your feet and keep on marching. The way you live, Michael, this is your future," he says, and pokes a thumb at his chest. "At least you still have your daughter. Why not enjoy that? And let her be. Enough pretending. You're not in Communist Russia. Maybe ten years from now she'll still come to visit. Maybe she won't come to visit . . ." But John Martin doesn't finish.

We know then that something has happened. The wind has come to a complete stop. It's no longer raining, and the air gets, suddenly, so charged that every sound, no matter how tiny, travels without the slightest distortion.

It sounds to me like my mother is calling us, this very moment, me and my sister, home for dinner.

"Hush . . . listen," John Martin says and the three of us lean forward against the windshield as if that would make us hear better.

A terrible gust smacks the side of the truck, like another truck, but much larger. Elli yelps and throws herself in my arms. The wind slaps us, left, right, left, and we can do nothing but sit there and take the beating. The whole truck is shaking, rattling, and any minute now it seems the glass will shatter. I cover Elli's face in my shirt and hold her very tightly against my chest. For some reason John Martin is punching the truck horn. He unloads, but the horn is barely audible against the slapping of the wind.

Then we see it—to the right of us, half a mile away: a white funnel stretched between sky and field, perfectly peaceful in its rage. Elli peeks up from my grip and now we are glued to that window and we are all children now, stunned, Elli's breath on my neck and even John Martin's breath, sharp and warm, sour with the smell of stale beer. It could kill us of course, this funnel of air, which is ridiculous to even consider. It could pass through us and wipe us clean from the earth, like we never existed, truck and all. Yet, we feel no fear—I can sense that—we feel only awe, and that is all there is to feel, no regret, no envy, no *yad*.

Then it's gone, decomposed into thinner wind, into sky and field. It begins to rain again, large drops that splash against the windshield and then bounce off it, because they've hardened in midair and turned to hail. Chunks the size of walnuts. They slam against the truck top, crack the windshield up in the corner.

And with the ice chunks, a black crow slams on the hood,

and then another, and we watch, frozen, as a flock of dead crows rain around us, their bodies splashing mud and water on the road.

This is the craziest thing we have seen, there is no doubt about that. But like before, we aren't scared—not even Elli, who's climbed on the dashboard and her face, flattened against the glass that divides them, is just inches away from the crow on the hood.

When the hail lets up, I step out into the rain, and Elli follows and then John Martin. We poke the crows with our feet, their necks at awful angles, their wings broken like the spines of little umbrellas. We keep moving, quiet with each other. I kick a crow lightly, like a football, and the crow, neck droopy, suddenly flaps its wings, three-four mighty flaps in the mud. I pounce back, trip on my own foot, and land flat on my ass.

Elli, of course, starts screaming. But soon, strangely, her screaming turns to laughter. John Martin, too, is laughing beside me, his big belly shaking. So, just to amuse them I run down the road, and kick my own heel. I land in the mud again and sit there for a while with the rain pounding, with my daughter laughing, with my hands up at the sky, waiting for something. Maybe a whistle.

I know that Elli wants to call her mother and tell her all about the rain and the tornado. Thank God there's no reception. But what about my mother? There are no tornadoes in Bulgaria, and that's a fact, so surely she'll fail to understand me. But I can try to make her *feel* at least. How cold the wind was, how shiny the feathers of the crows. It's true, she hasn't seen the Texas sky, but I have seen it. It's true her hair was never soaked with Texas rain, but mine is dripping rivers. She doesn't need her eyes to see my world. Neither do I to see the things she sees. My blood runs in her veins and hers in mine. Blood will make us see.

XI.

"One evening, just when my great-grandmother is about to breast-feed the baby, the earth begins to tremble. The sun is still an hour away from setting and Ali is still out with the herd. My great-grandmother, the baby in her arms, runs out to the meadow.

"A black wave eats the hills in the distance and approaches quickly. As it moves closer, my great-grandmother realizes soldiers are marching toward her. Five thousand janissaries, the great sultan in the lead, riding on three horses tied to one another with golden ropes so as to carry his enormous weight. And on a horse in front of the sultan, she sees Ali Ibrahim, disfigured, beaten nearly to death. His hands are tied, and bloody tears roll down from his blinded eyes.

"Panic seizes my great-grandmother. The baby sleeps in her trembling arms and only mewls quietly from time to time. The forest, the peaks, the gorges, are all too far away; the meadow spreads under the cloudy sky. My great-grandmother understands that she can never outrun the soldiers, so back in the house she lays the baby in the crib and kisses her farewell. She opens the seven locks that chain the chest and takes out Ali's sword. Again— the chill, the painful cries. Just then, Ali calls out from the meadow.

"'Run to the Mountain!' he shouts. 'Take the baby and run!'

"Light like the morning mist, my great-grandmother steps out of the hut. She stands before the sultan, before the five thousand soldiers, before Ali, who has fallen from the horse and now weeps in pain. The tall grass reaches up to her waist, the dark clouds crawl across the sky, the wind smells of dust.

"My great-grandmother plants the yataghan in the ground, then gathers her hair and ties it behind so her face is uncovered.

"'*Az bez boy se ne davam!*' she says to the sultan: 'I will not let myself go without a fight!' She grasps the sword handle again with both hands and lifts the weapon. Instantly, the sultan waves at the soldiers to seize his prize. But the soldiers cannot move. They have seen my great-grandmother's face and now those lustful pyres burn them.

"Five thousand men—all madly in love. So much want in one place turns the clouds to rock, and they fall upon the army in solid, glassy chunks. When all the clouds have fallen, silence descends upon the meadow.

"Ali writhes before the sultan's horses. Even though most of the janissaries have been crushed to death, there are still enough left to take my great-grandmother away.

" 'Seize her!' the sultan shouts, and kicks one of the soldiers, a janissary. The man stumbles forward, breathing heavily, sweat running down his cheeks. My great-grandmother holds tight to the yataghan, whose tip now dances in the air with every tremor of her arms. The jannissary steps closer, almost touches her apron—then falls at her feet.

"My great-grandmother raises the sword. *Slay him*, it whispers, thirsty. But then another voice whispers. *It is your blood you spill as you kill him. Bulgarian blood.* My great-grandmother drops to her knees. At last two dazzled soldiers pick her up amid the mad shouts of the sultan. 'Bring me my bird!' he screams. 'Bring me my prize, my trophy, my bride!'

"Then the Mountain wakes up.

"The wind stops blowing. The soldiers pull hard on my great-grandmother but can't move her—she is fixed to the ground. The Mountain is holding her back. Thick, supple stalks of grass have entwined with each other, in living chains that twist around her feet and waist, her chest and shoulders.

" 'Give me my prize!' the sultan shouts. With great effort he dismounts his horses. But when he pulls on my great-grandmother, the Mountain pulls back. He pulls hard; the Mountain pulls back harder. The sultan takes Ali's sword and cuts the living chains. When he is done, he grabs my great-grandmother and throws her over his shoulder. He passes Ali in the dirt and spits in his blood-washed face, then seats my great-grandmother on the riderless horse.

" 'Let's see what the most beautiful woman in the world looks like,' the sultan says, pulling back her hair, once again loose.

"Two empty eyes stare at him from a pale and empty face. The lips have no color, the cheeks have lost their rosy shade. The Mountain has drunk her beauty away, to preserve it.

" 'So much ado for this?' The sultan frowns. He mounts his three horses with assistance and spurs them on. 'Lead her to the palace,' he commands. 'Bathe her in rose water and milk. Then I'll look at her again.' "

•

"No one knows why the soldiers never set the house on fire. I've heard on a few occasions that they did try. Yet, every time they brought a burning torch to the thatch roof, a strong wind blew from nowhere and snuffed the flames.

"They leave Ali Ibrahim lying broken in front of the hut, an easy prey for wolves and a feast for the crows. The baby cries fitfully inside, but the soldiers abandon her, too.

"Then silence descends upon the Mountain. For a while, not even the barking of dogs can be heard as the nearest houses are more than a day's walk away. When the sun has finally gone behind the peaks, the baby starts crying again. Ali crawls his way through the meadow. Bright spots twist before his blinded eyes; the scent of his beloved woman is still in the air. At the threshold he lets his head fall on his chest. He feels death on his lips.

"The sheep start bleating. Their bells sing in the night, and the tall grass rustles under light steps. A bucket splashes: someone has milked a sheep and is bringing the milk toward the hut. Distant whispers. Dancing shadows. A cold hand rests upon Ali's shoulder.

" 'Come, my child. Come, Sunshine. Let's go inside. The baby is hungry.' "

•

"And so this story ends. Many have told it before and many have sung about it. It is in the air and in the water, in the valleys and in the steep hills. And up in the Mountain you can still hear that lulling—the voice of a woman, soothing her children in times of despair, in times of darkness."

ACKNOWLEDGMENTS

I must thank, in somewhat chronological order, the following people, without whom neither this book nor its author would have been possible:

Agop Melkonian, who read my first stories, saw something in them and from then on treated me not as the sixteen-year-old geek I was but as his equal, a writer. I wish he could see this book.

My English-language teachers at the First English Language School in Sofia: Mrs. Yordanova, Mrs. Stoeva, Mrs. Vasseva. And Ms. Boyadjieva, who, during our first lesson, asked me to form a sentence in English: "The apple is on the table." But she could have asked me to compose a sestina and I might have done a better job.

Mrs. Marie Lavallard and the Foundation for the International Exchange of Students at the University of Arkansas, without whose support I could have never afforded to study in the United States.

Ellen Gilchrist, who has always been a champion of me and my writing and who first taught me that "writing is rewriting." My first creative writing teachers: Adam Prince and Mary Morrissy. Chuck Argo, without whom I might never have thought of writing about Bulgaria. John DuVal, whose friendship and wisdom helped me through difficult times. Davis McCombs, for his kindness. Molly Giles, for her generosity and editorial honesty. Donald "Skip" Hays, who taught me much about story, structure, character, and served as a minister at my wedding. His wife, Patty, who so generously hosted the ceremony. Kathleen and Collin Condray, Beth and Peter Horton, for their hospitality. Dr. Slattery, who never made me teach a morning class! My psychology professors Dr. Lohr and Dr. Freund. My old boss Mike Williams.

My dear friends in Arkansas who, lucky me, are too many to thank individually. My friends and colleagues in Denton, for all their support. My Bulgarian friends who stuck by me across continents and years: Botzata, Boyan and his family, Ivcho, Oto, Traycho and Tsveti.

My agent, Sorche Fairbank, who believed in the stories from the very beginning, for her friendship, editorial help and encouragement.

The editor of this book, Courtney Hodell, who saw promise in the stories before they were ready, and did not tire until they were; who taught me much about writing, and, as a side effect, tormented me greatly. You have my deepest gratitude.

Mark Krotov, who was always ready to help. Marion Duvert, Amanda Schoonmaker, Wah-Ming Chang, David Chesanow, Michelle Crehan, Jonathan Lippincott, Jennifer Carrow, Debra Helfand, Brian Gittis, Hanna Oswald and everyone else at FSG who worked so hard to make this book possible.

Brett Lott, Donna Perrault and the staff of *The Southern Review*. Paula Morris, Sabina Murray, Heidi Pitlor, Salman Rushdie, Andrew Blechman, Hannah Tinti. The Walton Family and the Lily Peter Foundations at the University of Arkansas and Bob and Louise Garnett for their support of my writing.

My wife, for all her love and encouragement.

My family back home, but especially my grandmas and grandpas. My parents. Обичам ви!

My dear Bulgaria, who I return to, always, in my thoughts. And forgive me, beautiful Bulgarian language, for telling stories in a foreign tongue, a tongue that is now sweet and close to me.

Thank you, kind reader, for reading.

A NOTE ABOUT THE AUTHOR

Miroslav Penkov was born in 1982 in Bulgaria. He arrived in America in 2001 and completed a bachelor's degree in psychology and an MFA in creative writing at the University of Arkansas. He has won the Eudora Welty Prize in Fiction, and his story "Buying Lenin" was published in *The Best American Short Stories 2008*, edited by Salman Rushdie. He teaches creative writing at the University of North Texas, where he is a fiction editor for *American Literary Review.*